Undeniable Desire

Will had forgotten how the contrast of smooth skin and pebbled nipple satisfied him and drove him crazy all at once, how she had been part of his first thought in the morning and his last thought before falling asleep in her arms, how he'd believed they'd always be together . . . and how much her betrayal had hurt.

That faded away as the intensity of his need grew. He wanted to take her back to his hotel and make love to her, to find out if she still made those little sighs and breathless mews of pleasure, to find out if time still stopped when he was inside her.

Mia suddenly pulled back, her pupils so wide her eyes looked black. "We probably shouldn't be doing this here," she murmured. "We're both old enough to know better."

And to know there was no going back to what they'd had before.

He'd been sent here to do a job and she was part of that job, whether he liked it or not. If she was guilty, he would take her down.

But until then, he couldn't turn away from her tentative smile or the reflection of his own desire in her eyes.

More acclaim for Michele Albert, the bestselling author who "puts the snap-crackle-pop into the mystery-romance!" (*Detroit Free Press*)

HIDE IN PLAIN SIGHT

"A dangerous man, a clever woman, and a twisty, high-risk chase that kept me up half the night . . . hot, hot, hot!"   —Julia Spencer-Fleming

"Amazing. . . . Good romantic suspense is always a pleasure."   —*Romantic Times*

ONE WAY OUT

"The outstanding Michele Albert's new adventure is roaring, and the romance sizzles. Settle in for a great ride."   —*Romantic Times*

"Exciting romantic suspense. . . . Action-packed. . . . Michele Albert provides a fine, exhilarating, way-out tale."   —The Best Reviews

"A fast-paced, suspenseful book that's impossible to put down. This book has a kick-ass heroine and a hot, yummy hero. . . . If you like suspense, mystery, and action mixed in with your romance, this is THE book for you!"   —A Romance Review

"Another winner. . . . *One Way Out* is a brilliantly paced story. . . . The chemistry between Alex and Cassie fairly sizzles off the page. . . . A wonderful, one-sitting read that touches both the heart and the funny bone. . . . Snap this one up—you won't be disappointed!"

—Contemporaryromancewriters.com

OFF LIMITS

"Wow! Take one smart, by-the-book, beautiful cop and mix well with one hunky, devilish bad boy: the perfect recipe for a delicious romp of a romance. . . . Michele Albert gives us not only a wonderful love story with some hot sex, but also two people who stand up for what they believe in. . . . Fun, sexy contemporary romance."

—Curledup.com

"Intelligent characters and scorching love scenes."
—*The Romance Reader*

GETTING HER MAN

"Whoa, boy! Michele Albert outdoes herself with this sexy, sassy, and exciting book." —*Romantic Times*

MICHELE ALBERT

TOUGH ENOUGH

POCKET BOOKS
New York   London   Toronto   Sydney

An *Original* Publication of POCKET BOOKS

POCKET BOOKS, a division of Simon & Schuster, Inc.
1230 Avenue of the Americas, New York, NY 10020

This book is a work of fiction. Names, characters, places and incidents are products of the author's imagination or are used fictitiously. Any resemblance to actual events or locales or persons, living or dead, is entirely coincidental.

ISBN-13: 978-1-4165-3139-5
ISBN-10:   1-4165-3139-4

This Pocket Books paperback edition April 2007

10 9 8 7 6 5 4 3 2 1

POCKET and colophon are registered trademarks of Simon & Schuster, Inc.

Cover design by Jae Song

Manufactured in the United States of America

For information regarding special discounts for bulk purchases, please contact Simon & Schuster Special Sales at 1-800-456-6798 or business@simonandschuster.com.

Acknowledgments

I wish to thank my agent, Pam Ahearn, and my editor, Micki Nuding, for their continued support and understanding. No book is published in a vacuum. I also need to thank my family for putting up with crazy schedules, moments of forgetfulness, the occasional drama, and understanding that sometimes creative people are a little weird. Hugs and kisses to you all!

TOUGH
ENOUGH

One

I HAVE A JOB THAT REQUIRES YOUR SINGULAR TALENTS.

Had his boss meant the acting talent, the B & E talent, or the running-a-con-on-a-con-man talent? Or all three? Frowning slightly, Will Tiernay punched in his security code, then pressed his thumb against the digital reader. A buzz and a loud click signaled that the door was unlocked, and he entered the inner sanctum of Sheridan Expeditions.

The third-floor suite offered a perfect view of Puget Sound, and the earthy colors and log cabin theme met all expectations of what the executive offices of a thriving adventure travel agency should look like—although Sheridan Expeditions was also much more.

The woman behind the large, curved reception desk stood as Will approached. Her sleeveless turquoise shirt and tan pants emphasized both the strong, lean lines of her muscles and her smooth black skin. Usually the desk was staffed by Barbie-doll-blond and blue-eyed Ellie—where did Sheridan find all these hot, kick-ass women?

"Hey," he said, smiling as a subtle perfume scent tickled his senses. "Will Tiernay here to see Ben."

The woman arched a brow over the top of her narrow oval glasses, which made her chilly reserve all the more sexy and classy. "Mr. Sheridan is in a meeting in the conference room. He's expecting you—and has been for several hours," she added politely if pointedly. "So you can walk right in."

Yeah, he was late, but so what? Given the difficulty of booking a flight to Seattle out of Rio de Janeiro with barely any lead time, he could've been a hell of a lot later. He gave her an equally polite nod, then headed down the hall to the conference room and pushed open the door.

And immediately ducked as the thick sole of an athletic shoe rushed toward his face.

Twisting, he raised his forearm to block another kick to his head, this one launched by a bare foot with pink toenails.

"Goddammit," Will snapped. "I got here as soon as I could!"

Being ambushed by the company CEO and his executive secretary was *not* an auspicious start to a new assignment.

Ben Sheridan, in sweatpants and a Seattle University T-shirt, loomed above him. Faint lines crinkled at the corners of his dark eyes and around his mouth as he smiled. "Just testing your reflexes. Making sure you haven't gone soft after all those surveillance jobs lately."

"No need to worry about that," Ellie said. In her gray leggings, baby pink tee, and ponytail, she looked like any young suburbanite socializing at the local fitness club. "That arm felt rock solid to me."

"I hate to think of what you two throw at the tough guys on the payroll."

"Oh, you're tough enough." She ran her hand along the muscles of his upper arm and made an approving sound.

"Ellie," Ben said, his tone amused. "You're petting him again."

"Because he's such a very pettable man." With a small smile, she pulled at Will's black suit coat to reveal the label. "Tsk-tsk. Brawling in Hugo Boss. Shame on you."

"I never *brawl*," Will said haughtily.

"Says the wolf in sheep's clothing." Ellie straightened his lapels, realigned the red silk tie, and gave his shoulder a light pat. "I don't know many men who look this good in a suit. It must be that tall, dark, and handsome thing. I bet you leave a trail of drooling women in your wake."

"Not that I've ever noticed—which is a damn shame." He couldn't help being charmed by Ellie's girlie cuteness; flirting came as naturally to her as typing a hundred words a minute and breaking noses.

Smiling, he turned to Ben. "The receptionist didn't look too impressed when she informed me that I'd better haul my tardy ass inside. Is she new? And what's her name?"

"Her name is Shaunda." Ben took the towel Ellie held out and rubbed it vigorously over his short, dark hair. "She fills in for Ellie, and no, I won't give you her telephone number."

Annoyed at having his ulterior motives nailed so fast, Will said, "I wasn't going to ask for her number."

"Of course you weren't," Ben agreed, exchanging looks with Ellie.

Smug bastard. "Since when is fighting with your secretary a meeting?"

"My company, my policies. She helps me with my physical training three times a week, so I don't get soft."

What a hardship, being rich and top dog *and* forcing oneself to spar with a beautiful blonde three times a week. "Who wins?"

"She does."

"Only because you're not really fighting," Ellie retorted. "It's because I'm a girl. He doesn't take me seriously."

"If I didn't take you seriously, you wouldn't be my bodyguard."

Ellie sighed. "I should turn Shaunda loose on you;

it's exactly what you deserve. But if she kills you, I'm out of a cushy little job."

"Speaking of cushy little jobs, how's the Art Guy?" Will asked.

Her smugly secretive female smile said everything and nothing. "The Art Guy is very happy. I make sure he stays that way."

"Good to hear," Ben said dryly. "Without him, all you ex-cop and ex-military Neanderthals would never learn the difference between art and porn."

The Art Guy was a professor who provided crash courses on art to Avalon rookies, often on short notice and at odd hours of the night. The Art Guy also provided amazingly detailed knowledge on how to spot and produce forgeries. Will had never asked if that knowledge came from research or from something more hands-on.

He'd easily passed the art briefings, since the love of his life in college had not only dragged him to countless museums and galleries but also talked about art a lot. It was surprising how much had stuck after all these years; even more surprising was that he'd found a use for it.

Wouldn't she be surprised if she could see him now.

"If keeping him happy is that important, I think I deserve a raise. Don't you, Will?"

Ellie's question broke across the less-than-happy memory, and Will glanced up to see Ben watching him with an enigmatic expression.

Caught off guard, Will took a moment to respond. "I agree. Better pay up, boss."

"I don't pay Ellie to keep the Art Guy happy. I pay her to guard my body."

"It's your money. But for the record, keeping Nolan happy takes a lot more effort than guarding you." She picked up her towel and left, the door closing behind her with a quiet click.

Will slipped his hands in his pockets, jingling keys and spare change. "I think Ellie got in the last word."

"She generally does." Ben cleared his throat. "You're late."

"I was on the other side of the equator when you emailed me. What's up?"

"I'm going to need my man of the hundred faces, so brush up on your acting skills." Ben flashed a smile. "I'm sending you to Boston."

The tension in that quick smile, which had been more like bared teeth, blunted Will's rush of anticipation. "Okay. Give me the details."

"A call came in this week from a contact at the Met, asking for our help." Ben pulled out a chair at the conference table for Will, then one for himself on the opposite side. "You've heard of Mal Toller?"

"Old money, lords it over a Boston law firm, and is currently playing publisher with some men's magazine he bought from an Italian corporation."

"That's him."

Will leaned back, his brows pulling together in thought. "He has a few nice paintings . . . plus a sweet little Byzantine collection, if I'm remembering right. The Eudoxia Reliquary alone is worth a small fortune."

"It's said to hold a bloody thorn from Christ's crown of thorns, which boosts its value even more—and then there's the curse. Some people will pay big money for that kind of thing."

Because some people are stupid. "Was the reliquary stolen?"

Ben shook his head. "Not yet, but here's the deal: Toller's been short on cash and decided to sell the collection to the Met. Naturally the Met was eager to acquire it. As part of the deal, Toller wanted top-of-the-line replicas made for display at his estate."

Nothing unusual in that. Will sat forward, resting his elbows on the table. "Where's the problem?"

"The problem is that Toller didn't go through the Met for the reproductions. He contracted with a private firm in Boston that's been in business for only a few years. Toller claims he's friends with the owner and wants to give his company a boost."

Will reached inside his suit coat and pulled out a notepad and pen. "I see where this is going."

"The company is Haddington Reproductions," Ben continued. "Hugh Haddington used to work for the Facsimile Service at the British Museum. He left four years ago to start his own business in the U.S., taking a couple of co-workers with him. The business is doing well, but not as well as Haddington would like. Getting the contract for the Eudoxia collection is his big break."

"Who am I hunting? Toller, Haddington, or both?"

"Haddington, since Toller is in Europe on a business trip. If it turns out Toller is involved, all you can do is turn the evidence over to local law enforcement. Haddington's two assistants aren't in the clear, either. The sudden urgency is because one of our guys in Rome is hearing rumors of a lot of Byzantine art about to hit the market, and one rumor specifically mentioned the Eudoxia Reliquary."

Meaning the Metropolitan Museum of Art, New York's most prestigious art museum, was about to get a bogus collection for the big bucks they'd paid to Toller, while the real pieces would be sold for even more money on the black market.

"Why me instead of the local cops?"

"We need someone experienced in white-collar crime who can improvise his cover as needed, and that would be you."

That "we" meant Ben was acting on orders from the top, but Will no longer wasted time speculating on the identity of the mysterious individual who gave Ben Sheridan his orders and funded his small, private army of mercenaries. Mercenaries with an eye for art—and if he weren't living the reality, Will would've laughed away such a crazy notion.

"I'll need all the information you've got on Toller, Haddington, and the Eudoxia collection."

"We're still working on that," Ben answered. "We've got Toller and the collection covered, but we don't have much on Haddington yet, and only the names of his two employees: Vanessa Sharpton and Mia Dolan."

Will looked up sharply. Mia wasn't a common name—but it wasn't really rare, either.

Ben drummed the tips of his fingers on the table, whether from impatience, nervous energy, or something else, Will couldn't say.

"No spouses or significant others listed yet, but I'd expect that to change. They're all British citizens, so call our friends at the Yard if necessary."

Will nodded. "Got it."

"Ellie will hand over what we have right now, and forward everything else by courier as soon as possible. She's also booked a hotel room and put together your cover. You'll be posing as a freelance journalist. Details are in the file."

"Alias?"

"You won't need an alias."

"Why not?"

Ben stared at him, unblinking. "Because you won't. Like I said, details are in the file. Pick up everything you'll need from Ellie, then Shaunda will drive you to the airport."

He should be used to traveling long hours for five

minutes' worth of information; it was the way Sheridan always operated. Once upon a time people delivered their important news by Federal Express, then computers came along and they used Outlook Express. But with the Internet a quagmire of security holes, Ben preferred to deliver actual information face-to-face—hence the enigmatic email to haul his ass to home base..

Will glanced at his watch. It would be at least a six-hour flight to Boston, and he'd already spent tedious hours in transit. "Do I get a company jet?"

"Yes, since I needed you there yesterday. Haddington will be expecting you around seven tonight. You've already sent him an email," Ben explained at Will's questioning look.

"How efficient of me." Will stood. "I'll talk to Ellie, then head out."

"Hold on. I'm not done yet." Ben frowned. "We have reason to believe von Lahr is involved."

Will sat back down.

Rainert von Lahr, the Bundeswehr-trained sniper who'd walked away from a promising military career and transformed himself into one of the most wanted art thieves worldwide. Bringing down von Lahr had been Avalon's Holy Grail for fifteen years; there wasn't a single person at Avalon who didn't want to be the first to nail the sonofabitch.

This was the reason Will was going in before the local cops.

"You know how good von Lahr is at moving small pieces. If he gets his hands on that reliquary, we may never get it back."

"No wonder my surveillance in Rio was a bust," Will said. "The bastard had already left."

"Did you find out where he was staying there?"

Recalling hours wasted in stuffy vans and dark hotel rooms—nowhere near the fabled beaches and kilometers of tanned female flesh—Will grimaced. "The intel was legit and he *was* using the condo, but he was long gone by the time I got there."

"And the woman?"

Wherever von Lahr went, there was always a woman about to take a big fall just as he disappeared into thin air. "Nobody's seen her or heard from her in the past six weeks."

"That doesn't sound good."

Will shrugged. "The lady was a player. If she turns up dead, the list of suspects will include more names than von Lahr's. Our few other leads didn't tell us anything we didn't already know."

"It was always a long shot." Ben squeezed the bridge of his nose and let out a long sigh, equal parts frustration and weariness. "But at least we know he's back in the game, after lying low for the last couple years."

Will had heard about the near-miss with von Lahr in Los Angeles, back in November. "Is it true Laughton quit?"

"It was something he needed to do. I respect that." Ben shifted, resting his elbows on the chair's back. "And now that we know for sure von Lahr's set up business in Brazil as well as Venezuela, I'll work on finding someone else to keep an eye on things down there."

"Okaaay," Will said after a moment. "So I'm not going back to surveillance once I'm done in Boston?"

"For now, no. There's something else I'd like you to work on between assignments. It's not a priority, but I have a personal interest in seeing it resolved."

Personal? Intrigued, Will leaned forward. "What kind of project?"

A stack of files sat at the side of the conference table, and Ben reached over and removed the top one. He slid the folder, with a soft swishing sound, across the smooth surface toward Will. "Take a look."

It contained copies of old typed and handwritten reports in Italian, although a few pages were in English and German. Will was fluent in Spanish, and his French and Italian reading skills were passable, but he'd have to break out a dictionary for the German.

A faded photograph sat on top of the reports, showing a young woman with long black hair. She had a pretty smile, but what caught his attention was how she looked right at the camera, as if she could truly see him. The wistful dreaminess in those dark eyes stirred old memories.

Shaking off the feeling, Will glanced through the

papers for the girl's name. He found it, along with a death certificate dated July 1943. She'd been only twenty years old.

"I'm getting the feeling Maria Balestrini didn't die of natural causes."

"Murdered. The case was never solved."

A hell of a cold case file—over half a century old, from a country half the world away. But how could he turn down a challenge like that? "Sure. I'll look into it for you."

Ben raised a brow. "It always surprises me, how you never ask the questions everyone else asks."

"If I did, would you tell me the truth?" Will asked mildly.

"Doubtful."

"Then asking questions would just be a waste of my time."

The flat, veiled expression on Ben's face was one Will recognized from his cop days: a warning flash of hard-edged power, a thrum of controlled violence, which came of a life spent looking too deeply into the darkness, of doing what should not have to be done.

The look was gone as suddenly as it had come. "Probably not," Ben agreed in an equally genial tone.

Will closed the file, shutting away the girl's disturbing gaze. "Okay, but if there's anything else I should know, now's the time to spill."

"Not much to tell. There's evidence that she knew

a man who disappeared in 1939, and there was a connection between that disappearance and another one nearly fifty years later. My first assignment for Avalon was to investigate what happened in both cases; we hoped solving the older disappearance would solve the newer one. Instead I just hit one dead end after another. I don't like failure. It eats at my peace of mind." Ben spread his hands in a there-you-have-it gesture. "Maybe a fresh look will uncover something I missed."

"Do I get the names of the people who disappeared?"

Ben shook his head. "Not until you need them."

"All right." Will mulled that over for a moment. "And how will I know when I need them?"

"I'll know."

The speaker phone buzzed, and Ellie's voice rang out: "Ben, there's a courier here with an urgent delivery. Do you want me to send him in or have him wait?"

"Have him wait. I'm almost done here." Once she'd disconnected, Ben turned back toward Will. "When I said *fresh*, I meant *fresh*. No preconceived expectations, like I had then. And keep in mind that her death *might* not have any relevance," Ben cautioned. "It's another long shot. They're always long shots in this business."

"I agree the odds don't look so good for solving a sixty-year-old murder. I'll have better luck at foiling dastardly plots to steal the Eudoxia Reliquary, curse and all." Will pushed to his feet. "Why do I always end up with the weird shit?"

Ben's smile warmed his eyes. "Because you're so good at it. Stay sharp. If von Lahr *is* involved, he's had time to bring in help. And the way things look right now, I might not have anyone available to back you up."

"Not a problem. We lone wolves in sheep's clothing prefer to work alone."

Ben didn't look as if that made things better. He stood up. "I want you to check in twice a day with Ellie or Shaunda. A missed check-in means trouble, and I'll respond accordingly. I have a feeling this could get complicated."

Will gave a derisive snort. "What's complicated about a bunch of greedy bastards trying to double-cross each other? Unless von Lahr decides to make a personal appearance—and I doubt we'll get that lucky—nothing will surprise me."

Two

"DO I HAVE A DATE-FROM-HELL STORY?" MIA DOLAN SET her tea on the café table. "Vanessa, *any* woman who's ever fallen in love has been stupid in love."

"Impossible." Vanessa Sharpton stirred a straw through the whipped cream and chocolate sprinkles of her mocha smoothie. "You have all the luck with men."

"Are we remembering the same past five years, here? My ex?"

"Philip was a lovely fellow. He just needed a keeper, not a wife."

As Mia had quickly discovered. Adorably absent-minded men made poor husbands. "You're also forgetting that guy from the BBC. And Jonathan."

Vanessa laughed. "All right, Jonathan was quite awful. But that's still only a few failures out of many, many more successes. My track record with men is far worse than yours."

Vanessa did have an unerring talent for choosing losers and deadbeats. It had even led to a big argument a few months back that resulted in Vanessa getting her own apartment and living with the boyfriend Mia had bluntly accused of sponging off her friend.

"You and Kos have been together for nine months now, so maybe your luck has changed since Hugh dragged us to Boston," Mia said. "You all but glow these days."

Vanessa's blush deepened, bright pink against her pale, blue-eyed coloring. In contrast, Mia had inherited all of her mother's exotic Maltese darkness and none of her American father's fairness.

"I think you're trying to distract me." Vanessa's eyes were bright. "Could it be you really *are* embarrassed to tell me this story?"

"What else are friends for, if we can't reveal our deepest, darkest secrets?" Mia leaned forward, elbows resting on the table, and cupped her chin in her hands. As the memory drifted back, a smile curved her mouth. "My worst date was my very first date with Will."

"Ah. The Ohio boy."

"Are you sure I haven't told you this one already?"

"Positive. I remember you telling me he was a big, strapping lad who liked short skirts and sex in the woods, but that's about it."

Oh, God. She'd forgotten about the sex in the woods. "I met Will barely a week after classes began. He was the cutest boy in the entire dorm, and when he asked me out, I almost died on the spot. I might have even squealed."

No matter how hard she tried to keep the big, sappy smile away, it kept slipping back. "He picked me up from work, and he was driving this ugly yellow car he'd borrowed from a friend. I almost didn't want to be seen getting inside it, but he was the perfect gentleman and ran around to open the door. At that point, what else could I do?"

"The male ego must be carefully nurtured," Vanessa agreed.

"It was hot and the car had no air conditioner, so we had the windows rolled down as we drove to the restaurant. I was nervous, talking so fast I was almost hyperventilating. I don't even remember what I said; I just remember how much I wanted him to like me, to think I was pretty and clever and sophisticated. Everything I wasn't feeling at the time."

Smiling, Vanessa toyed with her whipped cream topping. "When do we get to the horror?"

"That would be when the cutest guy at Ohio State pulled up to the restaurant, and I told him it was the nineties and women could open their own car doors. I got out, and when I locked the door, I realized I hadn't rolled up the window."

Strange, how she could close her eyes and still remember the bright blue sky, the smell of traffic and hot asphalt mingled with a mouthwatering charbroiled burger scent, and the warmth of the car leaking through her little black dress. "So I stuck my hand inside the window and started rolling it up."

Vanessa blinked. "From the outside?"

"Uh-huh . . . and the window was almost at my armpit before I realized the flaw in my plan. I can't even begin to describe how stupid I felt."

Vanessa laughed. "Did Will say anything?"

Mia took a sip of her tea. "He never let me live it down, the bastard."

Vanessa pointed her straw at Mia. "You're smiling as you say that."

"Oh, I know. He was such a sweet guy. Too nice for me, as it turned out, and we had nothing in common. He was a total philistine when it came to art, but I loved him like crazy anyway." The smile slipped a little. "He was my first . . . my first *everything*."

Until the offer to study in Venice had arrived, and Will had pressured her to accept. Long-distance relationships rarely worked out—especially when the girl was immature, selfish, and puffed full of unrealistic dreams. She'd betrayed Will's trust in the most painful way possible, and he'd never forgiven her for it. Regret still ached, even after all this time.

"And then there was Lorenz," she added. "And Mathieu, and Philip, and now I'm sitting here with you in a Boston café, totally man-free."

Why did that make the last twelve years sound so underwhelming?

Mia stood, brushing the thought away. "We should get back before Hugh calls. I swear, that man will give himself a heart attack before he turns fifty."

After paying their checks, they headed back to the workshop. It was only three blocks away, but the April day's warmth had faded with the setting sun, and Mia regretted not taking her coat.

Vanessa touched Mia's arm. "You did the right thing."

"I never regretted going to Venice. It's just . . ." She trailed off, trying to put those nebulous little tugs of emotion into words. "We were talking about getting married. We were much too young, but it doesn't excuse what I did, and I wish . . . Well, it doesn't matter anymore. Sometimes we get a chance to make up for mistakes; sometimes we just have to learn to live with them."

"I know," Vanessa murmured.

"I wonder how differently my life would've turned out if Will and I had gotten married." Mia let out a long sigh. "Good thing we didn't, though. I was always chasing after some grand fantasy, and Will was Mr. Solid and Steady. I'm sure he's got a nice middle-management job, is happily married to a nice woman and raising a crop of nice kids in a nice town in Ohio."

"Nice is . . . nice. It's something I wanted for a long

time, to find someone I could be with for the rest of my life." Vanessa smiled wistfully. "It doesn't seem too much to ask for, and I don't understand why it's so hard to find."

"It's *not* too much to ask for. Don't ever think otherwise."

"Does anyone's life ever turn out the way they expected? Even people who don't come from a family of mad bastards like mine?" Vanessa shrugged. "I think most of us make do with whatever comes our way. That's as good as it ever gets."

A man in a suit bumped into Vanessa as he passed, knocking her off balance. She would've fallen had Mia not grabbed her, but the man never even slowed down, let alone apologized.

Mia scowled and spun on her heel. "Hey! You could've at least said 'Excuse me,' asshole!"

"Mia, don't," Vanessa said as the businessman flipped the finger in their direction. "It's okay. Come on."

Still scowling, Mia stalked down the sidewalk, hardly noticing others giving her a wide berth. "Why the hell don't you ever stick up for yourself?"

"Why should I? That's what I've got you for."

Startled, Mia wasn't sure how to interpret that cool statement until she saw Vanessa's smile. "Well, you should've at least *glared* at him."

They reached the unassuming single-story brick building that housed Haddington Reproductions. Security grids covered the windows, and the front and back doors were protected by a very expensive alarm system, as was the door that led from the reception area to the workshop. Sometimes, like now, there was even a guard on duty.

Mia sighed. "Home sweet home. You almost done with the reliquary?"

"Getting there. I'm having trouble with the inlay; the colors keep coming out too bright." Vanessa grinned. "It's the Curse of the Eudoxia Reliquary. Woe and misfortune unto those who touch it. Even a fake."

"The curse doesn't seem to have done Mal Toller any harm," Mia pointed out wryly. "If you want, I can give you a hand when I'm done with the earrings."

Jewelry constituted the bulk of the Eudoxia collection, and since that was her area of expertise, Mia had been working on a steady stream of varying items while Vanessa struggled over the little reliquary.

"I don't know why Hugh's been such a pain in the ass," Mia added. "We're on schedule, and— Hey, it looks like we have a visitor."

"That's not Mr. Toller's Benz."

Thank God. Toller was a lecherous prick who always found an opportunity to brush up against her backside when he visited the workshop.

"It must be that journalist Hugh said would be visiting this week. I didn't think we'd see him until tomorrow." Mia punched in the security code for the back door, then entered, Vanessa at her heels. "Maybe this will improve Hugh's mood. He loves being the center of attention."

As the door shut behind them with a solid thump, Mia saw Hugh by the vault with a tall, dark-haired man who stood with his back to them. She admired what she could see of him, as well as the fine cut of his suit. She hoped the front looked as good as the back. If she had to be pestered while on deadline, it would help if the pest was attractive.

Hugh wore his standard baggy black pants, black shirt, and ever-present black fedora. He caught Mia's eye and smiled.

"Ah, there you are," his deep voice boomed cheerfully. "It's about time you two got back. This is Mr. William Tiernay, the freelance journalist who's doing a piece for *Antiquities Review Magazine*. He's here to write a feature about our work on the Eudoxia collection."

Mia's breath stopped in her throat before the man even turned around. Heat rolled over her, and her heart beat so loudly she could hardly hear Hugh. The entire room spun down to a narrow, focused point that included only the man's face.

No matter how many years passed, she'd never forgotten the strong jaw and cheekbones, the firm, full mouth, or those dark eyes beneath impossibly long lashes.

"Mr. Tiernay, these are my two assistants, Mia Dolan and—"

"Will?" Mia interrupted, her voice an octave higher. "Oh, my God . . . it *is* you!"

Three

WILL FROZE, STARING AT THE WIDE-EYED WOMAN IN front of him. *Well, it's been twelve years, idiot. What were the chances she'd still be Mia Shaeffer?*

A split second later, red-hot fury filled him. He was going to fucking kill Ben Sheridan. He'd *known* and hadn't said a word—unless "you won't need an alias" counted as a warning.

Shaking her head in disbelief, Mia said, "I just . . . I can't believe this!"

Instinct kicked in then, forcing back the shock and anger. This was a role like any other, nothing more than improvising and smooth talking. Taking a quick, head-clearing breath, he said, "Hello, Mia. It's been a long time."

She was even more beautiful than he remembered. Generous curves filled out her black cargo pants and red silk sweater, though her curling dark hair was now shoulder-length rather than falling to the middle of her back. And her eyes . . . the same wide, dreamy-soft brown eyes dominated her heart-shaped face, with its single dimple on the right cheek and full mouth that smiled so easily.

That mouth now curved up in a shy smile. She hesitated, then hugged him lightly, lips brushing across his cheek. Before he could think better of it, Will hugged her back.

He was *hugging* one of his suspects.

He'd forgotten how she'd always fit against him just right, the top of her head coming right below his chin—and she must've forgotten about their last conversation, all the hateful things they'd said to each other. Otherwise she never would've dared touch him like this.

Mia eased away, her smile fading as he let her go and took a step back toward much-needed emotional safety.

Haddington cleared his throat. "I take it you two know each other."

"Will's an old friend from my days at the uni." She glanced at the tall, blond woman who'd come in with her, who still stood by the door. "And an old boyfriend. I'm . . . well, *shocked* doesn't cover it." Turning to Will, she said, "You're the last person I ever expected to see again."

No shit. "Yeah, it still surprises me sometimes that I ended up in the art business." That, at least, was the absolute truth.

"When I last talked with you," Mia said, "you were going to teach high school."

"And when I last talked to you, you wanted a career in museum conservation."

And a boyfriend who "understood" your needs and your dreams.

The sharp bitterness took him by surprise; he'd sworn he'd put aside the anger and blame years ago, and moved on.

"And here I am creating legal fakes, instead." She briefly dropped her gaze. "Not quite what I'd planned, but I have a certain talent for it. Gotta go where the talent takes you."

Will hoped it hadn't taken her to the wrong side of the law. In the short time he'd spent talking with Haddington, the man had struck him as too transparent to concoct any kind of scheme. The slender blonde radiated a nervousness typical of the shy and awkward; though pretty, next to Mia she faded into invisibility. His first impression was that she didn't look the type to plan or pull off a major art heist, either.

Yet within the week, he'd expose one of them as a thief.

After a moment, Will said softly, "You haven't changed much."

"I wish—but I'm sure that's not true." A faint blush colored her cheeks. "You, on the other hand, have grown into a very handsome man. And it *is* nice to see you again, Will."

Awkward as hell was more like it, judging by the expression in her eyes.

"What an amazing coincidence . . . bloody *amazing*," Haddington said, beaming with undisguised delight. "You two will have a lot to catch up on, then, won't you? Since you've already talked to me, Will, please feel free to use my office if you'd like to get reacquainted with Mia. Vanessa and I can get back to work while you talk."

"Thanks, but that won't be necessary." Relief flashed across Mia's dark eyes, and Will added, "I'm beat. I've been in airports and planes for almost two days straight, and I was thinking of keeping things brief today and getting down to business tomorrow morning."

Initial shock and potential complications aside, the fact that he and Mia already knew each other could be useful. If nothing else, it would make asking necessary questions that much easier.

With that in mind, he turned back to Mia. "Maybe we could get together tomorrow for breakfast, before you start work?"

The blonde sighed behind him, and Mia suddenly smiled. "That would be perfect. There's a café about three blocks from here called Bella's Bistro. How about I meet you there at seven?"

"I'll be there. It'll be great to have a chance to catch up with each other."

Amazingly, he meant it—and along with the realization came a stab of guilt. Dismissing it, he turned to the quiet blonde, who was watching him with undisguised curiosity. Like Mia, she was dressed casually, wearing jeans and a plain white shirt.

"My apologies, Ms. Sharpton, for not introducing myself." Smiling, he held out his hand. "It's a pleasure to meet you."

She took his hand, squeezing it quickly before pulling away and stepping back. "No apologies required. I'd be distracted, too, if I were in your place. And please, call me Vanessa. We're not very formal here."

Haddington clapped his hands, his droopy brows making Will think of a basset hound in a fedora. "Excellent. Glad that's all settled. Now, then, you two can get back to whatever you were doing. Shall I start the grand tour, Will?"

Glad for the chance to put a little distance between him and Mia, Will nodded. "Yes, please."

The tour didn't take long. Haddington Reproductions provided an appropriately artsy reception area for clients who didn't want to risk getting paint or sawdust on their suits. The workshop was dominated by big wooden benches, computers with massive monitors, and power tools separated from the workstations to reduce noise and dust contamination. Safety goggles sat by the drill press and table saw, the sander and lathe, and the wax-casting station looked messy and well-used. The whole area smelled of wood, hot wax, paint, wet clay, glue, and oiled machine parts.

There wasn't a horizontal or vertical surface that hadn't been used for storage. Rolls of canvas hung from the ceiling, suspended over a cutting table as in a fabric store. Tall shelving units lined the back wall, each holding dozens of clear plastic bins in various sizes, full of paint tubes or jars or cans, brushes, chisels and spatulas, and a jumble of art-related tools. A bookshelf outside Hugh's office was crammed full of art and art history books.

A bench, computer desk, and microscopes for detail work equipped each workstation, and Will located the source of the pungent scent of freshly cut wood. Lumber for frames and other projects was stacked against the back wall, beside the large vault bolted to the concrete floor.

There were no windows in this area, and Will didn't notice additional cameras, not even by the vault. Still, the security was impressive; its only real flaw was that it focused on keeping unwanted people from getting inside. When it came to keeping something inside from getting out, it was all but useless.

Inside jobs were a bitch. There wasn't much any museum, gallery, or estate could do to protect itself from betrayal by a trusted insider.

"What's in the vault?" Will asked.

"Anything we need to keep secure, of course," Haddington answered, giving the bulky metal of the vault door a fond pat. "Right now we're working on three reproduction projects. One's a standard copy of Old Masters for the CEO's office at a new investment banking firm, another is a small collection of Greek vases and figures for a traveling exhibit to inner-city schools—we're doing that one on a tight budget that's proving to be quite the challenge—and the Eudoxia collection."

"For which the budget is limitless," Will said.

"Mal's paying us for the best of the best, and that's what we're here to deliver." Hugh moved away. "The vault's also where we keep gold leaf and silver, as well as rougher gemstones for projects that require them. We contract out to local jewelers for any actual cutting: it saves time."

"That's a specific skill?"

"Yes, and I'm not any good at it. Nor is Mia or Vanessa."

"But they have their own skills."

"Oh, yes. Vanessa is trained in art and can reproduce anything in paint or inlay from Neolithic to pop culture. Mia is my jewelry and metals expert. We get a *lot* of requests for jewelry reproductions, which keeps her very busy."

Will glanced at Mia. She smiled at him, then returned her attention to a pair of gold and pearl earrings he recognized. Lady Eudoxia had been a jewelry addict; not much different from any modern teenage girl who all but lived in a mall.

"And you?" Will asked. "What's your area of expertise?"

"A little of everything, though wood carving and sculpting was my forte at the British Museum. I help out wherever I'm needed."

"So is Vanessa working on the reliquary?"

Will knew she was, but he wanted a closer look. When Haddington nodded and headed around the partition to stand inside Vanessa's work cubicle, Will followed.

Will instantly picked up on the tension that hummed around the woman. "Do you mind if I watch?" he asked.

"I'm not used to it, but I don't mind. I'm nearing the final stages now. The reds on the petals here aren't quite right. I'm having a little trouble with them."

He'd have to take her at her word, because what sat on her bench looked to his eyes identical to the pictures in the file. The reliquary was an amazing piece: barely three inches long and only an inch deep, dominated by a colorful cloisonné panel of the crucified

Christ on the front with a stylized floral border. The hinges were edged in gold niello. A fragile sliver of wood attached to a sharp thorn, darkened by what some believed to be the blood of Jesus Christ himself, was still nestled within the inner compartment of the original.

A fake, like most relics from those days, but it made for a good story. The legendary curse, and the strange deaths of a number of its owners since its discovery in 1876, only added to the notoriety. The reliquary was by far the best sound bite in the funerary goods of a wealthy, privileged girl who'd died in childbirth when she'd been only nineteen.

Some people babble when nervous, but Vanessa Sharpton seemed the quiet type. He'd have to nudge her along to get her to talk. "This must've taken you a lot of time."

"Yes, it's been quite the project. I had a couple false starts and few uneasy nights before it all started to come together." Her long, thin fingers trembled as she patiently sifted through red paint chips. She looked over at him. "It's funny, but Mia was just talking about you before we walked in."

"Vanessa!"

Will glanced at Mia, then back at a pink-cheeked Vanessa. "Really? What did she say?"

"Maybe I shouldn't have said anything. It wasn't all that—"

"We were swapping stories about dates from hell," Mia interrupted. "I told her about our first date, when I tried to roll up the window, but—"

"—stuck your arm inside the car to roll it up. I remember that." The memory flooded back with an intensity that took him by surprise, and he couldn't help smiling.

She'd been wearing a sexy black dress, and he'd wanted to touch her so bad it had hurt. Her flustered response, her self-conscious smile . . . damn if he hadn't fallen in love with her right then and there. As naïve as he'd been, and ruled by his dick, he'd never stood a chance.

"Figures." Mia's glum voice cut across his thoughts. "Of all the things to remember, it would be that one."

"I thought you were cute." He met those dark, heavy-lidded eyes, and for a moment he completely forgot about Haddington and Vanessa. "That's what I remember, anyway."

He remembered the sex, too, which had been excellent. There'd been many good days before things had soured—and all of it was ancient history, he reminded himself, useful now only if it could be turned to his advantage.

"Sorry," Will said to Hugh. "I know I'm not here to talk about college days."

Haddington appeared disappointed that the personal

detour had ended. "Back to the boring work thing, then?"

Will laughed. "Boring? How can you, a man who spends hours working with two such beautiful and talented women, say that?"

Haddington chuckled and pushed up the brim of his fedora. "There is that."

"I bet their husbands are jealous of all the hours you spend locked away back here with them."

"Neither lovely lady is married. Not that they would have anything to do with an old bore like me anyway." In an exaggerated whisper Haddington added, "You might be interested to know that Mia is romantically unencumbered. Vanessa is, sadly, quite taken."

Despite Haddington's statement, he could still be involved with one of his employees—or both. Will had seen too much over the years to dismiss any possibility. If Vanessa Sharpton had a boyfriend, he'd need investigating as well.

"Any more questions, then?" Haddington asked. "Or are you done for the night?"

"I've soaked up enough information for today. I'll be back tomorrow with lots of questions, though."

After collecting his briefcase, Will nodded at Mia—and he could feel her gaze on him until the door shut behind him.

Outside, in the crisp evening air, he let out a long

sigh, feeling the tension in his shoulders finally ease. Mia's presence put his cover at risk, but she'd also handed him a tailor-made role. All he had to do was slip into it and play it through to the end.

If she was guilty, he'd still do the job he'd come here to do, personal feelings aside. If she was innocent, there'd be no harm. Maybe her feelings would be hurt when he suddenly disappeared, but she'd get over it.

"Karma," Will muttered, getting into his car. "And payback's a bitch, baby."

Four

BEN SHERIDAN RESTED HIS FOREARMS AGAINST HIS OF-
fice window, the glass cool against his skin. The sun was
setting over Elliott Bay, painting the sky in fading stria-
tions of purple-blue and orange, and the deep, muffled
blare of a ferry sounded in the distance.

Behind him, his monitor spilled light across his
darkened office, the email still incandescent in its ac-
cusation and anger:

> *These are people. They are not walking weapons*
> *that you point and shoot at your whim. You will*
> *not send out one of my operatives on a personally*
> *difficult assignment without their full knowledge in*
> *advance. Tiernay has earned his chance to say no.*
>
> *Once upon a time, you had a conscience. It's*
> *time you found it again.*

And once upon a time he'd been out there working, fighting, and getting dirty along with his people. Now he was leashed in an ivory tower, the one who had to make those trips to tell parents, a wife or husband or kid, that their loved one wasn't coming home. He was the one who had to make the final decisions, the one who had to play mediator when one of their people fucked up beyond all belief, who had to be on hand 24/7 to respond to anything from a disaster to a simple question.

For all intents and purposes, *he* was Avalon—which made him not only responsible for human lives and priceless pieces of art and history but also a highly visible figurehead. So far there hadn't been any trouble his bodyguards couldn't handle, but one of these days, that would change.

Von Lahr was up to something; he'd felt certain of it ever since the L.A. incident, when the fugitive they'd cornered had managed to play Avalon and von Lahr against each other. His people had gone in blind, but von Lahr had shown up knowing that it was a trap.

His presence in L.A. that night felt personal, more of an attack than a swat at an obstacle in his way. Ben had no facts to back up his suspicions, only a strong gut instinct, but it was one more reason why he couldn't allow himself to be distracted with guilt over Will Tiernay.

Tiernay was the best suited for the assignment, regardless of whether he'd have to deal with an old girl-friend who might've sold out her boss. Despite the playboy persona he cultivated, Will could be counted on to keep out of trouble—unlike a few others on Ben's unofficial payroll.

Outside his office, Ben heard the rapid clicking of fingers on a keyboard as Ellie worked on quarterly reports for the *other* business, the official one. Sheridan Expeditions needed his management even while he organized a small army of men and women around the world, enforcing laws most countries didn't have the resources to enforce on their own. It wasn't that the police didn't care when priceless art and artifacts went missing, but the loss of luxury goods simply wasn't as important as murders, rapes, and missing children.

But the world had changed in the hundred years since Avalon had been formed. The criminals had changed, and the way they did business had changed. Working in the shadows was no longer efficient or practical. If ever there was a right time for mercenaries to go legit, that time was now. Operating this way was like fighting with one hand tied behind his back.

Unfortunately, he didn't have the power to change how Avalon operated.

The phone rang. Ben turned from the window, waiting as Ellie answered. A moment later she poked her head past the doorway, looking a little worried. "Will's on the secure line. He doesn't sound happy."

No, he wouldn't.

"That's the call I've been waiting for. When I'm through, we can quit for the night."

She nodded, quietly closing the door behind her.

Ben walked to his desk and picked up the phone. "Sheridan."

"You sonofabitch."

Briefly closing his eyes, he said, "So I've been told."

Five

WILL SAT ON THE EDGE OF HIS HOTEL BED. "DON'T TRY to tell me you didn't know about her."

There was a brief hesitation. "No, there's no point in denying it now."

Will leaned forward, resting his elbows on his knees. "Jesus Christ, Ben—why didn't you just tell me?"

"Because I couldn't afford to have you say no. I don't have anyone else to spare, and even if I did, you're the man for this job. Besides, it was a long time ago. If she's half the woman you remember, then she's not involved and you have nothing to worry about."

"You had no right to keep this from me." Will tamped down a fresh rush of anger. "The second she saw me, my cover was compromised."

"And you handled it, didn't you?" Ben asked.

Will recognized the attempt to defuse the situation. "I trust you to send me into a situation with all the facts I need. If I can't trust you to be straight with me, then we have a problem."

"I would never send you in without information if doing so would endanger you or others. Your life wasn't threatened. The worst was that now you know you have a personal connection to a suspect, and you're pissed about it. But look on the bright side: you didn't have to act surprised to see her."

Leave it to Ben to reduce genuine shock and anger to minor inconveniences. Yes, his reaction to Mia had been more real than any act, but that still didn't make the man's manipulation acceptable.

And if he sensed a whiff of hypocrisy in that thought, it wasn't something he could afford to look at too closely.

"Do something like that again, Ben, and you'll find yourself short another body on the payroll."

"Understood. Is there anything else to report?"

Will couldn't tell Ben's mood from that flat, even voice. "Not yet. The security is solid, but that doesn't matter for an inside job. I'm meeting Mia for breakfast tomorrow, and I'll work on finding a way to get inside so I can look around and set up surveillance."

After a moment's silence, Ben asked in that same flat tone, "Are you going to be able to do this?"

"Kind of late to be asking me that."

"It has to be asked."

Sitting up straight, Will rubbed at the ache between his brows. "Yes, I can." And it was true, the initial shock aside. "Once a cop, always a cop. I can still see that thin white line of goodness and virtue. When will the courier get here with the rest of the information?"

"It'll be there by noon tomorrow."

"Have them leave it at the front desk. I'll pick it up when I get a chance." With nothing else to add, he said, "I'll check in tomorrow."

"All right. And Will, I am sorry that she's involved in this."

"Yeah. So am I," Will said, and hung up.

He tossed his suit coat onto the chair by the small table in the corner. The tie followed, then his shirt. Taking a beer from the minibar, he sat on the bed and opened the Haddington file Ellie had given him.

Nothing new turned up in the second reading. Hugh Haddington was a forty-eight-year-old overachiever who was very good at the restoration and reproduction part of his business but less skilled in the running of it. Vanessa Sharpton was thirty-six, born and raised in London, and trained at the University of London. He now knew she had a boyfriend, and he could easily get the man's name from one of the three. He also knew Mia had been married and apparently was now single.

Will leaned back, recalling the pleasure and wariness in her eyes—and the reality of what was at stake hit with a sudden, unpleasant jolt. Rubbing again at the knot of pressure gathering behind his brows, he put the file aside.

Too restless yet to sleep, he pulled out the folder on the Balestrini murder. As he browsed through it, he found nothing to change his initial feeling that solving this girl's murder would be nearly impossible. So many people had disappeared during those war years, and millions more had died. All the world had gone crazy, and the strangulation of one girl in an obscure Italian village would've hardly made a blip.

Except to her family. After this long, it was easy to forget that she'd been someone's daughter, someone's sister, someone's friend. In a way, it was good Ben had given him the project. It would help him remember why he'd gotten into law enforcement.

As he mulled over Ben's explanation, something about the timing of that second disappearance nagged at him. Something he should remember, but he couldn't fight through the fuzz of exhaustion to puzzle it out.

After continually nodding off as he tried to decipher a report written in Italian, Will gave up for the night. He stripped, shut off the lights, and collapsed facedown.

The air conditioner hummed, and from outside came the whoosh of passing cars. Sleep hovered on the edges of his awareness, lapping closer and closer, but his mind wouldn't let go.

His thoughts kept circling back to Mia—that first date, and how another week had passed before she'd let him kiss her. He remembered the first time they'd made love, and how nervous he'd been. From the very start, he'd known she was impulsive and ambitious, but he couldn't imagine her ambition ever crossing over to thievery.

Of course, a lot could happen in twelve years. People changed. He was a glaring example of that.

Will rolled over to his back, not liking *that* line of thought. He forced himself to concentrate on the hum of the air conditioner, and when his physical weariness finally overpowered his restlessness, he slipped into a deep, dreamless sleep.

Will arrived at the café a half hour early and spent the time formulating a plan to get past the security at Haddington. He needed to set up a few inconspicuous monitoring devices to help him keep track of computer use, phone calls, and after-hours activity. He'd considered asking Hugh for a temporary security pass, but that would raise too many questions. If he couldn't find a way in within the next day or two, he'd try that route as a last resort.

A young mother in a business suit sat with her toddler at the table next to his, stopping for a breakfast snack on the way to day care. As the mother talked on her cell phone, the little girl squirmed on the chair, coloring her place mat, picking at a muffin, and working on a glass of milk. The girl kept turning toward him, and although he liked kids well enough, the staring was getting to him.

Will tried a smile. Maybe that was all she wanted and then she'd get back to her crayons. The girl blinked, giggled, and whipped her face away. Then she turned toward him again and waggled her fingers.

Christ. It would be a long wait if the kid was going to play peekaboo the entire time. Cute went only so far.

"Hi," she said.

"Hi," he replied, smiling in spite of himself. "What's your name?"

"Jen-fur."

"Did you like your breakfast?" Will asked, pointing at the mess that had been a large blueberry muffin.

By this time, the mother had noticed her daughter flirting outrageously with the lone man at the next table. With a mixed expression of wariness and ruefulness, she said "Hold on a sec" to whomever she was talking to on the phone, then pulled her daughter back around to face her.

"Jennifer, eat your muffin and mind your own business. It's not nice to disturb other people when they're eating breakfast."

"But he's not *eating*," the girl pointed out. "He's drinking coffee."

"Same thing, for most people." The woman smiled at Will. "Sorry about that. This child knows no fear."

Will smiled back. "Not a problem."

The mother returned to her phone call, and shot her daughter a look so stern it would've stopped *him* cold. With one last grin at Will, the kid resumed scribbling over her place mat.

Once, he'd expected his life to turn out like this: married and juggling career and parenthood. *Everyone* had it expected it of him and Mia, the perfect couple.

Then the perfect couple had derailed into the perfect mess. She'd been his first love, his first heartbreak, his first lesson that the world wasn't always fair, even when you tried to do the right thing and played by all the rules.

It embarrassed him to remember that last phone call. He'd *cried*, for Christ's sake, his voice raw with pain, repeating "How could you do that to me?" over and over.

Now he couldn't imagine living that old dream. It was one thing to mix fatherhood and a city commute but another when the commute was to the other side of the world. What would it be like for his kids if he had to talk about homework from hotel rooms in Rio, Istanbul, Seoul, or Paris? Would that be fair to any kid, or a woman he cared about?

People managed it, though; he knew of operatives in Avalon who had families—

And why the *hell* was he even thinking about this?

It had to be delayed shock—or his subconscious warning him to consider his options unless he wanted to spend the rest of his life alone in dark, empty rooms passing the hours waiting and watching.

Like now, waiting for the woman who'd turned his

life upside down twelve years ago. If he wasn't careful, she'd do it all over again.

The second Mia arrived, Will picked her out in the breakfast rush, shamelessly taking in the sight of her before she spotted him.

Her dark hair was still damp from the shower, and she wore just enough lipstick and blush to play up her full mouth and high cheekbones. Her olive-tinted skin looked flawless, except for that childhood scar beneath her right eye. Somehow that little flaw transformed her wide-eyed, heart-shaped face from pretty to interesting.

Her black pants hugged the round curve of her rear, and the burgundy sweater accentuated the swell of her breasts. They were fuller now, and he couldn't help wondering how they'd fill his hands, if the touch of his tongue was still enough to set her off, arching her back and making those soft little sounds—

Just then, Mia turned and caught sight of him as he shifted uncomfortably on his chair. Recognition lit her face, and as she came toward the table, dread swept over him, burying that unexpected rush of lust.

Time to earn his paycheck.

Six

WILL STOOD AS SHE REACHED HIS TABLE, AND DESPITE her jitters, Mia couldn't help smiling. "I see you still have those old-fashioned manners."

And the same boyish smile that had stolen her heart at eighteen, although nothing else boyish remained. The man before her was older, harder-edged . . . Why did men always seem to look *better* as they aged?

"Have you been waiting long?" she asked as he pulled out a chair for her.

"Not long at all."

He wore a dark gray suit with a black shirt and black jacquard tie, and he looked so handsome that it took all her willpower not to stare. "Are you trying to blend in with us arty folk in arty black?"

"Purely coincidence."

His voice sounded distinctly cooler than it had yesterday. Not a good sign. But then, what did she expect?

"It's a nice suit. Life's been good to you, I take it."

"I've developed an appreciation for the finer things."

"Growing up can have that effect on a person."

As he sat, her jitters bloomed into unease. Once she'd been able to tell his mood just by looking in his eyes, but that no longer held true. She'd give anything to know what was going through his mind right now.

Then again, maybe it was better not to know. "So," she said. "Tell me what you've been up to all these years."

"Work and more work, mostly." He flashed a quick smile, and her tension eased a fraction. "After graduation I went into journalism, and there were a lot of jobs in different places. Eventually I started doing work for *Antiquities Review Magazine* and a few others, and the years have been good ones. How about you?"

Mia tipped her head to one side, brow raised. "Wait a minute, that was *far* too abbreviated. At least tell me how your parents are doing. And your brother?"

She hadn't noticed a wedding band, but couldn't quite bring herself to ask if he'd married.

"My parents are fine. Still living in Toledo. My brother is married and has three little girls. I think they've given up trying for a boy." He caught the waiter's attention and signaled they were ready to order. "Hugh said yesterday that you'd been married."

Looking away, Mia nodded. A lot of people had ex-spouses, but she hated admitting to failure of any kind.

Nor was it something she liked to talk about, and especially not with *him*, the major mistake of her life.

"Philip was a conservationist at the British Museum. We met while we were both visiting the Louvre, and got married a few months later. We divorced after a couple years. Irreconcilable differences. The usual."

"No kids?"

Mia shook her head. "Just a ferret. I got custody."

He smiled at that, which knocked loose a little more of her tension. After placing their orders, he asked, "So there's no man in your life right now?"

"Not at the moment, no." Her face warmed, and she glanced away from his direct gaze to fiddle with her napkin. "And you? Seeing anyone?"

Will shook his head. "Not really. Work's been a priority lately."

"I understand how that goes," Mia said with feeling. "It's funny, but I always imagined you would be settled down by now with a nice little family. I was the vagabond, not you."

He shifted, as if uncomfortable with the direction of the conversation. "So now you're in the U.S. again. Does it feel good to be back?"

"Oh, yes. I loved living in Europe, but it's great to be home again."

"Your co-workers probably feel homesick, though."

"Maybe a little. Hugh is close to his family, and he has a lot of friends in London, so of course he misses that. Vanessa is glad to be as far away from her family as possible. Not a lot of happy memories there for her." At his questioning look, she hesitated, then added, "It wasn't a good situation. Substance abuse, lots of emotional issues."

"It happens," Will said. "Too bad for her, though."

"She got out and never looked back, but that sort of thing stays with a person. You'll have noticed she's not very assertive."

Will nodded. "It was generous of Haddington to take you both with him when he relocated. You must enjoy working for him."

This definitely wasn't how she'd imagined their reunion conversation to unfold. She hadn't been sure what to expect, but it hadn't been . . . well, shoptalk. "Is this an interview? Or off the record?"

Something in her voice must've hinted at her disappointment, because he sat forward and covered her hand with his. Only then did she realize she'd twisted the napkin into a long, sharp point. His hand was warm, and it completely enveloped her own.

"Sorry. I just wanted to know what you've been up to, what life's been like. And yes, all the questions are off the record."

His hand felt . . . nice, more than it should have, and she slipped her hand away. Several awkward seconds passed, then he picked up his coffee.

"I love the work," Mia said, to cover the moment.

"It's not what I'd planned on doing with my life, but I can't say I have any regrets."

Except one, now sitting in front of her. All those times she'd wished for a chance to try to make amends for hurting him, and now that the chance had presented itself, she didn't know if she had the courage to take it.

"Things are going well, and the work we're doing for Toller will help boost our reputation a *lot*," Mia said, hoping that he didn't notice her nervousness. "I'm settling in nicely. I have an apartment about seven blocks from here. I shared it with Vanessa until she moved in with her boyfriend. Hugh lives downtown, but I like being able to walk to work."

"So you and Vanessa have been friends for a long time?"

"Oh, yes. We met at the museum in London and hit it off right away. People don't always understand why, since we have such different personalities." And sometimes people hinted it was a case of her wanting to take care of people, the way she'd "needed" to manage her ex. "I'm the stand-in for Van's aggressive self, since she'll do anything to avoid a whiff of conflict. People tend to take advantage of her, and I hate seeing that."

Will looked amused. "I take it her boyfriends have to meet your approval."

Mia shrugged, a little embarrassed. "Not really, although Vanessa gets on my case about it every now and then. What can I say? I always was the bossy type."

"Those bossy vagabonds building castles in the air. Nothing but trouble."

His words stung. She might've brushed it off as oversensitivity on her part had his eyes matched the smile.

Steeling herself, she put down her coffee. "I owe you an apology."

His gaze shifted away. "You don't owe me anything, Mia. It was a long time ago."

"That's doesn't matter. I treated you terribly. I didn't mean to, but at the time I thought telling you would hurt you. It never occurred to me that *not* telling you would hurt you even worse, or that if you called when . . . God, I was so stupid back then."

It didn't matter how much time had passed—she'd never forget how her heart had seemed to stop beating when Lorenz answered her phone. Will had been on the other end, and it wasn't possible to explain away a man in her bedroom at 4:00 AM, Venice time. Especially since she'd stopped returning Will's calls and answering his letters. It was an awful way for him to find out, and the call had gone from bad to a thousand times worse.

"I think I'd convinced myself if I just stopped all contact with you, the problem would magically go away. It's hard to understand how I could've felt that way; I was certainly old enough to know better."

Time crawled, the silence between them all the

more difficult because of the surrounding din of voices. Mia forced herself to look up from the napkin, which she'd mangled again.

Will was watching her, frowning slightly. "I'm not going to say it didn't hurt, but we were just kids. You were living so far away, and it would've happened sooner or later. If I'd been in your place, I can't say I would've acted any differently."

"That's . . . a very generous thing to say."

"Not at all. It's the truth."

Oddly enough, she'd wanted him to be angrier; his calmness only added to the guilt. "I betrayed your trust. That's the worst thing one person can do to another. You'd *never* do something like that, I know it."

Emotion shadowed his eyes, gone so quickly that she couldn't tell what it had been. He leaned back, then shifted, and as he opened his mouth Mia added quickly, "You don't have to say anything. I know it doesn't make any difference at this point, and for all I know, you've long since forgotten about me."

Will sighed, focusing on some point behind her. "No, I didn't forget."

"I didn't intend for this to be so uncomfortable, but it was something I needed to say—if only because ignoring it would've made things difficult for you here." She hesitated, then added softly, "If it helps any, I thought about you a lot. You were always the one—"

"—that got away," Will finished. "I know."

Surprised, she didn't know what to say and was grateful that the waiter arrived with their breakfast. Will had ordered the real deal: eggs, bacon, and toast. She'd ordered only a cranberry-orange muffin. It was a monstrous muffin—the café's specialty—but his meal looked and smelled downright decadent. She envied his ability to pack away food like that and still look hard and lean.

Noticing her gazing longingly at his plate, he offered her a forkful, which she waved off, embarrassed. "No, thanks. It looks wonderful and smells even better, but I can feel my hips expanding just watching you eat."

She couldn't get over how much he'd changed, physically. It wasn't just maturity adding strength and self-confidence, either. Something else kept snaring her attention, though she couldn't put her finger on it.

Had he always been this heart-stoppingly handsome? She remembered him being cute, but no one would call him cute now, not with those dark looks, the broad set of his shoulders and harder lines of his face. She still envied those long lashes, and his mouth was . . . A sudden, unsettling urge to trace her finger along his bottom lip swept over her. What other changes were hidden beneath that expensive suit?

The thought warmed her uncomfortably, and she looked away, shaken. As she picked at her muffin, Will started asking about the details of her job. After a while, as the awkwardness eased between them, she tired of the questions about her and asked, "What's it like, being a journalist?"

He shrugged. "It's all about asking the right questions, although that's not always as easy as it sounds."

Then he asked more questions about her time at the British Museum, and Mia got the hint, loud and clear, that he didn't want to talk about himself.

Maybe this was "off the record," but the conversation wasn't personal. Not for him.

After finishing breakfast, Will led her to his rental car. "I know it's only a few blocks to Haddington, but my car's here, so we might as well take it."

"We'll be there before everybody else. There won't be a lot to keep you entertained."

Will flashed her a wide, easy smile. "I won't mind spending more time alone with you."

Startled by his abrupt change in mood, Mia didn't answer. Did he mean what she thought he meant? If so, where had *that* come from? He'd been polite and friendly all along, but in a cool, distant way.

Maybe her blurted apology had cleared the air between them, but she still needed time to get her thoughts—and her feelings—about Will straight.

Mia was quiet during the short drive to the shop. After Will parked, he walked with her to the back door. Acutely conscious of him beside her, trying not to dwell on the flutters of a very inconvenient desire,

Mia punched in the security code and then pulled on the door handle. Since the door was reinforced steel, it took effort to haul it open, and she was glad for Will's help.

"If you'd like, I can show you what I've been working on," she offered. "Or I could make coffee and we could talk some more."

"How about both?"

Will continued to stand very close beside her. Nervous, her hands shaking, it took her three fumbling tries to find the light switch.

He *had* to know his effect on her, unless he was blind. If he stayed this close to her all day, it would take all her concentration to keep her focus on her work—rather than wondering if twelve years was too long to wait for makeup sex.

Seven

WILL WATCHED AND MEMORIZED THE SECURITY CODE
Mia entered. As soon as she went off to make a pot of
coffee, he jotted the sequence down in his notepad.

Too easy. Obviously it had never occurred to her
that letting him watch her open the door was a
breach in security. He wanted to believe it meant she
was innocent but knew better than to rely on that
alone.

Thanks to her talkativeness—and her trust that he
was the journalist he'd claimed to be—he knew much
more about everyone at Haddington. By noon he'd
have the rest of the files from Sheridan, and then he
could get serious about figuring out which one of them
he was hunting.

"Do you have a coffee preference? Hugh stocks a va-
riety, with Colombian his favorite."

"That sounds fine. Thanks."

Will shoved his hands in his pockets as she turned away.

Trust.

The word kept popping up: in his angry conversation with Ben, in Mia's apology, and then again when she declared he'd never be capable of betraying a trust.

In her eyes, he was still that naïve kid who'd made her the center of his little universe. Her assumption angered him, but it also made it easier to work his way inside her trust and make short work of his assignment. He'd be the old Will again, full of enthusiasm and conviction and optimism, wanting nothing more than to have a good time and be a good guy.

"Do you mind if I watch you work?" he asked when Mia settled at her workbench.

"Not at all," she said, pulling back her hair and securing it with a colorful tie.

He pushed the guilt away as he sat beside her. Whatever happened, happened, and he wouldn't have to deal with the fallout. When his work was done he'd simply disappear, "riding into the mist" as they called it at Avalon. He appreciated the irony, since the old Arthurian legends were about knights in shining armor, not mercenaries.

"You sure? I don't want to make you nervous."

"Why would I be nervous?" Her voice was light and easy, but he didn't miss the slight flush of color on her cheeks.

"I made Vanessa nervous."

"Men in general make Vanessa nervous. Give her a few days to get used to you, and she'll stop stuttering and looking everywhere but at you."

"So Vanessa is working on the reliquary because she's the paint and inlay expert?"

"Exactly." Mia bent over the earrings he'd seen yesterday, adjusting the gold settings for two large pearls. "And it's the most valuable and complicated item in the collection. She's been slaving over it since we began. In that time, I've essentially reproduced the entire jewelry collection."

He watched for several minutes, then asked, "Are those pearls real?"

"Yes, and it wasn't easy finding near matches to the originals. Sometimes we use synthetic jewels and gold leaf or a composite metal, but in this case it's all real. Toller wanted quality replicas."

Will leaned closer for a better look. The jewelry *was* amazing, intricate and elegant, and he realized she wasn't just a copyist but also an artist. "I had no idea you were so talented."

"It's funny—I was supposed to be a museum bureaucrat. I had no idea there was an artistic bone in my body."

"But you were always making things. In that apartment we had, you painted every room, and sewed curtains and slipcovers for the furniture."

"That's because we could only afford garage sale furniture. I wanted to make the place look less like the dive it was."

It had been years since he'd thought about the apartment they'd shared. Try as he might, he couldn't recall anything but the good times. "Yeah, but there were all those knickknacks and stuff that you made out of what looked like junk to me. I'd say all the signs were there."

"As the saying goes, we see what we want to see." She glanced at him. "Sometimes we don't see the truth even if it's right in front of us."

Shit! Had she figured out . . . ?

No. It wasn't possible. His alarm faded, suspicion rising in its place. He might not like it, but years of training to pick up body language and verbal cues were too deeply ingrained for him to ignore the warning signs of subterfuge, secrecy, and guilt.

Just then, the back door opened and Hugh Haddington strode in, wearing loose-fitting black pants and shirt and his fedora sitting at a jaunty angle.

"Hullo," he called. "Here early, are we? The coffee smells splendid. So what are your plans for the day, Will? More questions?"

"Lots of questions." Will stood with a genuine smile. Maybe it was the relentless cheerfulness, the droopy basset hound eyes, or Hugh's sense of style, but he found himself liking the guy.

Yet one of them *was* guilty: the cheerful and ener-getic Haddington, or the shy and amazingly talented Vanessa Sharpton, or Mia—he couldn't forget that, even for a second.

"What's the look for?" Haddington demanded. "You can't have questions for me that are as serious as that."

"Sure I do," Will replied lightly, slipping into the good-buddy role. "In fact, the biggest, most serious question of all."

Mia glanced up, smile hovering, but didn't say any-thing.

"What's that?" Haddington said, coffee cup in hand, looking faintly puzzled.

"C'mon, Hugh," Will said. "The question everyone wants to know is whether or not you ever take off that hat."

Haddington blinked in surprise as Mia laughed and said, "I've wondered that myself. I think maybe he even wears it to bed."

"Are you mocking me?" Haddington tried to sound offended, but he was grinning.

"Not at all. Because if you *do* always wear it, then the next big question is, how do you keep it on your head when one of those nor'easters blows in? Glue? Staples?"

"Magic," Mia said. "It's an enchanted hat."

Vanessa arrived right then, a little breathless, and said, "Who has an enchanted hat?"

"We're talking about Hugh's fedora," Will said.

"Oh." Vanessa frowned as she tried to puzzle it out.

Mia caught Will's eye and grinned. "Don't strain yourself, Van. We're thinking he never takes it off for a magical reason—like maybe he keeps the secrets of the universe inside his hatband."

"*You* think it's magic," Will said, easily picking up the teasing rhythm. "I was thinking glue or tape."

"Oh, that's so dull. Where's your imagination?"

"You're both absolutely insane." Hugh suspiciously eyed his coffee. "Is there something illegal in this?"

"But *why* are we talking about Hugh's hat? I missed something, I know it. I always do," Vanessa said with a sigh. "Still . . . I think I like the idea of secrets of the universe much better than glue. Not practical, but grander. More romantic."

And from there, the conversation derailed completely as Hugh, befuddled, listened to Mia spin tales about his hat, each more fantastical than its predecessor.

Will stood by and listened. God, yes, that imagination. She'd been imaginative in the bedroom as well. He vividly recalled the night she walked out of the bathroom with homemade pasties on her nipples and a fake grass hula skirt and pretended she was a stripper. All because they'd gotten into a fight the night before, when she'd found out he'd gone to a strip club with a couple of his friends.

Flummoxed by the sight, he'd taken several minutes to realize she'd made the pasties out of poster board and pasta shapes that she'd colored with Magic Markers.

"What are you smiling about?" Mia asked, once Hugh had disappeared into his office to answer a call.

He leaned toward her and whispered, "Pasta pasties."

Her eyes went wide, then she burst out laughing, a full-chested laugh that rippled over him with a sweetness that damn near ached. "Oh, my God. I'd forgotten about that."

"I never will. Even when I'm an old, old man, I'll still remember."

She blushed, and he found her response surprisingly . . . endearing. "I'm not surprised. I looked ridiculous. The horror of it must be burned for all eternity onto your retinas."

"You were the most beautiful girl I'd ever seen," he murmured. "You still are."

"You always were the romantic one, Will," she said, looking away. "And sweet."

Guilt rushed back with a vengeance. Annoyed, and realizing it was time to put some distance between them, Will left to talk with Vanessa. After mentally noting details about the reliquary as she worked on it, he spent more time asking Haddington questions, letting the man ramble on. Then he excused himself for lunch and headed back to his hotel.

As promised, the courier package was waiting for him at the front desk. Back in his room, he ordered a hamburger from room service, stripped off his coat and loosened his tie, then propped himself against the headboard to start reading through the report.

It gave him addresses, dates, basic facts. Still no obvious warning flags beyond what he already had: Haddington was teetering on the edge of solvency and had a taste for the finer things life had to offer; Vanessa Sharpton showed characteristics of a personality prone to subversion—Christ, the woman had a long history of loser boyfriends—and then there was Mia.

He couldn't find any hints at a motive in her files. She was financially secure and didn't even have a parking ticket, let alone a list of calls to the police concerning abusive situations, as there were in Vanessa's file.

Of the three, Mia should be on the bottom of his list of suspects, but his determination to think objectively about her made him look even harder for something.

The only mark against her was that she'd wasted no time in moving in with the Italian guy she'd been sleeping with when she dumped Will. She eventually left for Paris and hooked up with an art professor, and from what Will could tell, her relationships with the Italian student and the French professor were long-term, serious affairs that had ended amicably.

Lucky them.

Will scowled, forcing back the anger. Their dramatic crash-and-burn *had* been a long time ago, and he *had* gotten over it. Seeing her again simply reminded him of a dark stretch of days—nothing more, nothing less.

Scowl deepening, he returned his attention to the file, looking for information on her ex-husband. The marriage to Philip Dolan was so short-lived that the report had nothing useful on him. The only vaguely interesting item was that the London constables frequently came to Dolan's assistance because he had a habit of locking himself out of his flat. Why Mia had married a guy like that, Will couldn't even begin to guess.

It was midafternoon when he left the hotel and drove past the addresses listed in the files. He wanted to get a feel for the neighborhoods, gauge if Vanessa or Mia was obviously living beyond her means. One thing he'd learned about white-collar crime was that there didn't have to be any motive beyond money for someone to dip a toe into larceny, petty or grand. Greed, financial desperation, a tempting moment of opportunity—it didn't need to be any more complex than that.

Mia's apartment and neighborhood looked nice but average middle-class. The same held true for Vanessa. Only Hugh had provided himself with a lifestyle that would require plenty of cash to maintain.

Will then made a quick stop at the nearest Old Navy store to buy a pair of black pants and a black sweater baggy enough to conceal a gun. It took longer than he'd expected to find a vintage clothing shop and run down a black fedora, and by the time he drove back to Haddington, it was late afternoon.

His to-do list now included breaking into the workshop, setting up surveillance, and finding out the name of Vanessa's live-in boyfriend. He'd found nothing on the man in the files Ben had sent—surprising, since it sounded like a long-term relationship. That lack of information disturbed him, and he hoped going through the workshop and its computers would remedy that.

Everyone at Haddington was hard at work, so after asking a few token questions of Hugh, Will sat at the coffee table and hauled out his laptop, pretending to write the article while setting up surveillance software and reporting back to Ben.

"Will you be here long?" Vanessa asked, a little after six.

"Probably for another hour or so, then I'll head back to the hotel. Unless you all kick me out before then."

"No, I meant will you be in Boston for long." Vanessa stood, leaning on the top of her file cabinet to see him better.

"As long as it takes me to get the information I need. Probably a few days or so."

She glanced at Mia. "Well, I think this is so romantic! I mean in a general way, even if the two of you
aren't still together," she added hastily at Mia's warning glare. Hugh, plugged into his iPod and lost in concentration, was oblivious. "Mia used to talk about you
now and then. She always made you sound like such a
lovely man."

"That's because I *was* a nice guy," he said lightly.

"Vanessa, please." Mia looked embarrassed.

"But isn't it like one of those movies? Where the
guy from the past shows up and—"

"This is real life, not a movie," Mia said coolly, turning back to the earrings. "Meeting Will again was a big
surprise, but I think we're past the novelty of it now.
Time to get back to our regularly scheduled program
and all that."

A flash of hurt darkened Vanessa's eyes before she
turned away, and Will looked over at Mia. What the
hell? She'd been in a good mood earlier, why the attitude now?

"Oh, don't look like that, Van! I'm sorry for snapping at you." Mia's apologetic voice cut across Will's
thoughts. "I have the start of a headache, and it's been
a long week."

"Then take off for the day." Although he hadn't been
listening in, Hugh had still noticed Mia's mood. He
pulled his earbuds free. "You're almost done, right?"

"I still have to apply the patina and—"

"And that'll hardly take you any time. If you're going to pick up the slack for Vanessa and me for the next couple days, you might as well take a break while you have the chance. Have you been to Boston before, Will?"

"Once or twice for short visits."

"Maybe Mia could show you around," Hugh suggested. "You could hit all the local spots like the Freedom Trail and Boston Harbor. Faneuil Hall Marketplace is a must-see. I imagine you've been to all the local art museums, like the Gardner?"

Vanessa wasn't the only romantic. Judging by her suspicious expression, Mia had sniffed out the setup as well.

"Yes, I've been there often." The largest unsolved art theft in U.S. history happened at the Isabella Stewart Gardner Museum back in 1990, and Ben would like nothing better than to beat the FBI to solving the mystery and bringing the missing paintings back home.

Well, he had a few hours to kill before he could break into the workshop tonight, and he could probably coax a little more information out of Mia if he played his part carefully enough. "That would be good," he said. "If Mia doesn't mind."

She didn't look happy, but she didn't look entirely displeased, either. "Sure. I guess I wouldn't mind a break."

"And the rest of you aren't going to be staying too late, are you?" Will asked. "I have a feeling Mia isn't the only one who could use a break."

"No late night for me today. I have a movie date with friends at nine," Hugh said. "Van, luv, you're not staying late, either, are you?"

"Kos is picking me up after he gets off work at seven."

Kos would be the boyfriend. And with everyone gone well before midnight, Will could slip inside earlier than planned. Searching and setting up surveillance would take time, and the sooner he got started, the better.

Will stowed his laptop back in his briefcase, then headed to Mia's cubicle. "Ready to do some sightseeing?"

She nodded. "As soon as I put away my things. Are you sure you want to do this?" she asked, lowering her voice. "If it's just to be polite or to humor—"

"Not at all. I'd like it if you would show me around the neighborhood, at least."

A few minutes later Will was alone with Mia again, outside in the cool April breeze and gathering dusk. "Are you okay? You seem upset about something."

She sighed. "I'm fine. I just . . . It's a little like living in a fishbowl all of a sudden, with Hugh's looks and Vanessa's questions, and I was feeling bad for you. You're here to do a job, not get caught in a rerun of some maudlin little affair that ended years ago when your girlfriend cheated on you."

"It wasn't maudlin and it wasn't little. We were talking about getting married."

"And, as you pointed out earlier, we were still just kids."

"That doesn't make what we felt any less real." They'd stopped by his car. "How about I drive you to your apartment, find a place to park, and then after you change or feed the ferret, we can go out for dinner?"

She looked surprised. "We met for breakfast. Dinner seems—"

"I need to eat. I assume you need to eat as well."

"When you put it that way." She shrugged as if it weren't a big deal, but every tense line of her body, every stiff motion, revealed her nervousness. "There's a restaurant about two blocks from where I live. It's family-run and small, but the food is good. We could go there."

Will walked around to open the door for her, waving away her protests. "I know, I know. You can open your own doors, but please humor me."

Her smile warmed her eyes and eased the tension in her face. "At least there's no chance of me subjecting you to another car window fiasco."

Although he knew where she lived, Will asked her for directions as he headed out of the lot. It took longer to find a place to park than it did to drive to her building, and he finally managed to squeeze into a spot at the next street, around the corner.

"So what's your ferret's name?" he asked casually as they walked up the stairs to the second floor.

"Caligula."

He stared at her. "*Caligula?*"

"My ex-husband's idea. I wanted to call him Noodle because they're such boneless little things, but Philip won." As she approached her door, she pulled keys out of her jacket pocket. "This is it. Come on inside."

He followed her in, and as soon as she turned on the light he spotted a sleek, white-furred animal curled up on an overstuffed couch upholstered in a dark floral print. It eyed them without budging an inch.

"Will, meet Caligula. Cal, this is Will."

The ferret closed his eyes, and Will grinned. "He doesn't look too impressed."

"Ferrets can be snooty sometimes." She made an effort to sound nonchalant, but her voice was still a little tight. "Have a seat. If you're thirsty, help yourself to whatever's in the fridge."

"I'm good, thanks." Will sat on the matching chair across from the couch as Mia headed down the short hall to her bedroom. The ferret yawned, pink tongue curling, then followed silently.

It was a spacious apartment, with a separate kitchen, dinette, and living room. As befitted an older building, it boasted a few extra decorative touches, plaster crown moldings along the ceiling and windows, which were taller and narrower than modern ones. Mia had always been something of a packrat, and the place was crammed full of books, art and art prints, knickknacks, and lots of pillows. It struck him as an eclectic blend of English cottage and shabby chic, with touches of the East in wicker and bamboo and brightly colored Indian silk pillows embroidered with mirror disks. Her approach to decorating seemed to be as unpredictable as her moods. Still, it gave an impression of comfortable warmth.

He got up to look around, partly out of curiosity. The living room window overlooked the busy street. A lot of people just home from work were out walking dogs. Across the street a young couple sat talking on a porch step, heads bent toward each other.

As Will watched, they kissed, bodies pressing so closely together it was hard to tell where he ended and she began. The boy had his hands under the girl's shirt, and the embrace was sweet and sensual, and stirred a need Will hadn't felt in a very long time.

Frowning, he turned away from the window, and a moment later Mia emerged from the bedroom, having changed into dressier pants and a black sweater set.

"You're not at work now. No need to coordinate with your boss."

"Maybe I'm color coordinating with *you*." She

flicked his tie. "When did you get so conservative?"

Will arched a brow. "You think I'm conservative?"

"It's a *very* nice suit, and you look great in it, but I remember how much you hated to dress up. Shall we go?"

Once outside, they headed down an older residential street, as quiet and well-maintained as one would expect to find in any nice middle-class neighborhood.

The cool breeze smelled of freshly mowed grass and lilacs, with a hint of rain in the gathering clouds.

Maybe it was the promise of spring and new starts, or seeing the young couple lost in each other, but the impulse to take Mia's hand was so strong, so natural, that it almost made him feel as if the last twelve years had never passed. Every time she brushed against him, her arm a hint of warmth through his sleeve, he knew she wanted him to take her hand as well.

Again, there was no reason not to. All he had to do was step into whatever part he needed to play—friend, lover, confidant—as he had done countless times before this.

But if he fell into the old role, how long would it take before Mia sensed it wasn't real? Worse, what were the chances that he'd play the role too well and lose sight of where the playacting ended and reality began?

"It's a beautiful night," she said after a moment.

"It is."

"Is fall still your favorite time of the year?"

He couldn't remember when he'd last taken the time to notice the changes of the seasons. "Yeah," he answered at length. "I think it still is."

"I'm glad."

When she smiled like that at him, that generous mouth still sparked heat, and those deep, dreamy eyes still pulled him in.

Bedroom eyes.

He'd lost himself in her eyes the very first time he'd met her. Even now, the years fell away and he wanted to lean forward and kiss her and—

"Will?"

Her voice cut through the lust-haze of his thoughts. "What?"

"Why are we stopping? The restaurant is—"

"We stopped?"

Her mouth slowly curved in a small smile. "Yes."

So they had, by an empty, shadow-filled park; the swing sets and teeter-totters, merry-go-round and play gyms, were all still and silent.

"I was thinking about work, not paying attention. Sorry." As he started walking again, he took her hand.

Warm and small, it felt just right in his. She didn't pull away, and after a moment he closed his fingers more tightly around hers, and she squeezed back.

"The park looks kind of sad at night, with no children," she said, then tugged at his hand and drew him toward the playground. "The restaurant isn't going anywhere. Are you in a hurry?"

"No."

The next thing he knew, she'd sat on a swing, and he started pushing her gently back and forth. The chains creaked and groaned, and her toes kicked up bits of sand with every pass.

From the swing she led him to the merry-go-round, and he went without protest, not sure of her intent but not minding, either. It was strange not to be operating with a plan or an objective, no race against the clock, just letting the moment play out.

He sat beside her, and they pushed with their feet until the merry-go-round began to circle lazily, providing a changing view from the dark patch of trees to streetlights and cruising cars and houses with their lamps glowing behind curtains and blinds.

A sense of peace settled over him, and as the temperature began to drop further, he became more aware of her warmth pressing closer against him.

"Are you cold?" he asked.

"A little, but I don't mind."

"Can't have that." He shrugged out of his suit coat and draped it around her shoulders. Then he wrapped his arm around her and pulled her against him, wondering if she was shivering because of the cold or because of something else. He didn't want to jump to any conclusions, no matter how his body was reacting to her closeness.

The swiftness of his arousal stunned him, as if he was eighteen all over again.

Mia sighed, resting her head lightly against his shoulder. "This brings back memories."

It took him a moment to find his voice. "It does."

And when she turned her face up toward him, it was the most natural thing in the world to lower his mouth and kiss her.

God, she still fit him perfectly, filled his arms and his hands as if tailor-made for him. The kiss grew urgent, deeper, and the sounds of passing cars faded away as the merry-go-round creaked to a stop. Will pulled her to him, legs straddling the seat, and as she pressed against his growing erection, he slid his palm along the full, heavy curve of her breast. Her soft sigh encouraged him, and he slipped his hand beneath her sweater and bra and cupped her breast, rubbing his thumb over her nipple. Her sigh became a moan, and she kissed him with a passion that made him forget they were in plain view of passing cars and anyone walking along the sidewalk. The darkness and his coat hid where he had his hands, but not that they were doing something.

He'd forgotten how the contrast of smooth skin and pebbled nipple satisfied him and drove him crazy all at once, how she had been part of his first thought in the morning and his last thought before falling asleep in her arms, how much he'd loved her then and believed they'd always be together . . . and how much her betrayal had hurt.

That faded away as the intensity of his need grew. He wanted to take her back to his hotel and make love to her, to find out if she still made those little sighs and breathless mews of pleasure, to find out if time still stopped when he was inside her.

Mia suddenly pulled back, her mouth gleaming from his kiss, her pupils so wide her eyes looked black. "We probably shouldn't be doing this here," she murmured. "We're both old enough to know better."

And to know there was no going back to what they'd had before.

It was the reminder he needed: that he'd been sent here to do a job and she was part of that job, whether he liked it or not. If she was guilty, he would take her down.

But until then, he couldn't turn away from her tentative smile or the reflection of his own desire in her eyes.

Eight

THE DIM EVENING LIGHT CONCEALED WILL'S EXPRESSION, but Mia didn't need to see his eyes to know what he was thinking. Kissing him was like going from zero to sixty in five seconds flat: exhilarating, scary, breathless. Irresistible.

And she wanted more, wanted it more than she'd wanted anything in a long, long time.

"You know," she said softly, "I'm really not all that hungry."

Will's sudden stillness told her that he understood exactly what she meant. A moment later, he said, "We could go back to your place and hang out. We can always get something to eat later."

"I'd like that."

Holding hands, they quickly returned the way they'd come. Mia was aware of every brush of his clothing and body against her, the heat of his proximity, the scent of his cologne clinging to the suit coat surrounding her.

"What are you thinking about?" Will finally broke the silence as they walked up the steps to her building's entrance.

"Wondering why wearing a man's clothes always feels so nice." She opened the door, and he followed her up the stairs. She motioned to his coat, struggling to explain this strangely sweet sense of possessiveness. "I thought I'd grown too old and cynical to feel this way."

He smiled. "You're only thirty-four, Mia. That's not old."

"It's a lot older than twenty-two. The world doesn't look the same as it did then."

"Is it supposed to?"

Inside her apartment, she turned on the hall light, then locked the door. It was hard to breathe normally with Will so close; the tiny distance between their bodies seemed almost more intimate than a touch. She wanted him to touch her, all of her, but at the same time she didn't, because then the sweet tension of waiting would be over.

"Maybe sometimes I wish it did. Life was a lot easier then, when I thought I knew everything."

He went still again, so briefly she wasn't sure if she'd imagined it, before he leaned closer and brushed her mouth with his. "There's something to be said for experience."

The look in his eyes sent a delicious shiver of anticipation rippling over her, head to toe.

He kissed her again, and this time there was no mistaking his hard-held edge of urgency as he hands slid beneath her sweater toward the back of her bra. By the time he had the bra unhooked, she had his shirt pulled from his pants, her breathing as fast and uneven as his.

Mia broke the kiss long enough to whisper, "Let's take this to the bedroom."

Once they were down the short hall and in her dark room, they fell onto the bed in a tangle of arms and legs and roving hands and hungry mouths.

His heated weight, pressing her into the softness of her comforter, further stoked her hunger, making it difficult to think beyond what it would feel like to have him inside her again.

"Wait," she murmured, rolling slightly until she could reach the nightstand. After pulling open the drawer, she rummaged around until she found a condom. "Just in case you didn't have any."

"I don't, but I'll make sure to plan ahead next time."

Within seconds Will had stripped off her sweater and bra. She undid his buttons as he kissed her, then pulled off his shirt and tie. A thought flickered of what else she might do with that tie, but she didn't have the patience for teasing games tonight.

Maturity had chiseled his body into that of a man, wide-shouldered and lean and powerful. She ran her hands over him, testing the strength, the sharper defined lines of muscles. When he brushed her hair away from her face, she caught sight of a tattoo on his upper bicep. That, along with the incredible body, was the last thing she'd expected to find on an art journalist who wore pricey suits. It surprised her enough that she pulled back and touched the tattoo.

"At the time, it seemed like a good idea," he said, smile flashing again as he kicked off the comforter. "It's a scorpion."

"For a Scorpio," she murmured. "I like it."

It emphasized the hard curve of his bicep. Though she'd loved his whipcord-lean body in college, this new look was *very* nice.

"Do you have one?"

"A tattoo?" Mia laughed and gave a little sigh when his chest brushed her bare belly as he moved lower, freeing her from her pants and underwear. "I'm needle-phobic, remember?"

"That's right." He ran a hand over her breast, and she shivered, eyes fluttering shut at the feel of his rougher palm across her sensitive skin.

"I did have a ruby nose stud. I let it go—mmmm, that feels nice—a couple years ago."

"I bet it looked hot. You've got the right face for it." His tongue followed where his fingers had been, and this time her sigh ended in a low moan.

He played his tongue and teeth over her nipple,

sending such a jolt of lust through her that she jerked upward with a gasp.

Mia's fingers dug into his shoulders, and she could feel his erection nudging against her through his pants.

That just wouldn't do.

She unfastened his pants, slipping them down his hips as he continued to lick and tease her breasts with his tongue. He raised his hips to help her, and she worked the pants down past his knees.

As if he could still read her needs and moods, she didn't even have to ask him for what she wanted. He grabbed the condom, then spread her legs and pushed inside, filling her with a thick, satisfying pressure.

Will started to move, and she whispered his name, eyes closed to concentrate on every sensation. The smooth glide of his skin, the tickle of the dusting of chest hair against her, the increasing rhythm of his thrusts flooding her with a hot, demanding rush of desire.

A split second later the thought scattered, lost in the powerful tremors of her swift orgasm. Will followed shortly with one final, grinding thrust, his head arched back, eyes shut tight.

She could feel the slight trembling of the arm muscles supporting him above her. Her legs were wrapped tightly around his hips, her hands clutching at his upper arms, and she could still feel him inside her.

He bent his head and kissed her, but didn't say anything.

As the heat of pleasure faded, uncertainty filled her, bringing with it an abrupt awareness that, in all the ways that mattered, Will was a total stranger.

What now?

Will rolled over to his back, and as he removed what was left of his clothes, he asked, "You okay?"

"Oh, yes. It was very . . . nice."

Brows raised, he propped himself up on his elbow. "Nice? It was just *nice*?"

"It was fantastic, Will, and you damn well know it. It's only that . . . well, we haven't seen each other in years, and then we fall into bed together within a day of meeting again. Is that normal?"

"It felt right to me." His gaze held steady, which soothed some of her anxiety. At least he wasn't avoiding her, making moves to grab his clothes and run for the hills.

"I can't help thinking in terms of unfinished business. Tying up loose ends."

Will gave a low laugh. "Mia, you think too much. And whatever it was, it was over too fast. You always *did* make me crazy in every way, good and bad."

In the dim light, she could've sworn there was a look of sadness that matched the somber tone of his voice.

"Mia, I can't stay." As she turned to look at him, he added, "I can't stay tonight, or at all. When my job's done here, I'll be moving on to the next one."

"Oh," she murmured, not sure what else to say.

"I just thought I should make that clear."

"Thank you. I appreciate the honesty."

And she did, despite the niggling disappointment. It was foolish of her even to imagine they might have a second chance together. After all that had happened, how could he ever trust her again?

"But until you have to go, we can keep busy. Right?" She touched his cheek, running her thumb over the slight, rougher stubble of his chin, then rubbed his lower lip. So full, so kissable. She leaned over, rolling him to his back, and ran her tongue over that lower lip. He made a low sound of interest, and when she kissed him, he opened his mouth and let her slip her tongue inside to play with his.

Sex would chase away whatever doubts and awkwardness they didn't want to face right now, and it was so easy to fall back to the way it used to be, even if it was unwise.

Mia straddled him, smiling. God, he was magnificent.

Earlier, she'd been too distracted to take a good look at him, and she made up for the oversight now. With a hum of appreciation, she slid her hands along his shoulders, along the sinews and muscles of his arms and chest. His body was toned and hard, his skin smooth where it wasn't dusted with fine, dark hair, and where his narrow hips met powerful thighs, his penis thickened and grew erect, rising toward her belly.

She didn't recall any of her other past boyfriends or her ex *ever* looking this damn good in her bed.

Grabbing his hips, she lowered herself onto his erection, leaning forward as he grabbed her bottom and pulled her down so that he pushed deep inside her. It was a different feel, a little sharper, and she gasped, moving slowly to draw out the pleasure.

Will stroked her breast, then covered her nipple with his hot, wet tongue, and the tug of his mouth, coupled with the thick glide of him inside her, was almost too much. She could already feel the orgasm building, and she closed her eyes to try to control it.

Her eyes flew open when Will suddenly sat up and pulled out of her. "Not so fast. Let's make it last this time."

Mia didn't protest. As hot as she was, he could tell her to do anything and she probably would without a second thought. She let him roll her to her stomach, and as he massaged her back, her bottom, and her thighs, she melted into the softness of the sheets, languid with contentment. She ached for his touch again, but he deliberately teased her, touching everywhere but where she most ached. When his fingers strayed to her inner thighs, closer and closer to where she wanted his touch, she arched her hips toward him in a wordless appeal.

"God, you're beautiful," Will whispered, his voice harsher. "So beautiful."

He slipped a finger inside her, his thumb massaging her clit, and rapidly brought her to a climax. While she lay there panting, limp-boned from the powerful spasms, he knelt behind her.

Legs spread wide, erection straining toward her, Will pulled her hips up tight against him and entered her in one hard, deep thrust. She gave a high gasp, shaking at the fresh ripple of pleasure. He bent, kissing along the line of her neck, taking her earlobe gently between his teeth. Then he kissed her in that sensitive spot just behind her ear and whispered, "Lean forward a little, and move your legs out. Like that, yeah."

Balancing on her elbows, she spread her legs wider and leaned forward slightly as Will's powerful arm wrapped around her, supporting her as he thrust. With his other hand he pinched and rolled a nipple, adding such a sharp spike of pleasure that she cried out, again and again, though she tried to hold it back.

"Don't," he said, and even the low, dark urgency of his voice was arousing. "I want to hear you."

As he pounded into her, teasing her breasts, she moaned loudly. All she cared about was riding the rising tension, higher and harder, hearing his ragged breathing behind her. When his hips began a frenzied rhythm, she knew he was close and she squeezed her eyes shut, focusing on that dark thread of lust that unraveled so sweetly, so sweetly . . .

She cried out again when her orgasm hit, and if he

hadn't grabbed her with both hands, she would've toppled forward. She sucked in air, holding his hands tight as he shuddered in release.

"Oh, wow," Mia managed to whisper, after a long moment. "I should thank whoever taught you that."

He laughed breathlessly. "Give me a few minutes, and I'll show you more. Then I really have to go—sorry."

Again, the sharpness of her disappointment took her by surprise. "It's okay; I understand. You're here to work, not play."

"Yeah." His voice was soft, and then to her utter delight, he pulled her close in a comfortable cuddle. "But don't remind me. I'm trying to forget that part."

Nine

WILL PARKED ACROSS THE STREET FROM THE HADDING-ton building, close enough to make a run for it if he had to but not so close that his car would catch the attention of the security camera or an employee, should one happen to drop by.

Considering the time, that was doubtful. He'd left Mia's apartment later than he should have—nearly 1:00 AM—then returned to his hotel to change into the clothes he'd bought earlier. Tonight he was Hugh Haddington, right down to the fedora, and he walked to the back door, black canvas bag in hand, as if he had every right to be there.

Security personnel would be used to seeing Hugh work late, so Will gave them what they expected to see. They wouldn't look too closely at anyone who resembled Hugh if they were watching the monitors at all.

He quickly punched in the security code, thinking about what he might find inside—and tried not to dwell on the fact that whatever he found might require him to turn in a woman he'd had sex with for the past few hours.

Swearing under his breath—the lack of sleep wasn't helping his mood any—Will waited for the click that signaled the lock's release, then pulled the door open and walked into the workshop without turning on the lights. With no inner windows, he didn't have to worry about passing police cars or security personnel spotting a light, but he couldn't be sure his insider wouldn't make an unexpected appearance.

With Hugh at the top of his list of suspects, Will searched his office first. It was as disorganized as Hugh himself, so the search would be slow. He browsed the email program, reading through a number of terse, anxious emails from Toller—Christ, the man was a nag—and as many placating emails from Hugh, but nothing raised any red flags.

Will next checked the internet browser history, finding the usual news sites and blogs and a few soft porn pages. Again, nothing suspicious. He then accessed the accounting software and browsed other files of interest. Hugh rarely used passwords, and when he did, he'd used the "remember me" feature. Someone up to no good would be a lot more careful than this.

After copying pertinent files to a flash drive, Will

pulled a key logger from his canvas bag and plugged it into the back of Hugh's keyboard. Small and unobtrusive, it would log all keystrokes and email, and all he had to do to read the data was plug the logger into his laptop's USB port. He also fixed a small, powerful listening device to the back underside of the desk. Finally, he searched the file cabinet and garbage.

Satisfied that he'd covered everything in Hugh's office, Will headed to Vanessa's cubicle. She was far more organized than her boss. Judging from her browser history, she liked to shop online and had a long order history with lingerie sites—some of her orders left him wondering what she was wearing under those jeans and shirts. It also looked like she was planning a trip to New York City that summer. She'd neatly sorted her email into subfolders that archived unremarkable business correspondence, except for the folder labeled "Kos."

Will clicked on that folder and found what he'd expected: highly personal emails between two lovers. After the lingerie orders, he wasn't surprised to see that Vanessa had an enthusiastic, blunt sexual relationship with this Kos.

Intruding into personal territory wasn't his favorite part of the job, but it was unavoidable. If she was innocent Vanessa would never find out, and if she was guilty, then she'd get what was coming to her.

The email headers also revealed that Kostandin Vulaj worked at Boston's Logan Airport as a baggage handler.

That would come in handy for smuggling small pieces of priceless art out of the country, and it was a trick Rainert von Lahr had resorted to several times in the past.

The name sounded Eastern European; as soon as he got back to the hotel, Will would page Ellie to check into Vulaj's background.

He turned off the computer, and as he shined his flashlight around the cubicle, deciding where to set up his surveillance equipment, he heard the unmistakable click of the security door unlocking.

He spun with a soft curse, then moved quickly toward the vault, where he could hide without being immediately seen if someone turned on the lights. As he slid behind the shelves full of lumber, killing the flashlight's beam, the door swung open, letting in a gleam from outside. A female figure walked into view.

Mia!

A heart-freezing second later, he realized the woman was too tall to be Mia.

A light snapped on, momentarily blinding him even in its dimness, and he saw Vanessa Sharpton standing at her workstation.

"Make it quick," a man ordered tersely. He had a distinct accent, and Will guessed this was the star attraction of Vanessa's hot little email fantasies.

"I *am* hurrying." She sounded tense. "I have to be certain the colors match exactly. It's important."

There was a chance that she had a legitimate reason

for being in the shop this late, but if that wasn't the case, she'd just delivered herself and her boyfriend into his hands.

"Hey," she said suddenly. "My computer is warm. Like someone just turned it off."

Shit. If they started searching, his hiding place wouldn't last long.

"Someone was here?" the man asked.

"Maybe Hugh or Mia stopped by for some late-night work. We are on a deadline, you know." Vanessa sounded calm but with an edge of unease. "I don't know why they'd need to turn on *my* computer, though."

At the sound of footsteps, Will squeezed back as far as he could behind the lumber. Through the board slats, he caught a glimpse of Vanessa as she moved to Mia's workstation.

"Her computer isn't warm. I'm checking Hugh's office."

"Careful," the man said, sharply. "Wait for me."

"It's okay, Kos. Just stay by the door."

Will tracked the squeak of athletic shoes on linoleum as she walked swiftly to the office. Inside, she switched on the light, and a moment later, she called, "I'm not sure, but I think this one was on as well. I can still feel heat."

"You think someone was searching the computers?"

"I'm sure it was only Hugh looking for a file. He's always losing something," Vanessa answered.

The lights turned off in Hugh's office, then the door clicked shut as Vanessa walked toward the vault.

Will pulled the Glock from his back holster.

"It doesn't look like anything was disturbed. I don't think it's worth worrying about."

"Ask about it tomorrow, to be sure."

"All right." Vanessa pulled on the vault door. Assured that it was locked tight, she headed back to her station.

Will silently let out his breath and slid the gun back into its holster.

"Now I'm even more nervous," Vanessa said. "What if Mia or Hugh comes back? We're getting close to the deadline, and if one or both of them starts putting in unexpected appearances, how will I—"

"Then take the reliquary with you," Vulaj interrupted, tersely.

"If I do, I'll have to make sure I get back in here before Hugh or Mia arrive. I won't risk that, not this late in the game. Just give me five minutes."

Will frowned. Why would she have to match colors for the copy at night when she could do it during the day without rousing suspicion?

Unless . . .

There were only two possibilities. Either Vanessa had already taken the genuine reliquary from the vault or she'd created a second reproduction without the Haddington logo that marked it as an official copy, and was now making sure the two copies were identical.

If that was the case, then she and Vulaj were likely planning on selling the second fake to make a little extra cash on the black market.

He'd seen this double cross of a double cross before—and if von Lahr had set up this job, he'd be pissed as hell when he found out about it.

As Vanessa worked, muttering under her breath, Will waited patiently, sifting through possibilities and plans. He needed to verify that there was a duplicate, since that would change the whole game plan, and breaking into her apartment would be quicker and easier than breaking into the vault.

"Are you done yet?" Vulaj demanded.

"Almost," Vanessa said softly. "Please, Kos. I'm working as fast as I can."

Will shifted in his hiding place, trying to get a look at Vulaj, and one of the boards slipped. He grabbed it instantly, keeping it from falling but not from clattering against the board beside it.

"What was that?" Vulaj demanded.

"I'm not sure."

The chair casters rattled, and the squeak of rubber soles came toward him.

Perspiration dotted Will's upper lip as he pulled his gun, his other hand still keeping the board in place.

He hoped like hell that he didn't have to shoot anybody. He doubted Vanessa was armed, but there were no guarantees about the nervous boyfriend.

Vanessa was close enough that he could hear her breathing, and her body blocked the light from her workstation.

That was probably what saved his ass. In the dimness, and amid the jumble of lumber, she couldn't clearly tell one dark shape from another, even though she was so close that he could've reached out and touched her.

After a few seconds that seemed much, much longer, she turned and headed back to her bench. "There's nothing here; one of the boards just shifted or something. Now hold on. I'll be done soon."

She was as good as her word. A few minutes later she turned off the light, and Will heard the back door close. He remained unmoving for several minutes, then cautiously emerged, gun in hand, in case anyone had stayed behind to see if someone had been hiding.

That's what he would've done, but apparently Vanessa and Vulaj hadn't considered that possibility.

Still tensed and alert, Will walked to Vanessa's workstation, shining the flashlight across it. The reliquary reproduction was on her table but moved to the other side.

It was looking more and more like his theory about the second copy was right.

"This," he muttered, "is going to get ugly as hell."

Ten

"THAT'S IT FOR ME TONIGHT, KOS," VANESSA SAID, moving aside the second copy of the reliquary. "It's after three. I need to get some sleep."

"How much longer until it's done?"

He slouched against the apartment's small kitchen island, arms folded across the front of his navy sweatshirt, jean-clad ankles crossed. His olive-tinted skin, shoulder-length black hair, and alert hazel eyes looked even more exotic framed by beige walls and countertops.

It always made her breath catch, caused something inside to twist into a little knot of anxious happiness, to see him. He was so handsome . . . too handsome to be with someone like her. She worried constantly that she was so much older, so much paler and washed out and boring compared with him, and she didn't know why he stayed with her.

Why he'd *sought* her, she knew. She'd figured it out

before he'd confessed it to her, a few months after they'd first had sex.

"Another day, two at the most." Finishing the one reproduction of the reliquary in Hugh's time frame had been challenging enough. Two had seemed impossible. Yet with Kos's support, she was going to make it. "I can barely keep my eyes open. If I don't get some sleep, I'm going to make a mistake."

"I know." He pushed away from the counter and walked toward her, shaking back the hair from his face. Not every man could carry off long hair; on Kos, it looked perfectly natural. "And I told you that you could do this, didn't I? I have more faith in you than you have in yourself."

He pulled her into a tight embrace, and she pressed her face into the warmth of his neck. The muscles of his arms and chest felt wonderfully firm and steady against her tired body, and she leaned fully against him, trusting him not to let her fall.

"Thank you," she whispered. "You always say exactly what I need to hear."

"When this is all over, I'll take you to wherever you want to go . . . anyplace in the world. We can stay at the best hotels, sleep all day and stay out all night. I'll buy you whatever you want," Kos said, running his hand slowly up and down her back, then beneath her sweatshirt. "How does that sound?"

"It sounds better than any dream."

Vanessa shivered at the rough touch of his callused palm against her skin. Loading luggage was strenuous work, and it showed in his hard, lean strength. There wasn't an ounce of fat on his body.

"Maybe I'll want to take you someplace quiet and private, where we can have all the hours of the day to ourselves," she said as a familiar, welcome heat washed over her.

He laughed quietly. "If that's what you want, that's what I'll give you."

"What I want is to stop feeling so bloody terrified, Kos."

"Soon." He kissed the sensitive spot on her temple, which always made her squirm against him. He liked it when she did that kind of squirming; she could feel it. "Everything is set on my end. All we have to do is make the switch and we're on our way. I'll keep you safe. Don't ever doubt that."

"You know I don't," Vanessa whispered.

Because what Kostandin Vulaj wanted, he always managed to get. He'd come to the United States only four years ago, straight from the upheaval in Albania and barely able to speak English. He'd lived in New York City for a while, running menial jobs for the local muscle, before relocating to Boston, where he'd hoped to find a better ladder to climb. Now he had a steady, decent-paying job outside that *other* work, and a place to call home. He'd had help along the way, of course, and Vanessa knew that "help" had strings attached—though Kos didn't talk about that, for her protection.

Cutting free from those strings was why he'd come up with this risky plan. The life he wanted with her, and the power and respect he wanted to claim for himself, couldn't be found here. He said South America would be better, and she'd agreed. Wherever Kos went, that was where she wanted to be.

A heady thing, to love a man who burned with so much ambition, who didn't just accept life "as is," the way she'd done too often in her past.

Kos slipped his hands under her bra, his fingers working her nipples, and that little rush of warmth crested hotly. She turned her mouth toward his and surrendered to his rough, demanding kiss.

"You too tired for this?" he asked, his voice thicker with desire.

She grinned. "Are you?"

"I can have you begging for mercy in five minutes."

"Is that so?"

Of course he could; she was halfway there already.

"Is that a challenge?" He arched a brow. "You know how I am about challenges."

Without warning, he bent, grabbed her by the hips, and set her on the kitchen table. She squeaked in surprise.

"Careful of the reliquary!"

"I'll be careful." He smiled as he slipped off her jeans and underwear. "And very, very focused."

She laughed breathlessly as he raised her legs and positioned her heels on the table's edge. She closed her eyes, biting her lip, the breath catching in her throat as his fingers stroked her, inside, outside, until she gasped his name, begging him to finish it.

He eased back, laughing softly. "That wasn't even two minutes."

She sucked in her breath sharply an instant later when he slid his jeans down and his erection brushed against her thigh. Then he took her hips and pulled her toward him, thrusting inside so deeply that nearly every mind-melting jolt of pleasure made her gasp.

God, she lived for this. When he was inside her, pushing her fast toward orgasm, she couldn't think about anything else. Fears, worries, guilt, insecurities . . . everything fell away until there was nothing but a hot, urgent need to have him bring her to her release.

She came almost at once, the rolling tremors following one after another, and Kos let out a low-throated moan and ground his hips against her as his orgasm shuddered over him.

"Fast and hard," she said, when she caught her breath. "The way I like it best."

Kos looked up, and she was lost in those green-brown eyes, the movie-star handsome face, how his full lower lip just begged for a bite. He gave her a long, lingering kiss, tongue caressing hers with a maddening slowness, then landed a light slap on her ass, grinning at her startled yelp.

"You've given me so much, all I want is to give you back something that's for you alone. If you liked sex best hanging upside down in a closet, I'd give it to you," he said.

She knew he meant every word and was so grateful for his presence in her life that she couldn't even find the words to express it. It was all she'd ever dreamed of, to have a man who loved her as much as she loved him, cared about what she thought and wanted, no matter how trivial or random. She tried to hold back her tears, but one slipped out.

"You shouldn't cry," Kos murmured, pulling her toward him so that she was cradled in his arms, her bottom on the table and bare legs wrapped tightly around his hips.

"It's all right." Vanessa turned her face in to his neck again, letting his dark hair fall over her skin, liking the softness of the ends brushing against her. "It's just . . . sometimes I'm afraid this is all too good to last. I was always so jealous of Mia, of how men acted around her. None of the other men in my life were ever so good to me as you are."

"Mia is nothing compared to you. You're the one with the real talent."

"Don't say that. She's very good, just at different

things." Mia had barely concealed her dislike and disapproval of Kos, so it wasn't surprising that Kos was hostile toward her. "And she likes you a little better now, I think."

It felt so good to be in his arms that she didn't want to move, although sitting bare-assed, still swollen and tender between her legs, made her feel oddly vulnerable, even in her own kitchen.

"As if I care what she thinks of me."

At his cold tone, Vanessa looked up. "You promised me she wouldn't be in any danger."

"And I'll keep my promise, if at all possible." He was frowning now, and Vanessa regretted bringing up the subject, because the mood plunged from warm and intimate to coldly distant. "You're certain she doesn't suspect anything?"

"I'm certain. And now that an old boyfriend of hers has shown up, she'll be so distracted that it'll be even easier to keep her out of the way."

Kos's frown deepened. "You didn't say anything about this boyfriend before."

"I've been a little busy," she said, more sharply than intended. "It's not a big deal, and I *did* mention it to you, actually. Remember I said there was a journalist who's doing a story on Hugh and the collection?"

Kos nodded and drew back, pulling up his jeans as he did so.

"So it turns out the journalist is her old college

boyfriend. They were supposed to get married, but she moved away and everything went bad. It was quite the surprise for her to see him after all this time. She's been out with him twice already, and I didn't even have to push hard to get her to leave early tonight."

"What's his name?" Kos asked.

"Will Tiernay." She didn't like the clipped tone of his voice, or the look in his eyes. She eased down from the table and picked up her underwear. "Is something wrong?"

"Do you have his contact info?" When she nodded, he said, "Give it to me. And get me his picture, too."

"How? I can't just—"

"Use whatever excuse you need, but I want his picture."

"I don't understand. Is he a problem?"

"He may be nobody important, but he's not a part of my plans. At this point I can't be too careful about the details."

True enough, and he was much more experienced than she was at handling these sorts of . . . details.

For weeks she'd resisted Kos's pressuring her to go along with his plans to steal the Eudoxia Reliquary, along with a portion of the rest of the collection, and smuggle it out of the country. She knew that doing what he asked was wrong, but Kos was right that rich people could always buy more art. Nobody would be hurt, and the two of them could live comfortably for a very long time on what they'd earn from selling the second copy.

And if she did her job right, Kos's partner would never know what they'd done. Vanessa believed Kos when he told her it was very important his partner not learn the truth, because the man sounded dangerous to cross.

She *couldn't* mess up; the mere thought of Kos coming to harm paralyzed her with fear. She refused even to think what she would do if something were to happen to him.

Vanessa carefully picked up the nearly complete reliquary, slipped it into its protective box—an emptied yogurt carton—and put it in the refrigerator.

"I'll get you the picture tomorrow," she said.

Kos kissed her and gently brushed aside a strand of her hair. "That's my beautiful girl. Let's go to bed. We both need the sleep."

Eleven

WHEN A KNOCK CAME SHORTLY BEFORE 6:00 AM, WILL wasn't surprised to see a cop outside his hotel room door. Ellie's call, warning him that he'd have an early-bird visitor, had come an hour ago.

The man standing in the hallway wore a navy suit that had probably fit better when he'd weighed ten pounds less, and his graying, dark hair didn't look as if a comb had recently touched it. His Boston P.D. detective badge was in plain view, and he held a file folder loosely at his side.

"Sergeant Detective Doug Morris. I got a call from Mr. Sheridan asking that I fill you in on Kostandin Vulaj."

Will motioned the detective inside. "Coffee? Room service just brought it up, so it's good and hot. There's also some fruit and pastries."

Morris grinned. "Ever hear of a cop who turned down free donuts?"

"I do believe I've heard that cliché a time or two," Will said dryly.

Once they'd sat at the small table, Morris said abruptly, "Vulaj has ties to the Albanian Mafia."

Will halted briefly in midreach for the carafe, then filled his coffee cup. "Shit."

Morris shrugged. "His activities in Queens weren't anything out of the ordinary, but these guys are slippery as hell to pin down. He had a few misdemeanor convictions but was smart enough—or lucky enough—to clear out before New York City's finest took down his boss. After Vulaj moved here, he seemed to clean up his act."

"But you don't think he's really clean?"

"Nope. He's been seen with the local guys. It's all in here." Morris tapped the file on the table. "They deal in the usual drugs, extortion, gambling, and prostitution, so I was surprised when Sheridan told me to look into Vulaj's history. Art theft and forgery are way outside his repertoire."

Will didn't miss the *told* rather than *asked*. Whatever kind of favor Morris owed Sheridan, it had to be a big one. "Vulaj is working for someone else on this one."

"I'll take your word for it." Morris leaned forward to pick out a Danish. "I've got a call in to the Feds for more information about Vulaj's activities in New York. We know that he has family connections to someone high up in organized crime in Albania, possibly through the Karagiannis clan. Vulaj's got a hair-trigger temper, too."

Will took a sip of coffee. "Ben's not going to be happy about the organized crime connection. Not that it comes as a big surprise; art's a steady moneymaker for them."

"You want help?"

"It might be good if a few people on your end are aware of the situation, in case something goes wrong. My orders are to wait until the suspect or suspects make their move, contain them, call in the locals, and then disappear."

"The usual M.O. for you people. The disappearing part, that is."

"Because it usually causes a problem if we're still around when local law enforcement shows up," Will said, keeping his tone neutral. "Especially in other countries."

"For the record, I believe the locals could've handled this one without Sheridan's interference."

"Avalon has a vested interest in the man giving Vulaj his orders. To get to him, we need Vulaj. You can't handle a hunt like this the way we can."

"No," Morris agreed, after a moment. "Wearing a

badge limits me in a way it no longer limits you."

Resentment clearly bubbled under the apparent friendliness.

"In the end, all that matters is that the bastards go down." Will finished his coffee. "If you would keep me updated on Vulaj, I'd appreciate it."

"And in return you'll do what?"

"The same."

"Don't fuck with me, Tiernay. If it weren't for the fact that I owe Sheridan, as I'm sure you've guessed, I wouldn't be here."

Will nodded. What the hell, he could afford to be generous. "Vanessa Sharpton, Vulaj's girlfriend, is the one on the inside that we're after. Haddington and the other employee, Mia Dolan, check out so far, and I have no reason to believe either one of them is involved. Once Sharpton finishes with the reproduction of the Eudoxia Reliquary, which is the key piece of the collection, Vulaj will make his move."

"And do I want to know how you came by this information?"

"Most likely not." Will smiled, amused by Morris's glare. "I'm estimating Sharpton won't finish before the end of the week. In the meantime, I have to determine if she's arranged to switch anything else. And if Malcolm Toller is involved."

Morris's brows shot upward. "If Toller is involved, how are you going to hand him over to us? It's one thing to spoon-feed a couple of petty criminals to cops who won't ask too many questions, but Malcolm Toller is a big name in this city. Seems to me that going after him will draw more attention to your outfit than your boss would like."

"Prosecuting criminals is out of my jurisdiction. All I do is set them up to take the fall. After that, it's up to you—and there are enough prosecutors in this town who'd jump at the chance of taking on a high-profile case. Only Vulaj will know if Toller is involved. Once he's in custody, make him a deal and get him to talk. It's not like he owes Toller any loyalty."

"Maybe. He's never been too cooperative under questioning before." Morris handed the folder over to Will. "I copied a few files for you, and there's a picture of Vulaj as well."

Will opened the file to see a decent color photo of Kostandin Vulaj. He was younger than Will had expected, almost ten years younger than Vanessa.

"A good-looking guy, eh? When he first moved here, he'd hang out in fancy bars and restaurants and hook up with older, wealthy women. We figure he was looking for a sugar mama. Now I'd say he was looking for rich women who also had art collections he could rip off."

"Instead, he got involved with Sharpton. Not a bad plan, though," Will said. "From what I've read about her, she came from an abusive home situation and does well for herself, except where men are concerned. She's prime pickings for a master manipulator. I'm assuming that was Vulaj's angle."

"I've seen her type too many times to be surprised." Morris stood. "You do what you people do, and I'll help out where I can. But if things move out of that workshop and into the streets, I'm taking over. I don't want any innocent people hurt."

"Neither do I, Morris."

"Good to hear." The cop headed for the door. "And watch yourself. I don't have to tell you these guys play rough."

Once Morris left, Will stashed the new file in his briefcase with all the others, headed to the hotel's parking garage, and then drove to the Haddington building. Now that Mia was in the clear, he looked forward to seeing her again.

But as he turned in to the parking lot, he reminded himself that all the hot, sweaty sex in the world wouldn't protect Mia from being caught right in the middle of a painful situation.

Ugly didn't cover even half of it.

Mia arrived at the workshop earlier than usual. She pulled out the earrings and started on the final stage, giving them an aged patina, all the while glancing toward the door leading to the reception area. She hoped Will would arrive before anyone else. She didn't trust herself not to act differently around him, and even a couple minutes to compose herself in his presence would decrease the chances of Hugh or Vanessa figuring out that she'd had sex with Will last night. She wanted to keep what had happened between the two of them, savoring it for as long as possible.

Still, the morning-after doubts were a bitch. She couldn't help wondering if he'd gone to bed with her out of some sense of obligation or, worse, felt sorry for her. His mood had changed so suddenly—one moment he was coolly polite, and the next he'd had his hands all over her. She didn't understand—and wasn't sure she wanted to.

She *did* think too much. She should just enjoy the time they had together and ignore those wistful little thoughts of how nice it would be if he could stick around.

"What has you all dreamy-eyed this morning, eh?"

Hugh's voice startled her into a little yelp.

"Sorry." She took her hand away from her chest, not wanting to look as foolish as she felt. "I didn't hear you come in."

"How could you not? It's not like I'm ever quiet, and that back door always makes a racket when it closes." Hugh's grin widened. "I hope whatever you did was astonishingly wicked and you are going to give me all the raunchy details."

"Not on your life," Mia retorted.

Hugh didn't look in the least abashed. "It has to do with that journalist, doesn't it?"

"Oooh, does it?" Vanessa piped up from behind Hugh. "Did something happen? I want details, too!"

Mia looked from Hugh to Vanessa—when had *she* come in?

Hugh must've picked up on her dismay, because he laughed. "Don't look like that. Vanessa came in at the same time I did. You didn't miss her beam in from outer space."

"Well, *we* obviously missed something, didn't we?" Vanessa asked.

Something in her tone sounded angry, yet she was smiling. Mia wished she'd gotten more sleep; her senses seemed to be playing tricks on her.

"We went out for dinner. Or we almost went out for dinner but ended up back at my apartment. Fade to black, the G-rated version." Mia couldn't help grinning at the two curious faces peering at her over the top of her cubby's partition. "There, are you happy?"

"Depends," Hugh said. "Are *you* happy?"

Mia's grin widened. "That's a definite yes."

"Then we're all happy, too." Hugh gave an exaggerated wink in Vanessa's direction. "Aren't we?"

"Oh, absolutely."

Again, the odd tone. "Are you all right, Van?"

"Of course." She headed toward the coffee table.

"Why wouldn't I be happy when your phenomenal good luck rears its sparkling little head again?"

Mia exchanged looks with Hugh, who shrugged. "PMS. Or maybe that pretty boyfriend of hers wasn't up to the job last night. Who knows what her problem is?"

"Her 'problem' might be tight deadlines and not enough sleep," Vanessa shot back tartly. Then, after a loud sigh, she added, "Sorry for snapping like that, Mia. I am happy for you, really. I'm also exhausted. I'm counting the hours until all this is over and I can relax again."

"Think of the big fat bonus you'll be getting for making that deadline," Hugh reminded her as he made a beeline for the coffeemaker.

"That's the only thing getting me through this week." Vanessa slowed as she passed Mia. "I *really* am sorry. Still love me?"

Mia laughed. "Of course. Go drink your coffee. That should improve your mood a little."

Vanessa started to move off, then hesitated. "Is he coming in today? Will, I mean."

"I imagine so. He said he'd be here when he left last night." Mia looked down. "He didn't spend the night. I was kind of disappointed, even though I know I shouldn't be."

"I'm sure he would've stayed if he could." Vanessa patted Mia on the head, as if she were a puppy. As Mia rolled her eyes, Vanessa added, "And that certainly was quick, wasn't it?"

"It's not as if we're complete strangers," Mia reminded her.

"Yes, but you haven't seen him in twelve *years*. That's a long time. People change."

"You're in quite the mood this morning."

"Just . . . a little concerned that you're seeing him through the memories of a younger girl, when he might not be who you think he is."

Mia opened her mouth to argue but realized Vanessa had a point and was only trying to help, just offering a boyfriend opinion the way Mia had done so often in the past. "You're right. He's not the same person, but neither am I—and I think I'm old enough to know better this time around. No unrealistic expectations."

With a last anxious look, Vanessa walked back to her desk. Then Hugh headed to his office to return a few calls before working on the finishing stages of his own project. Left alone again, Mia tried to concentrate on getting the patina on the earrings just right, but her mind kept circling back to Will. She was beginning to wonder what was keeping him when she heard the door to the reception area open.

Will walked into the workshop with a confidence that made him look like he'd always belonged in this room. He probably managed that little trick wherever he went, and Mia had a hard time reconciling the man who radiated such power and self-confidence with the easygoing boy she'd fallen in love with.

All right, so he'd changed, and Vanessa was right. But some of those changes were definitely for the better. Not only did he look incredible in suits but he'd developed a lot more control and patience in bed.

And then he was in front of her, filling the entire space with energy and vitality . . . and wearing a strange expression.

"Is anything wrong here?" he asked, his cautious tone pitched just for her ears.

Wrong? She stared at him in confusion, wondering if he'd always rattled her ability to think coherently and she'd simply forgotten it. When she glanced at Vanessa for help, she saw the reason for Will's question: Hugh and Vanessa were looking at him the way one would stare at an exotic animal in a zoo.

"Cat's outta the bag, mate." Hugh tipped the fedora in a salute, then gave an exaggerated thumbs-up motion.

"Ah," Will said. "I see."

"Um, sorry." Mia stood, heat spreading up her chest and neck to her cheeks. "I've never been very good at these things."

"Meaning that she wears her emotions clear as day on her face," Hugh said, as if Will needed clarification. "And that we're a relentless bunch of hectoring gossips."

"Hugh," Vanessa said, her tone gently chiding. "You're embarrassing them."

"Not at all." Will leaned toward Mia, smiling. "And since we don't have any secrets, nobody will mind this."

The gleam in his eyes broadcast his intentions, and Mia leaned forward, not caring about their audience. He kissed her thoroughly and possessively, as if he hadn't spent hours kissing her last night.

When she broke away, breathless, she caught Hugh's wide grin. Vanessa looked startled as she said, "Wow."

"Agreed," Hugh said. "So now that our prurient curiosity has been slaked, it's time to get back to work. What do you have planned for today, Will? Questions? Observing?"

Mia hoped Will would say he needed to "observe" her, but her jewelry projects were not nearly as flashy as a reliquary with a legendary death curse. She sent him a look that said she couldn't wait to get him alone again.

"Hold that thought," he said quietly. "Maybe we can get away for lunch."

"Count on it." Anticipation colored her tone, though Mia spoke quietly so that only he would hear.

When he left, it seemed as if he took all the bright and sparkle with him. Sighing, she bent back over the earrings and picked up a pair of gloves.

Will spent much of the morning with Hugh, asking questions as Hugh worked on the chalice. Mia kept him in her field of vision, watching him in action. She didn't know any journalists, but maybe it was a routine part of his job to keep up a steady stream of easygoing conversation, guiding Hugh toward the topics he wanted to discuss without Hugh even realizing he was being efficiently managed.

Just like he'd done with her the other morning at Bella's.

Then they got to talking about London, and Hugh, unabashedly homesick, was caught up in local sports, the best pubs, strange encounters on the Tube, the Royals, and girl watching in Trafalgar Square.

With a jolt of shock, Mia remembered Will asking her if Hugh or Vanessa was homesick. It might be a coincidence that Will had brought up the subject now; it didn't have to be a calculated intent to get Hugh to talk even more freely.

Unease filled her, but she quickly dismissed it. That sort of behavior wasn't like Will. Vanessa's earlier comment was only making her look for ulterior motives where none existed. And since when did anyone need a "motive" for being nice to a homesick guy?

Whatever the reason, bringing up London had certainly endeared Will to Hugh. When she went to ask Hugh to approve her patina, he and Will were arguing about which stores in London had the best men's department.

"Just listen to you." She grinned at Will, then turned

to Hugh. "I remember when he lived in jeans and T-shirts, and I had to bully him to do his laundry."

Footsteps from behind announced Vanessa's arrival, and as Will glanced at the other woman, Mia saw the warmth leave his eyes. Puzzled, she turned.

Vanessa held up her digital camera. "Do you mind if I snap a couple of shots?"

"I'm the one who's supposed to be taking pictures," Will said. "It goes with the territory."

"This isn't about the interview. I know Mia would love a picture of the two of you together."

"Maybe later, Vanessa," Will said.

Surprised by his response, Mia glanced at Will.

"I'm afraid I won't take no for an answer," Vanessa insisted. "If you won't do it for Mia, then how about one little picture for posterity's sake? It's not every day a journalist does a feature on our work. We're always the invisible people."

Was it Mia's imagination, or was there tension in Vanessa's voice? "Honestly, Will, why is it a big deal?" she asked. "Just let her take the picture."

"You're right. Sorry," Will replied, looking at Vanessa.

"Good man," Vanessa said lightly, bringing up the camera. "Now, put your arm around her and smile."

Will hesitated, so briefly that Mia wouldn't have noticed had she not been alert to the strained undercurrent surrounding them.

"One picture," he said with finality as he slipped his arm around her waist and pulled her against his warm chest, surrounding her with his intoxicating scent of warm skin and expensive cologne.

It would've been a nice, cozy moment, if tension wasn't crystal clear in the hard lines of his muscles.

What on earth had him so upset? And why was Vanessa being such a pest? It wasn't like her at all.

"Say cheese!" Vanessa ordered cheerfully.

Twelve

IT HAD TAKEN ALL VANESSA'S COURAGE NOT TO BACK down in the face of Will Tiernay's resistance—but that very resistance convinced her that Kos was right to be concerned. The man might not be a journalist at all, and that possibility made her push him harder.

She suspected he hadn't refused outright because he had no good reason to do so, and Hugh and Mia would've started asking questions. Why would Will want to avoid raising questions if he was legit?

Her stomach knotted with a queasy fear, she headed back to her bench. If this anxiety continued much longer, her nerves would snap and she'd make a terrible mistake. Maybe even the kind of mistake that would get Kos hurt. Or worse.

She sat at her computer and quickly uploaded the photo, emailing it to Kos. As she hit the Send button, Will looked over at her.

Vanessa froze at his cold, narrow-eyed stare.

Maybe Mia's Ohio Boy had been sweet years ago, but that had obviously changed. When she went back to work, her hands were shaking so much she kept messing up the cloisonné on the corner.

Why did this have to happen now, when she and Kos were so close to getting what they wanted? Anger rose, forcing the fear away and steadying her hands enough that her fourth attempt at the corner succeeded. An hour passed in frustrating slowness as she waited for Kos to call, her dread mounting.

To calm herself she stood, stretching the tension-cramped muscles in her shoulders. A moment later, her phone rang. A glance showed it was Kos's cell phone, and she snatched up the headset. "Did you get my email?"

"Yes." His voice had that clipped, tight sound that had so worried her last night. "We have a problem. I'll pick you up for lunch and fill you in. Stay away from Tiernay and avoid talking to him."

Fear froze her in place; then she forced herself to lean back against her desk casually, looking at the phone and hoping Will wasn't watching her. "What's wrong?"

"I don't know who the hell Tiernay is, but I got a feeling he's no journalist. His cover checks out, but when I asked Ari to dig deeper, he found out that Tiernay used to be a Seattle cop."

"Oh, my God," she whispered. It was all she could

do not to give in to the sudden weakness in her knees and sink to the floor.

"He was a detective for the Seattle Police Department until about three years ago, but after that, he disappeared. Ari couldn't find any recent addresses. The phone number you gave me forwards to an answering service."

"What should I do?"

"Right now, nothing. Just stay away from him as much as you can. Try to act normal about it. I don't want you tipping him off that we're onto him."

Vanessa had a feeling she'd already blown the "act normal" part with the impromptu photo session.

"Did you hear me, Vanessa?"

"Yes," she managed to whisper.

"I'm going to give my partner a call this afternoon and ask his advice. He'll know what to do. Meet me outside in an hour."

"Yes," she repeated.

After Kos cut the connection, Vanessa held the headset for a moment longer, then slowly put it down.

A cop!

Before she could stop herself, she looked across the workshop—right into Will Tiernay's dark eyes, staring at her with the sharp intensity she'd seen once on a hawk as it guarded its kill. Then he smiled, and icy fear slid down along her spine as he approached, coffee cup in hand.

"Mind if I watch you work on the reliquary again?" he asked, leaning over her partition.

Stay away from him.

Vanessa couldn't see any way to do that, unless she wanted to cause a problem. Without meeting Will's eyes, she said, "No, I don't mind."

"Good!" He came around and sat on the empty desk chair. "Looks like we could both use a coffee refill. Be a dear and do that?" His voice was pleasant, slightly teasing—and clashed with his cold eyes.

Outside all civilized, inside . . . all predator.

Vanessa held his gaze as long as she dared, then grabbed their cups. "Of course. Happy to help."

As she walked away she could feel his eyes on her, raising the fine hairs on the back of her neck.

Thirteen

Zákynthos (Zante), Greece

RAINERT VON LAHR LEANED AGAINST THE WHITE-washed villa wall that held the lingering warmth of the sun, sipping a glass of wine as he admired the view from the balcony. The villa sat high on a hill, and below stretched the white sands of a beach, empty except for a few tourists and island natives walking along the shore in the darkening colors of sunset.

From the kitchen off the patio came the sounds of running water and rattling pots and pans, as Rovena prepared dinner for him. Her daughter sat on the deck at his feet, playing with ragged-looking fashion dolls.

Anna was five, her fingers too clumsy to handle the miniature clothing, and she made a frustrated sound. When she looked up and saw him watching, she held out a naked doll in one hand and clothes in the other and said something to him in an earnest voice.

Though his Greek barely went beyond the basics, he understood that she wanted help. He pushed away from the wall, put his wineglass aside, and then hunkered down to her level.

"Give it to me, then," he said with an encouraging smile and held out his hand.

The little girl beamed as she handed over the doll and clothes. As he struggled to push nonbendable legs into a pair of pants, the phone rang inside. Glancing over the girl's wind-tousled, dark curls, he saw Rovena pick up the phone—and then she turned and met his gaze through the window.

So the call was for him. It had better not be bad news. He'd all but closed the deal on the reliquary, and if Vulaj had fucked up there'd be hell to pay, even if he was Rovena's favorite nephew.

"Here you go." Rainert handed the dressed doll back to Anna, then stood as she thanked him very prettily in German. It made him smile.

He walked into the villa, and as Rovena handed him the cordless phone she said, "It's Kos."

He waited until Rovena went outside, shutting the balcony door behind her. Then he said, "Yes?"

"I think we have a problem."

Holding back a sigh, Rainert rubbed at his brows. "What kind of problem?"

"There's a journalist here to interview Haddington, but the guy's not checking out. He used to be a Seattle cop."

Rainert's wine-drowsy mind cleared in an instant. One of the things he most appreciated about Vulaj was that the man was always direct. Sometimes, though, it caused him to overreact. "An ex-cop could still be a journalist."

"Yeah, but this one is a blank for the past three years. It's like he left the police force and dropped out of sight. That's not right."

"I agree this sounds like a problem." One called Avalon. "Does this man have a name?"

"William Tiernay."

It didn't sound familiar, but Avalon fielded a small army of operatives, most of whom he'd never heard of, much less encountered.

"What do you want me to do, Rainert?"

He let the silence lengthen, and even across the Atlantic and Mediterranean, he could all but feel the pulse of Vulaj's uneasiness. "Is the reliquary reproduction completed?"

"Almost. Vanessa thinks she'll finish it up by the end of the week."

"What else is done?"

"Dolan's done with all the jewelry except a set of earrings, and she'll finish that today or tomorrow. Haddington is running behind on the chalice. I'm not sure he'll be done with it by the end of the week."

Rainert mulled over the information, tapping his fingers absently on the countertop. If they had to move early they'd lose the chalice, which would be unfortunate because he already had a buyer lined up. "Can you hold out until the chalice is done? Or do you feel there's an immediate danger to you or your woman?"

"Tiernay doesn't know yet that we're onto him."

"That's good news."

"I'm not sure what this guy is waiting for, but—"

"Kos. I've told you about Avalon. This is probably one of their people. If that's the case, then he won't make a move until *you* make yours. And understand that he's going to want to use you to get to me."

"I'd never talk, Rainert, I'm—"

"Even if you did, by the time they got here I would be long gone, and your aunt would be left to deal with the problem. You're in a tight situation, all right, and as I see it, you have several options."

Rainert leaned back against the sink, grabbed a couple of fat black olives from the colander, and popped them in his mouth. "You can kill Tiernay and draw attention to everyone in Haddington, including your woman."

"Vanessa. Her name is Vanessa." The other man sounded stiff, prickly with outraged male pride.

Rainert grinned and picked up more olives. They were always much better when fresh. "But if you kill

Tiernay, you'd better be ready to run. And if you do that, and lose the Eudoxia Reliquary and the other pieces, I will not be happy."

A brief silence followed as Vulaj took all that in. "I don't want to screw up the deal, or kill Tiernay if I can help it. The cops are less likely to care about stolen art than a dead body."

"You learn quickly."

Except for that tendency to overreact, Vulaj showed talent and promise—and there was something about him that reminded Rainert of himself when he'd been a lot younger and more reckless.

"That leaves you with a last option, which is to get him out of your way," Rainert said. "Either hurt him badly enough to put him out of commission for a few days or find some other way to force him to back off. Remember: if he's with Avalon, then he's not a cop. He probably has a temporary tie to the local police, but he can't operate like one. This is both good and bad for you, as I'm sure you can imagine."

Another silence followed, so long that Rainert began to wonder if they'd lost the connection.

Then Kos said, "I think I see a way out of this, but it won't be easy. We'll need extra help getting out of the country. I won't be able to go with the original plan."

Unfortunate. The original plan had been beautiful in its practicality and simplicity.

"I told you who you could contact for help if you needed it. Do you still have that information?"

"Yes."

"Good. Then I trust you to handle the situation. Do you expect a delay in getting the goods to me?"

"Maybe a day or two, no more than that."

Rainert popped the last olive into his mouth. "Let me make this very clear, Kos. If this man is working for Avalon, he is going to be a danger to you—but don't panic. Don't overreact and do something stupid."

"I know. I'll take care of him. Count on it."

"If you don't, then you and I will have a problem."

He disconnected and walked back outside. It had grown darker, and he could no longer see the beach. Rovena sat beside her daughter, stroking the little girl's hair as she played quietly with her dolls.

"Is everything all right?" Rovena asked.

Rainert retrieved his wine and sat on a patio chair across from her. "There are . . . complications."

He wasn't sure how many details he should give her. She was close to her nephew, and she might get emotional over the thought of him in danger. Then again, she came from a tightly knit clan with long ties to Albanian organized crime and had married into the Greek equivalent. She understood how the business worked, and its risks.

He added, "It looks like Avalon has arrived."

Rovena's dark eyes widened. "So soon? But how—"

"I don't know," Rainert interrupted, anger rising—which pissed him off even more. He'd been enjoying the view and the domestic mood of woman and child and cooking food. It was a nice fantasy for a fantasy kind of island. "They know the way they always seem to know. I tell you, Rovena, those people are beginning to irritate me."

Rovena studied him, a faint frown pulling her brows together. She was a beautiful, mature woman, with thick dark hair, lush lips, and even lusher breasts, but she was also married to a man who wouldn't think twice about killing him if he so much as looked at her in the wrong way.

A pity. The best way to get out of these dark moods was sex.

"Perhaps," she said at length, "you should find a solution to that problem."

Rainert leaned back and finished off his wine. "It's something I've been thinking about."

"Then it's time you stop thinking about it and act on it. If anything happens to Kos, I will not be pleased. Nor will my husband."

The mild threat didn't bother him; he'd heard worse many times before. When one swam with sharks, one learned to deal with sharks and to act like one. "I won't be pleased, either. I like your nephew. I have big plans for him."

As he relaxed back in the chair, he unbuttoned his

shirt to the breeze, slightly gratified to see Rovena's gaze flick toward his chest. He wouldn't touch her, but temptation added a hint of spice to the resistance.

"Stop that," she said curtly. "You will not disrespect my husband in his own home."

Rainert smiled. "You looked."

"This is not the time for your games!" She huffed in annoyance, then her lips curved in a barely there smile. "Ah, you are such a bad man. One of these days you'll cross the wrong woman, and I hope I'm there to see it."

"And you are such a cold woman." As anger sparked in her dark eyes, Rainert grinned and fastened one button. "Okay. No more games. You're right; it's time I did something about Ben Sheridan and his little army."

Fourteen

WILL STOOD IN THE LOBBY OF VANESSA SHARPTON'S apartment building wearing a Wilson's Exterminators uniform and holding a clipboard with official-looking forms that he pretended to read while listening to three older men talk.

The apartment was brown brick and blocky, 1980s vintage, with three stories. Off the lobby ran a hall to the first-floor apartments and a stairway leading to the upper floors. The lobby contained a few tired tan chairs and a wall of mailboxes. Numbers only, no names, but he already knew Vanessa was on the second floor, in Number 208.

He wanted a look inside Number 208, even more so since Vanessa's skittish behavior earlier had tipped him off that something was wrong. A quick check on the tiny recorder he'd taped beneath her desk had picked up her half of the conversation with Vulaj and confirmed Will's suspicion: they knew he wasn't a journalist.

Higher stakes always brought a rush of excitement and challenge, and he lived for that rush, that edgy tingle of heightened awareness. The greater the risk, the sharper the colors and sounds, the more alive he felt.

He glanced from under the bill of his ball cap at the three gossiping men, who were showing no signs of leaving anytime soon. Since they'd let him inside the building without asking any questions, they might prove useful.

"Excuse me," he said. "I'm here to see this guy about a roach problem, but I can't figure out how to pronounce his name. Kon . . . Kost—"

"You mean Kos Vulaj. He lives with his girlfriend in two-oh-eight," said the tallest of the three, who was wearing a jazzy fishing-print shirt over his jeans. "But he isn't here. I saw him leave about forty minutes ago."

Just what Will wanted to hear. "How about the girlfriend?"

"She works during the day," said the bald-headed man in the golf outfit. "Sorry, but I don't think anyone's home. You better talk to someone in the office."

"I'll go knock on their door first, just to be sure. If no one answers, I'll find the building manager. Thanks."

"No problem," said the tall man. "If it's roaches, kill 'em all dead. I live down the hall from those two, and I don't want any cockroaches in my apartment."

Will headed up the stairs. Until now, he hadn't been sure of Vulaj's whereabouts. Vanessa had left Haddington for lunch and come back looking even paler. He'd waited a half hour after she'd returned before he excused himself to go back to his hotel to write.

Instead, he'd changed into the set of clothing he took with him wherever he went: a generic worker's uniform of navy blue pants and shirt, complete with interchangeable company logos for the shirt and ball cap, and a selection of tools to make it look real.

In a matter of minutes, he could transform himself into a security guard, cable TV repairman, or electrician. Even though he was no longer a cop, he still drew on the aura of authority and the knowledge that few people questioned anyone wearing a uniform, and even fewer asked for identification.

He also had Vanessa's keys, which he'd lifted from her purse after he forced her to refill their coffee cups.

After slipping on a pair of gloves he let himself inside the apartment, one hand in his pocket gripping his switchblade.

No dog rushed out to bark, no angry guy ran at him with a gun, no woman started shrieking. The apartment was still and empty.

And well-kept. No clutter like that at Mia's place; no dust bunnies congregating in corners. A generic, beige one-bedroom apartment, but there were touches of Vanessa in the colorful art prints hanging on the walls, the equally colorful pillows on the couch and recliner, and the vase of yellow and pink tulips on the kitchen table. The TV, DVD player, video game console, and computer were all the latest—Will suspected they were Vulaj's doing rather than Vanessa's. He couldn't quite see her playing Vice City.

Several framed photos of Vanessa and Vulaj lined the top of the bookcase. They looked like any other happy couple, which gave Will pause. He hadn't considered that Vulaj might have formed a genuine attachment to Vanessa; he'd assumed the guy was using her. It didn't affect his work here either way, but it was a factor he hadn't anticipated.

Will began in the bedroom. Since he already knew about the exotic lingerie addiction, nothing in her dresser drawers came as a surprise. The closet revealed that both Vulaj and Vanessa preferred casual clothes and Vanessa didn't hog all the closet space—but there was no second reliquary.

Not that finding it would be easy: there were too many places to hide a three-inch-by-one-inch box.

The bathroom held the typical toiletries, all neatly arranged on shelves. Inside the medicine cabinet were common over-the-counter drugs, a box of condoms, and Vanessa's container of birth control pills.

Hurrah for bad guys who practiced safe sex.

He checked Vanessa's makeup bag, her boxes of tampons, the box of tissues, and shook the bottles of shampoo and conditioner. He also checked the toilet to see if the reliquary was hidden inside the tank in a waterproof box.

No luck.

The search of the living room, where he pulled back cushions and tested for false bottoms in drawers or hollowed-out books, also turned up nothing.

That left the kitchen, which would take more time. He glanced at his watch. He had at least an hour before Vanessa would leave work for the day, but Vulaj could come through that door at any second.

One of his ex-girlfriends, when facing the pending arrival of unexpected guests, would stash dirty dishes in the fridge crisper bin or inside the oven, assuming those were the last places anybody would look.

So those were the first places Will checked, assuming Vanessa might use similar feminine logic. The oven was empty, and as he headed to the refrigerator, he had a sudden thought of what Mia would think of him if she could see him now.

Not a welcome thought, and he forced it back by focusing instead on trying to figure out what had tipped off Vulaj, or Vanessa, about him.

Ellie had provided him with an excellent cover, complete with a portfolio website, fake articles, and an answering service, but internet searches and caches were among the few things in the world Ben Sheridan couldn't bend to his will or eliminate with a simple, brutal efficiency. Someone with enough know-how and patience could find the kind of information that would likely scare the shit out of Vanessa Sharpton.

Will had been involved with several high-profile cases on the Seattle P.D., which was why he always worked with an alias. While that would've been pointless given Mia's presence, the lack of one gave an extra edge to the bad guys, and he didn't like it. If Vulaj knew he wasn't a journalist, the first thing he'd do was try to get rid of Will, one way or another.

The crispers were empty of anything but fresh fruit and vegetables—safe sex *and* healthy eating habits.

Irritated, Will stood back just as the click of a key in a lock sounded behind him.

He slammed the refrigerator shut, grabbed the clipboard, and quickly slipped down the hall toward the bedroom.

The apartment door opened and closed, and he heard two men talking in another language.

Will's gaze swept the small room. He wouldn't fit under the bed. The window was open to let in the spring air, but he wouldn't have time to remove the screen and climb onto the fire escape.

Dammit.

He headed to the closet, opening it quietly. Inside, he moved to the farthest corner of Vanessa's half, pulling a nearly floor-length garment bag in front of him. His shoes were visible if someone looked closely enough, but with any luck, it wouldn't come to that.

Vulaj and the other man continued talking, presumably in Albanian, and Will went still at the mention of his name.

Tiernay. Clear as a bell.

It didn't sound as if either man was heading toward the bedroom. Will strained to catch their movements, their conversation. Someone went to the bathroom, then returned to the living room.

The talking grew louder, more heated. Will considered using the argument to cover the sounds of climbing out the window but decided it was still too risky. He remained in the closet until he finally heard the apartment door opening again, then slamming shut.

Will waited a few minutes longer, listening for any indication that Vulaj had stayed behind, then carefully emerged from the closet, knife in hand.

He couldn't be sure Vulaj wasn't coming back, so he went to the window and removed the screen, then climbed out.

The fire escape was on the rear of the building, overlooking the apartments' parking lot—and Vulaj stood below him beside a large black SUV, arguing with a skinny man wearing baggy jeans and a knit cap.

Will slipped back into the bedroom and replaced the screen.

He ran for the front door and stepped into the hall,

relieved to find it empty, then locked the door. As he headed quickly down the stairs he dropped Vanessa's keys, then stripped off his gloves and shoved them into his pockets.

Once he hit the main floor, he brought up the clipboard, grabbed a pen from his shirt pocket, and pretended to check off boxes as he went through the lobby. Two young mothers stood chatting by the mailboxes, babies in their arms, but they hardly gave him a look as he passed by.

As he stepped out of the building, he saw Vulaj heading his way.

Will looked down at his clipboard, keeping the bill of the ball cap low to hide his face, and continued toward the sidewalk at a leisurely pace. He wrote nonsense on the form with firm strokes of the pen as he passed Vulaj.

Once his back was to the man, he dropped the clipboard to his side and quickly crossed the street. As he did so, he turned his head enough to get a peripheral glimpse of the building—and spotted Vulaj walking back the way he'd come, gazing after him.

The man was sharper than he'd given him credit for.

Will kept going and turned at the first corner he came to. Then he picked up his pace; not running, which would bring unwanted attention, but moving fast. He took a few more detours, and after fifteen minutes he went to his car.

There was no sign of anyone having tried to follow him, or anyone looking for him, either.

Inside the car, he yanked off the ball cap and threw it down on the seat with a low curse, then laughed softly.

A close call, but he'd enjoyed every minute of it.

Fifteen

WILL WEDGED HIS CELL PHONE BETWEEN HIS SHOULDER
and ear, listening to it ring as he shoved the folded
uniform into his suitcase.

"Sheridan."

"I'm going to need help. Vulaj and Sharpton know
I'm not a journalist."

"Not unexpected."

Will forced his anger down, still pissed that Sheridan had put him in this position. "The situation is es-
calating."

"I've got a call in to Claudia. She's been following a
series of thefts from small galleries and museums that
don't appear to be connected to anything major, so I can
afford to pull her out for a few days. She's in Philly now,
and I'll get her to Boston tonight. Keep your phone on."

"Will do."

"Anything else you need to report?"

"Nothing new since the last call. I'll keep you posted. Thanks for pulling someone in to help me out."

"It's what I'm here for. I want all my people to come home safe."

The call ended, and Will stared at the phone for a moment. What the hell? Had that been an actual glimmer of sentiment in Sheridan's voice?

He shut the suitcase, then checked his appearance in the mirror. He'd changed into the suit he'd been wearing when he first saw Mia, but with a gold-and-gray striped tie. The suit looked great; *he* looked like he hadn't slept in the last twenty-four hours. Which he hadn't, come to think of it, except for a quick doze before dawn.

Christ, it had been a long day, and it was only going to get longer. Seeing Mia would be the one bright spot, and he picked up his pace as he headed toward the hotel parking garage.

The garage was gloomy and smelled of car exhaust and gasoline, and his footsteps echoed loudly as he walked toward his car. Another set of footsteps echoed as well.

He picked up the sound just as a hulking, man-shaped shadow separated from other shadows. A split second after that, a club swung toward his head.

Will lunged back out of range. The man wasn't Vulaj; he was powerfully built, dark-haired, dressed entirely in black.

With enough space between them to maneuver, his attacker didn't rush him again. Instead he circled, club raised and ready, waiting for Will to make a mistake. Will moved in unison, a partner in a slow dance of violent intent under the dull lights. There was no fear in the other man's dark eyes, only the watchfulness of a predator waiting its chance to strike.

If Will went for his gun, the man would attack—and he wasn't sure he could clear the holster in time.

Adrenaline kicked in, a wild rush of excitement and anticipation. Will darted to the side, trying to get behind the man, and barely missed another swipe of the club.

The man recovered quickly and forced Will back toward an empty parking spot, where he slipped on a patch of leaked engine oil and went down. He rolled to his feet in a crouch, raising his arm protectively over his head as the club swung toward him at a blurring speed. He managed to deflect it, but the blow still made contact with the back of his skull.

Pain exploded, and he stumbled backward, shaking his head to clear it.

Goddammit! That hit had been delivered with killing intent.

Will reached for his gun, but the man swung again and again, so fast that he had to raise both hands just to block each attack.

Breathing hard, Will ducked the next swing, spun,

and kicked for the knees. The man dodged, but the effort left him off balance long enough for Will to grab the club and wrench it free from the powerful grip.

He hurled it away, hearing it crack against concrete, and then he went at the man bare-handed, cold rage driving him.

Will pinned his larger assailant against a parked car, but the man fought like an animal. Will couldn't gain enough of a grip to do more than keep the man's fingers from gouging his eyes and fists from pummeling his head.

Then the man knifed his knee up toward Will's groin. Will twisted aside, taking the impact in his hip, but it cost him his advantage. The man rushed forward and rammed Will against the wall, slamming his head back so hard that his vision swam.

While he slumped, gasping for breath, the other man pulled his arm back. As the massive fist hurtled toward Will, he dropped down along the wall, and knuckles and concrete connected with a wet, crunching sound.

The man growled "Fuck!" and swung at Will with his other fist. Still dizzy, Will hadn't expected a southpaw punch and barely ducked fast enough to avoid it.

Away from the wall Will had room to maneuver again, and he delivered a flurry of blows, sending the other man reeling back against a car. Will moved after him with an intent to finish this fight, but his assailant launched forward, head down like a battering ram.

Will went down on his back again, this time with enough force to knock the wind out of him. Before he could suck in air, the man straddled his chest and wrapped both hands around his throat.

Will rammed the palm of his hand upward into his attacker's jaw. The grip around his neck loosened enough for him to rear up, grab the man by his hair, and drive his head into the wall with brutal force.

"Got you now, you sonofabitch!" Will rammed the man's head into the wall again.

A car door slammed, and a woman screamed, shrilly.

It was all the distraction his assailant needed, and he rolled off Will's chest, scrambled to his feet, and then took off at an unsteady run.

The woman screamed again, and kept screaming, and Will reacted instantly to the threat. He ran toward the woman and called out, "It's all right! That guy . . . he tried to mug me, but I scared him off. Stop screaming, for Christ's sake! It's hurting my head."

She abruptly shut up. He could see her clearly now, a pretty Asian woman crouched behind a silver Honda Civic, the right knee of her panty hose torn to reveal scraped skin, her eyes wide with fear.

Will slowly raised his hands. "I'm not going to hurt you. The mugger's gone. He ran out that way." He pointed, and the woman's gaze followed as she slowly stood.

"My God, I thought somebody was going to be killed! Are you sure you're all right? You're bleeding!"

No shit. And his head ached like a bitch where it had taken the glancing blow from the club *and* been smacked against concrete.

"Aside from a few cuts and bruises, I'm okay."

"We need to call the police. Maybe they can catch—"

"No," Will said sharply. At her startled look, he added more calmly, "I'm on my way to an important meeting, and I'm not hurt, nothing was stolen. I can't afford to be late. But you should report this to the front desk so they can increase the security around this place. Do you want me to walk you back to the lobby?"

She looked desperately grateful for the offer. "Please. I'm still so scared, I'm not sure I can walk."

Will gave her a soothing smile. "Sure you can. Is that your suitcase? Let me help you with it." He lifted it and kept up a steady stream of small talk until the color started to return to her face. Once she was in the lobby, he handed over her suitcase.

He briefly considered going up to his room to change his clothes—again—but decided against it, in case the cops showed up and detained him. There was a box of tissues in the car; he'd use that to wipe away most of the blood. He'd clean up at Mia's; all he had to do was tell her he'd been mugged and she would fuss over him.

The thought cheered him up considerably.

Back in the dim garage, his smile vanished. This

was Vulaj's work, the little bastard. But now that he'd had time to think it over, Will wasn't so sure that his bulky attacker had intended to kill him. If he had, it would've been more efficient just to shoot from the shadows.

Will put the car in gear and headed down the ramp, keeping an eye out in case his attacker was lurking for a second attempt.

There was no sign of the man, and Will switched his focus to spotting any tails. The last thing he wanted was to bring trouble to Mia's door.

Except that it was probably already too late to avoid that.

The realization hit with an icy jolt, setting off the pounding ache in his head.

Swearing under his breath, he reached in his coat for his cell phone—the display had been cracked in the scuffle—and called Morris's number. There was no answer, so he left a terse voice mail: "Tiernay here. Call me back. It's urgent."

Sixteen

"Oh, my God! What happened to you?" Mia stared at the cuts and bruises on Will's face, the splatter of blood on his shirt. "You were so late, I was worried, and now you show up looking like—"

"Some asshole tried to mug me," Will interrupted. "I wasn't in the mood to cooperate."

Wincing, Mia touched the oozing cut on the side of his mouth. "You must be hurting. Do you need to go to the hospital? I can drive you if—"

"No, I'm okay," he interrupted again. "I've got a few cuts and a hell of a headache, but nothing's broken."

"I can't believe you came here! You should've called and let me know what happened, and we could've gotten together later."

"I'm here because I want to be here. I needed to see you."

Mia hugged him tightly. "Did you call the police?"

"Yes, but the guy was long gone. Don't hug me too tight . . . you don't want what's all over this suit to get on you." He ran his hands slowly down the curve of her back, then eased her away. "If you don't mind, though, I'd like to take a shower. And maybe you could point me toward a box of Band-Aids."

How many men fought off a mugger, then got in a car and drove to see a lover as if nothing had just happened?

"Of course you can use my shower, but first you sit down right here." She pushed him onto the sofa, and he gave only token resistance. "I'm going to look you over to be sure." She pointed her finger at him as he opened his mouth. "No arguing. Just humor me."

She briskly got him out of his coat, wondering what he had in the pockets to make it so heavy, then pulled off his tie and unbuttoned his shirt, making a *tsk* sound. "This suit's in bad shape; I'm not sure it's worth trying to repair. Maybe I can get the blood out of the shirt. I'll throw it in the washing machine while you're in the shower."

She ran her fingers carefully over his head and found a large, sticky lump. He made a low sound as if trying to hold back a groan, and she pulled her hand away. "Will, that doesn't feel like 'nothing.' You could have a concussion—"

"I've had concussions before and know the signs. I'm okay. Really."

"You've had concussions often enough to self-diagnose?" Mia blinked, confused. "Will, what on earth are you—"

He suddenly leaned forward and kissed her, hard and hungry and with a lot of tongue. She gasped for breath when he pulled back, and caught the sparkle of amusement in his eyes.

"Mia, the best thing for me right now is you."

He couldn't be serious. "You don't mean sex, in the shape you're in?"

"Why not?" He gave her a slow grin, full of promise. "I *know* it'll make me feel better, and it'll probably make you feel better, too."

When he kissed her again, arguing suddenly made no sense. It was his body; who was she to say he wasn't up to the job? And from what she could feel now, as she leaned forward with her belly pressed against his groin, he was more than ready.

"All right then," Mia said, stepping back as he stood. "Go take a shower . . . and give me what you want me to put through the washer."

To her surprise—and appreciation—Will stripped down right there in the middle of her living room. How did a journalist maintain a lean, hard-muscled, physique like that? In the low light of her bedroom, he'd been utterly swoon-worthy. In the brighter light, and even a little roughed up, she had a sudden urge to rub up against him and purr.

"You'd better get in the shower fast." Mia laughed. "Because if you stay here looking like that, you'll never make it there."

"Yeah, yeah . . . promises, promises."

He grinned, which made her wince again to see the cut on his lip, then turned and headed down the hall, taking his suit coat and pants with him.

She gave him a few moments of privacy before following him to the bathroom, where her compact washer-dryer combo was. She could see him behind the frosted shower door, the lines of his body shadowed, leaving her to imagine the water on his skin, gleaming along muscles and sinews, dripping down his chest, his belly—

The room suddenly seemed much hotter.

"It's just me," she said, over the sound of the running water. "I'll get you some towels."

"Forget the towels. You just get naked in bed."

"What about the Band-Aids?"

Will opened the shower door and poked his head out, dripping water on her bathroom floor, and looking utterly adorable.

"Sure—can't have me bleeding all over your sheets." He waggled his brows at her. "Want to play doctor?"

Mia laughed again. "Deal. But you still get a towel. I don't want you dripping water all over my sheets, either."

His playful energy had instantly reduced her to a

giddy, light-headed blob of feminine lust—and she didn't care.

Grinning, Mia left a couple of big, fleecy towels on the sink counter, then took out the first-aid kit and re-treated to the bedroom. She turned on only the bedside light, and from under its dark linen shade the bulb glowed with an amber warmth.

She slipped out of her clothes but left on her white lace bra and thong. He'd have fun getting her out of her slinky things—which she'd allow only after he'd been properly doctored.

Her resolve on that was tested the second Will walked into the bedroom naked, rubbing his hair with a towel until it stood up spiky straight. The golden light enhanced the lean contours of muscle and sinew, and the contrast of boyish smile and tousled hair with raw male power left her breathless.

His smile widened. "White lace. Very nice."

"Thank you." She patted the bed beside her. "Now come here and let's make you feel better."

"I'm halfway there already."

Mia eyed him; the truth of his statement was blatantly displayed.

He sat beside her as she opened the first-aid kit, and Mia spent a good half hour tsk-tsking over Will's cuts, putting antibiotics and Band-Aids on some. Most of the cuts *were* superficial, though there were deeper cuts on his forehead, as well as the side of his mouth.

When she finished, she handed him three tablets of Tylenol Extra Strength and brought a glass of water from the kitchen.

"That should help with the headache."

"I'm already feeling a lot better." He reached over and caught her hands, pulling her closer. She scooted between his thighs, flushed with desire. "Though the white lace is nice, it's gotta go."

She draped her arms around his neck, resting her cheek against his damp hair as he nuzzled her cleavage and dropped soft kisses on the swell of her breasts while his busy fingers unfastened her bra.

A moment later he had the bra off, and his hot tongue circled her taut nipples, shooting a sweet pang of need through her, head to toe. Her fingers tightened in his hair, but she quickly let go, remembering the tender bump.

As he teased her nipples, he slid his palms along the curve of her bottom, then slipped a finger under the thong, rubbing her clitoris until her legs went weak and shaky.

"Hold on." Mia pulled back, giving him a long, lingering kiss on his mouth before kissing the line of his jaw, the exquisite curve of his neck, then down his chest and belly to the erection jutting toward her. She closed her hand around his shaft, working it up and down in a hot friction, rubbing her thumb across the sensitive head. Then she bent and took him in her mouth.

Will made a low sound of pleasure and moved his hands to her head, helping to guide her movements as she licked and sucked the hard length of him until she sensed he was ready to come. Then she kissed her way back up his chest to his mouth. His kiss was hard and hungry, surprising in its intensity.

Seconds later he'd stripped off her thong, pulled on a condom, and then thrust inside her. He was too close to the edge already, and his hips moved in a rough, unrelenting rhythm. It took just seconds before her orgasm built toward climax, and as she started to pant, he pulled her legs over his shoulders and thrust deeper until she came with a high gasp of pleasure, only a moment before he followed.

With a groan, Will rolled off her and sprawled back on the bed, an arm over his eyes, still breathing heavily.

Mia snuggled closer. "How's the headache?"

"Still there, but I don't care anymore." He let out a long sigh. "Thanks for that."

"Mmmm, totally my pleasure." She ran a finger lightly over his ribs, the corded muscles of his belly, and then up to his scorpion tattoo. "I don't suppose you can stay the night this time?"

"God, I wish I could. But no, I have a really tight deadline on this job."

"It's okay; I understand," she said, as she had last night, and tried not to sound disappointed.

She must've failed miserably at it, though, because

he rolled over to his side and looked right into her eyes. "I *am* sorry, Mia."

She lowered her face to his shoulder, turning toward his neck until she could gain control of her emotions again. Going all teary-eyed on him would be embarrassing. "You've probably noticed by now that I like having you around again."

"I started noticing a little while ago, yeah." He sounded amused, his voice muffled as he pressed soft, nibbling kisses along the side of her breast. "Until my brain exploded when you went down on me."

Her orderly thoughts scattered at each little kiss, and she shifted. "Will, I'm trying to be serious here."

His hands were already beginning to roam over her skin, lower and lower. "So am I."

"Where will you go once you leave Boston?"

"Assignments can take me anywhere. I just go where I'm told."

Mia gave up, too distracted to ask more questions. A part of her suspected he did this deliberately, but right now she didn't care why. She closed her eyes, sighing as a heavy languor of pleasure stole over her, and tried to guess by the touch of his breath where he'd kiss her next.

"It's so strange," she said, her voice husky and dreamy. "I keep feeling as if hardly any time has passed and that things should be just the way they were. I know it's not possible, yet it still feels that way."

"I know."

He pulled her legs up, then pushed her knees apart. Eyes squeezed shut in anticipation, she whispered, "You feel like that, too?"

"Yeah. I do." His breath was warm against her belly.

Mia arched her hips as his tongue brushed lightly against her, desire wrapping her tightly in its coil again. The sighs turned to gasps, then moans as he flicked his tongue rapidly over her while sliding several fingers inside, filling her with wonderful pressure.

"Beautiful," he whispered, and the feel of his breath on her damp, heated flesh sent her over the edge. Release came on strong, pulsing waves, one after the other, but even then he didn't stop, and kept licking and sucking and teasing until she came again. Lying limp on the damp sheets, gasping for breath, she didn't say a word as he rolled her over to her belly and pulled her hips up to meet his, sliding into her on a smooth, hot friction, so deep that she gasped out his name.

If she was going to die of pleasure, at least it was a sweet way to go. He played her body; knowing what felt best, knowing how to make it last for them both, building the pounding need to make it end as slowly as possible.

Mia moved her hips to meet his, fingers grasping at the pillows, panting so loudly that she could hardly hear the roar of blood pounding in her ears, or the harsh, urgent sounds Will made behind her. He was struggling to keep control, withdrawing almost completely, then entering her again slowly and deeply, and every time he thrust inside her, she moaned.

"I love how you feel in me," she managed to whisper. "Oh, God, it's so good . . ."

His long, slow thrusting rhythm suddenly changed and he moved harder, pulling her as close as he could, his fingers hard on her hips, and she didn't care that it hurt a little, she only wanted what he could give her.

Will came first this time, driving into her in a mindless need; then he reached down and touched her sensitive flesh, causing her to climax, too.

Mia fell facedown on the bed with a long sigh of utter contentment. The mattress dipped as Will collapsed beside her. When she had the energy to move again, she tipped her head toward him and found him watching her.

"I feel much better now," he murmured.

For a moment, she thought he might say something, then he sucked in a long breath and closed his eyes.

It reminded her of his earlier evasiveness, and she wanted to ask why he kept distracting her whenever she asked questions. But he looked so exhausted, she decided it could wait.

The sex probably should've waited, too. Feeling a little guilty, she leaned over and kissed him softly. "I think you need to get some sleep."

"Actually, I'm hungry. You got anything to eat?"

"It so happens I picked up a few things before you came over." She took in the shadows carved under his eyes, the darkening bruises. "Can I make you something?"

"Would you mind?"

"I can handle heating up a pizza and twisting the caps off of a couple of beers."

"Sounds like heaven to me."

"Good. I'm going to clean up and put your clothes in the dryer. When the pizza's ready, I'll come get you."

After taking care of his laundry, she had a quick, hot shower. On her way to the kitchen, she peeked into the bedroom and smiled at the sight of him still sprawled, gloriously naked, in her bed.

Mia thought he'd dozed off, but as she pulled the pizza out of the oven twenty minutes later, Will walked into the living room. "That smells good."

"Sausage and mushroom. The classics."

Wearing the boxers he'd pulled from the dryer, Will sat on the couch, arms along the length of its back, every relaxed, satisfied inch of him looking like he belonged there.

Stop, an inner voice warned. *Don't go there.*

Mia turned away until she had her composure firmly back in place, then brought over the pizza and beer. He straightened, making room for her, and draped an arm over her shoulders with a casual possessiveness that made her go warm. She opened their beers, and handed him his before raising hers in a toast.

"For old times' sake," she said.

He clinked the bottle against hers but said nothing.

A tickle of unease surfaced again, but Mia ignored it as they ate quietly, leaving not a single slice.

"You should probably get going," she said, snuggling close to him again. "It's late."

"I know, but I don't want to. I like this," he said, echoing her earlier thoughts. "I like being here with you, eating pizza and drinking beer. It feels nice."

With her head resting against his chest, she listened to his voice rumble deeply inside. "I was an idiot to ever let you go."

He laughed softly. "Sometimes you make me sound like I was some kind of saint. It's nice to revisit the old me, though. It's been a long time since I thought about who I was then, what I wanted."

"Besides lots of sex?"

"That hasn't changed, true."

"So what have you been doing all this time? You really never answered when I asked the other day. Where's home?"

Mia tensed slightly, waiting for him to dodge the question, but he answered, "I live in Portland when I'm not roaming around for work. It really does take me all over the world, sometimes for months at a time."

"How come you never got married? I can't believe

there weren't legions of women waiting to snap you up."

Will shrugged. "No time or opportunity, I guess. There was a woman I was involved with for a long time. We met in Columbus, and when she got a job in Seattle I decided to go with her. I already knew the long-distance romance thing was risky. We split up anyway, but when she left Seattle, I stayed."

He added, "I never forgot you, Mia. I moved on, but there was always this small part of me that never let you go."

The melancholy in his voice brought a lump to her throat. "I never forgot you, either," she whispered. "A girl never forgets the first man she fell in love with, the first man who taught her how nice sex could be. No matter what, he always holds a special place in her memories."

An awkward silence settled over the room, so she added more lightly, "Until he shows up in her life again. Reality is a hell of a lot nicer than a memory."

Will eased up from his slouch to finish off his beer, but he pulled her close as he did so. It was as if he didn't want to let her get too far away from him, despite how he kept telling her he couldn't stay. A photo of her parents sat on the coffee table, near where he'd set his bottle. He picked it up, looking at it briefly before returning it.

"How are your mom and dad?" he asked. "And your sisters?"

"My parents are doing fine. Dad's retired now and driving my mom crazy. All my sisters except Susan are married."

"When I last saw Susan, she was what, seven or eight?"

"Yep, and she hasn't changed as much as you'd expect. She's still charming and spoiled rotten. She's going to Ohio State. It's like a family tradition or something. Except for Elizabeth—she was the rogue and went to USC."

"That sounds like Elizabeth," Will said, smiling. He'd liked her; she'd had a mutinous streak of spunk that appealed to him.

"She married a dentist and is living the good life, with two kids. Both boys, and they keep her plenty busy. Poetic justice, considering how she drove my folks crazy."

"How come you never had any kids?"

Mia shrugged. "The timing was never right, or the guys weren't quite right."

Discussing these subjects, even casually, made things between them feel more serious than was wise. It frightened her almost as much as it made her happy.

"So how long have you known Vanessa?"

The abrupt shift took Mia by surprise. "Mmmm, five years now. Why?"

"Just wondering. You seem really close."

"Oh, yes. We even lived together for a few years.

Our personalities are really different, but somehow it always worked to our advantage. Well, except when I'm being overprotective."

"That must be interesting when she brings home a boyfriend."

Mia felt a blush warm her face. "I don't usually like most of them because they're such bastards to her, and it pisses me off that she makes excuses for them. But this latest one doesn't seem as bad. She's happier than I've ever seen her, which makes me a little nervous. If he flakes out on her, picking up the pieces isn't going to be pretty. If that happens, though, I'll be there for her. That's what friends are for."

Will didn't answer, and Mia couldn't quite pin down the expression on his face. Wariness, perhaps, reminding her of the odd tension she'd sensed between him and Vanessa earlier. What had that been about? Will had no reason to dislike Vanessa; he hardly knew her—although he kept asking questions about her. "Speaking of Vanessa, why—"

"Why is a very good question," he interrupted, kissing her. "Why are we even talking about her? Why are we talking at all? How about one more for the road?"

He didn't mean beer, and she blinked in surprise. "Are you trying to distract me on purpose?"

His brows shot up. "Well, yeah. We don't have a lot of time, and I want to make the best use of what we do have."

Now she felt stupid for bringing it up. "Never mind. I just . . . sometimes I was feeling like you don't want me asking questions."

"Sorry." He ran his thumb over her bottom lip. "I'll try not to do that again. Okay?"

Mollified, she leaned on him. "Okay."

"So what do you say to one for the road?"

"Why not?" Mia laughed. "Right here, on the couch."

"Then you'd better move the rodent. I'm not making love to you while a rat watches me."

"Love me, love my ferret—and he's *not* a rodent."

But she relocated Caligula's cage and rediscovered the joys of making out on a couch, which she hadn't done since she was in high school.

Before Will left, he kissed her and promised to come by early and pick her up. "I'll even make breakfast," he added.

"You don't have to do that."

"You made me pizza. My turn to return the favor."

"When you put it that way, how can I argue?" She pulled a key chain off a hook on a shelf by the door. "I'm not a morning person, so let yourself in. Careful not to lose it, though; it's the only spare key I have left."

Seventeen

"Is something wrong?" Vanessa asked from the hallway, blinking as her eyes adjusted to the light.

Of course something was wrong. *Everything* was wrong. Their entire situation had gone from wonderful to abysmal in a matter of hours. She'd gone to bed a little while ago, desperate for sleep, but Kos was still up, moving restlessly around the apartment.

"Just thinking. You should go back to bed."

She'd told him about Will Tiernay's intimidating behavior, which had upset him, but he'd been furious when she mentioned she'd dropped her keys on the way to work that morning. She didn't understand why that was more of a problem than Tiernay: a neighbor had found the keys and turned them in at the rental office; the super had called, and she'd picked them up. Hardly a big deal.

But then Kos said he suspected someone had actually

stolen her keys without her realizing it, and broken into
the apartment. It was possible; Will had forced her to
leave him alone at her desk. She'd looked over the
apartment but hadn't noticed a thing out of place.

"I'm having a hard time sleeping while you're pac-
ing around like this."

Kos rubbed at his brows and let out a sigh. "Sorry."

"Do you want to talk about it?" She walked to him,
slid her arms around his waist, his skin warm against
her bare breasts. "Is there anything I can do?"

"You're doing everything you need to do. This is a
problem I have to take care of myself."

"I take it you're referring to Tiernay."

"Yes."

The threat he represented had gnawed at her peace
of mind all day. "What are you going to do about him?"

"I'm not sure. I tried the quick and easy solution
first, but that didn't work out."

Judging from the scowl on his face, the "quick and
easy solution" was off-limits for discussion, and it wasn't
something she even wanted to think about. "So do you
have other options?"

"A few." Kos kissed her absently on the top of her
head, and she melted against him. Pathetic to react like
that to such a simple gesture, but her hunger for even
the most basic affection was never satisfied, even now.

After a moment, she added, "Remember, you said
you wouldn't do anything to Mia."

"Her being with him makes things more difficult. But I'll do everything in my power to keep my promise." Kos kissed her again. "You have to understand, though, that if it comes to a choice between her and you, I'm going to choose you."

His words both thrilled and terrified her, but she had to trust him. At this point, she had no other choice. It was too late to turn back.

"Maybe we should just take what we have and run with it now."

Kos shook his head. "I can't do that. I have my part in a deal to see through, and all we need is a few more days. If we're careful, we can still pull it off just like we planned."

"Why isn't he moving against us, if he knows?"

"Because we haven't done anything yet that the cops can use to prosecute us."

The word chilled her, reminding her of the finality of her choices. She had no regrets—or few, if she were honest with herself—but it still frightened her. "There's the second copy of the reliquary. Wouldn't that get us into trouble?"

"No. Until we switch the replicas with the real pieces, they don't have anything. I don't think Tiernay knows about the second copy, either. Once we make our move, though, things become difficult. The biggest mistake right now would be to panic and settle for less. Be strong, Vanessa. Remember?"

"I remember." She smiled faintly. *Her*, strong—an oxymoron if ever there was one.

The plan was a simple one. They were taking only a select few pieces: the reliquary, the chalice, and several necklaces and pairs of earrings. Kos's partner already had buyers lined up for those items. After they sold the second reliquary on their own later, they'd have all the money they needed to start over fresh.

"So you're saying I'll need to put up with Tiernay watching me, knowing that he knows. That's not going to do much for my peace of mind."

"Can't be helped. I have a few plans in place to keep things balanced in our favor, though. So keep on doing what you're doing, and leave the rest to me."

"Did your partner give you any advice on what to do?"

It felt strange to talk about a man she hadn't met and didn't even have a name for. Kos had flatly refused to tell her, saying it wasn't safe for her to know.

"He said killing Tiernay would cause too much trouble, and I agreed."

Suddenly weak-kneed, she leaned against Kos. "Please. No killing. That man terrifies me, but you said we could do this *without* killing anybody."

"And we will. I don't want to kill, either. It's bad for business."

To say the very least!

"So what is this alternative plan?" Vanessa asked,

half afraid of his answer. "Can you tell me about it?"

"I'm still thinking it over. Until I get it all straight in my head, I'm keeping it to myself."

It disappointed her that he wouldn't share even this much, but considering how bad she was at lying, it was for the best. When the time was right, he'd explain.

"And we're not going to talk on the phone at Haddington anymore. He may have mics or cameras around. Check tomorrow if you get a chance; look for anything suspicious. We'll meet at our place for lunch and talk then."

"Okay," Vanessa whispered. "But I'm feeling way over my head here."

"It's almost over. You just need to be strong for a little while longer."

Swallowing, she said, "Then I'll leave you to your thinking and go back to bed. Tomorrow's going to be a rough day. And the day after that probably even worse."

When she gave him a fierce hug, his muscles stiffened in surprise, then relaxed as he returned the hug. "You be careful," she whispered. "It's you he's really after, not me."

There were a lot of places Will wanted to be at two o'clock in the morning, but on surveillance in a dark car across the street from the Haddington building, with nothing but the cold dregs of coffee to keep him alert, was not one of them.

The guilt and unease dogging him didn't improve his mood, either. He hadn't realized how close Mia was with Vanessa; she would be deeply hurt when this was all over.

Ben would tell him not to sweat the little details, that nothing mattered but to get the job done and to get it done right. Will believed in Avalon's mission, and even the questionable methods Ben sometimes used to achieve those ends, but he couldn't harden himself to the consequences the way Ben could.

When had being one of the good guys become so damn complicated?

The world *needed* groups like Avalon. Law enforcement agencies didn't have enough money and personnel to deal with art theft and looting, and while most of the criminal underworld wasn't too smart, every now and then a Rainert von Lahr came along. Von Lahr had flair and vision, wielding the same skills that shot ambitious executives to the tops of their companies, and he knew how to use the limitations of international law enforcement to his advantage.

Von Lahr and others like him had to be stopped, and it was a fight that would never end. Because when one was taken out, another oozed out of the shadows to take his place.

But that wouldn't make a damn bit of difference to Mia when she learned of Vanessa's betrayal. There'd be no avoiding the hurt. Even worse would be the moment she figured out why he'd really come to Haddington—and that what he appeared to be, had said to her, had done with her, was all part of an act.

I betrayed your trust. That's the worst thing one person can do to another. You'd never do something like that, I know it.

The irony was so perfect that he would've found it amusing had it not stung so much.

"Payback's a bitch, boy," he muttered.

Christ, his head ached—and he found himself wishing Vulaj or Vanessa would try to sneak into the Haddington building right now, because he could *really* use the distraction.

His cell phone vibrated, and when he answered a woman's voice said, "Hey there, beautiful, it's Claudia. I'm in town. Where are you? I tried calling you a couple of times earlier, but you didn't answer. I guess you were, ah, occupied."

Apparently Ben had clued her in, which annoyed Will, even though it was within Ben's rights to do so. "I'm at Haddington, watching the back door."

"Why? I thought you'd be spying on the mafioso wannabe and his ladylove. Ben said they're your targets."

"Since Avalon doesn't have cloning technology yet, I picked the place that needed watching the most. The Eudoxia collection is in the vault. Vulaj and Sharpton aren't likely to skip town without the originals. And if they did, then they wouldn't be our problem any longer because von Lahr would take care of 'em himself. Elementary, my dear."

"As charmingly sarcastic as ever. Where exactly is this place? Ben's directions were kind of vague, and I'm not real familiar with Boston."

After giving her directions, he added, "Thanks for getting here so fast, Claudia. I owe you one."

She snorted. "Just doing my job, beautiful, but I'll keep your offer in mind. I'm on my way. Stay outta trouble, and don't do anything I wouldn't do."

"That won't be difficult," Will replied dryly. "I never do what you do."

"Oooh, that almost hurts. If Ben hadn't told me to be nice to you, I'd give you serious shit for that."

With an effort, he held back his retort. "See you in a few," he said, then he cut the connection.

Claudia Cruz wouldn't have been his first choice for backup, since everything about the woman pissed him off. But she was more than competent, and already the tension in his shoulders was easing, the ache stubbornly throbbing between his eyes fading.

Twenty minutes later, a car pulled up behind him. He drew his gun to be safe, and from his rearview mirror watched the approach of a shadowy figure. Passing under the streetlight, the shadow transformed into a tall, slender woman in jeans and a sweatshirt, the solid black of her clothing a stark contrast to the brassy short hair, dark eyes, and full lips outlined in hooker red.

It was Claudia, all right, in man-eater Technicolor.

She rapped on his window, and when he lowered it she leaned inside, grinning. "Hey, there. What happened to your pretty face?"

"One of Vulaj's buddies jumped me."

"Must've hurt. So you gonna let me inside the car, or what?"

"Say please."

"Fuck you."

"Considering the source, that's close enough." Will unlocked the doors, and she walked around and dropped into the passenger's seat, filling the car with a heavy floral perfume.

"What were you doing in Philly?" he asked.

"Chasing shadows and playing peekaboo with an asshole Fed."

Will pitied the poor Fed.

"There's some nutcase hitting little no-name museums and second-string galleries, making off with chump change, but even chump change starts adding up." She made an impatient gesture. "Unfortunately, he or she is smarter than the average nutcase. No clues, no apparent motive to resell. I hate the artsy-fartsy freaks that horde their sparklies. It's damn hard to catch 'em."

Like him, Claudia was one of the few ex-cops on Ben Sheridan's mostly ex-military payroll. She'd left the force under shady circumstances that she'd never explained, Ben had never elaborated upon, and Will had never questioned. But she was as smart as she was ruthless.

"I'm going to need you for surveillance."

"I figured as much. Who am I surveilling?"

"I have the building here under control, and I can keep an eye on Sharpton during the work hours, but I need someone to keep tabs on Vulaj and watch Sharpton's apartment."

Will quickly brought her up-to-date on what he knew, as well as his suspicions. "I got inside to look for the second reliquary, but Vulaj showed up before I could finish the search. I didn't have time to set up equipment inside, and he's onto me by now, so I won't get another chance."

"Ambitious little worms, aren't they?" Claudia said. "But not too smart. When von Lahr figures out what they've done, he'll strangle them in their own guts."

"More than likely he'll just shoot them. From a distance." Will stretched, trying to ease the numb tingle in his ass. "But yeah, I get the sense Vulaj is running on ninety percent adrenaline and ten percent brainpower. Makes him even more dangerous."

"Whatever. Creepy calm or apeshit crazy, we do what we gotta do." Claudia yawned. "Oh, and by the way, Ellie has a message for you. She says you're not supposed to fight in your good suits. Ben won't pay out for a tailor on any more expense reports."

"What?" He stared at her, confused by the abrupt change in subject. "When did—"

"And Shaunda thinks you're a sleazy mofo for almost hitting on her. But for the record, she thinks you're hot, too. Direct quote, by the way."

"What the hell? Did the three of you get together for lunch and gossip?"

"Something like that, yeah."

The thought was terrifying yet fascinating—in a car wreck kind of way.

"From the looks of you, Ellie should've passed on the message sooner. She gives your common sense way too much credit."

Will briefly closed his eyes. He could stay calm; he *could*. No more incidents with the two of them trying to shout each other down. "Knock off the editorializing. I'm not in the mood."

"Are you ever?"

"Claudia—"

"My bad, I forgot to be nice. So give me what you got on Bonnie and Clyde. And if there's anything else I can do, let me know. Like maybe stay close so you don't get beat up again."

"I don't need that kind of backup."

"Don't be stupid about this, Tiernay. Vulaj tried to have you killed tonight."

At her sudden seriousness, his annoyance faded. "I

doubt he was trying to kill me. If that's what he wanted, they would've just shot me."

"So what are you saying, that they were trying to scare you away by caving in your skull with a club?"

"I think they were trying to get me out of the way for a good long time, and if I happened to kick it eventually, they didn't care. An assault gets less attention than a homicide."

"I can think for myself, thank you very much," Claudia said impatiently. "And you're splitting hairs here. Vulaj is onto you, and you need someone to watch your back. He's gonna try to take you out again."

"I don't think he'll risk outright murder."

"He may not know you're Avalon, but he at least suspects you of being an undercover cop. I wouldn't put outright murder past him."

"He's not ready to make a move yet, I'm sure of it. If he bails now he loses the reliquary and everything else, and that spells no money and one very irate von Lahr, who's not exactly the forgiving sort. If he can juggle a few more plates for a few more days, then he's clear. So we can play along. And I won't give him a second chance at me."

"Sounds like you've got a plan."

"Several. One is finding a way inside that vault to check on the reliquary. The second involves me putting the squeeze on Sharpton today."

Claudia grinned. "That'll piss off Vulaj."

"And goad him into acting stupidly, if I'm lucky. That's why I need you to keep a close eye on him." He passed her the file Morris had given him, along with Vanessa's address. "And on your way over there, I'd appreciate it if you could check up on someone else for me."

"Sure. I'm here to assist, so let me assist away. And at the risk of stating the obvious, you look pretty bad. What are you going to say when people ask what happened?"

Will shrugged. "Someone tried to mug me and I fought them off. It's what I told Mia earlier."

"Mia," Claudia repeated with a sly grin, stretching out the first syllable so it was a catlike sound. "Such a pretty name. And I bet she's sweet and pretty, too, because that's your type, isn't it? I take it she's the 'someone' you want me to check up on?"

"Yes, she is. Where are you staying?"

"Same hotel you are," Claudia said. "So what's the address for this chick that you're banging when you should be watching your ass?"

"Claudia," Will said from between his teeth. "Knock it the fuck off."

"Truth hurts, doesn't it? Men." She sniffed. "You always think with your dicks, when you think at all."

"Careful, now. You wouldn't want anybody accusing you of being sexist."

"If you can call me a ball-busting bitch just because I'm an aggressive female, then I can call you a dick-brain. Equal opportunity insulting and all that."

Will laughed; he couldn't help it. "You have your moments. It doesn't mean I like you, but I do appreciate you."

"And some days, that's all a girl really needs to hear." Claudia grinned. "Now, what's this sweet thing's address and why am I checking up on her?"

He gave her the address, then hesitated. "I want to make sure she's safe."

Claudia regarded him for a long moment, her gaze knowing, but to his surprise she didn't push it. "Okay. And be careful yourself."

Eighteen

MIA WOKE TO THE SMELLS OF BREWING COFFEE, FRYING eggs and bacon, and buttered toast. At first she thought it was a gloriously self-indulgent dream, then she heard a loud clang and male cursing, and memory flooded back.

"He wasn't joking," she mumbled and glanced at the alarm clock on the bedside table.

7:00 AM.

She swung out of bed and shuffled to the bathroom to make herself look a little less scary. She brushed her teeth, splashed water on her face, and ran her fingers through her hair, then peered at herself in the mirror. Not bad, all things considered; he was just going to have to make allowances here.

Wearing an XXL Jack Sparrow T-shirt, she went out to the kitchen. Will had draped his suit coat over a chair and stood at her stove in a crisp white shirt, flipping eggs. The coffeemaker was in its final throes, hissing and spitting, reminding her she needed to give its innards a good cleaning soon.

"Mmmm, when you said you'd make breakfast, I was expecting donuts or Pop-Tarts. I'm almost positive this is a bacon-virgin kitchen," she said as he turned. "You're spoiling me."

His eyes crinkled as he smiled—the bruises and cuts didn't look as bad, but they were still a bit of a shock first thing in the morning—and then his gaze took in her sleep-tousled hair and the obvious fact that she didn't have a bra on. She wasn't wearing underwear, either.

"You look great," he said, turning back to the stove. "And that raspy sleep voice is a turn-on."

She smiled to herself, eyeing his broad back. Bacon was nice, but nothing beat a man who cooked *and* delivered multiple orgasms. "Is that so?"

"Everything about you turns me on. Now, sit down at the table before I forget myself and end up burning your bacon."

Mia sat, yawning, as he placed a cup of coffee in front of her, along with a plate of perfect sunny-side up eggs, bacon, and a slice of toast buttered just right.

"I could seriously get to like this," she said, staring at the steaming eggs.

"So could I." He sat across from her and dug in with an appetite worthy of a man twice his size. A sheepish expression crossed his face when he noticed her watching him. "After the adventure in the parking garage and hours of great sex, I'm *really* hungry."

Amused, Mia took a bite of her eggs—and briefly closed her eyes, savoring the taste. "Mmmm, excellent. I had no idea you could cook."

"Don't be too impressed. This is the *only* thing I can cook, aside from macaroni and cheese from a box."

"Sounds like you still live on a college student's diet."

"I've given up Ramen."

"Thank God." Mia shuddered.

When she finished, he collected her plate, rinsed their dishes, and stacked them in the dishwasher—actually *in* the dishwasher, not the sink.

A crazy urge to chain this man to her bed for all eternity took hold, and Mia marched over to the sink, grabbed his face, and pulled him down for a long, deep kiss. He kissed her back with equal enthusiasm, and he tasted so much like coffee and butter that she had to nibble on his lip.

When she pulled back a moment later, he asked, bemused, "What was that for?"

"For putting the dishes in the dishwasher."

"Damn." His brows shot up. "What'll you do to me if I vacuum the floor?"

She gave him a sexy grin. "Try it and find out." In no hurry to leave his arms, Mia settled closer against him. "Are you coming in to work with me?"

"Might as well. It's not like we'll be fooling anyone that we didn't spend most of last night together."

Mia gently touched the cut by his mouth. "When Hugh sees you, he's going to assume we had a most interesting night of it."

Will laughed. "Don't worry. I'll set him straight that it was willing sex."

Then he kissed her again, palms sliding down her back to her bottom, rubbing along the curves—and going still as he realized she wore nothing beneath the T-shirt. He growled deep in his throat and pulled up her shirt.

The next thing she knew, she was naked and backed against the counter, his pants and belt buckle hit the floor with a loud thump, he'd lifted her legs around his hips, and then he was pushing inside her, hard and urgent. It wasn't the most comfortable position and the counter pressed into her back, but within seconds she stopped noticing. Even to her pleasure-hazed senses, her moans and sighs sounded loud enough to wake the entire building.

Then she came, and couldn't have cared less if her cries woke all of Boston.

It was over almost as quickly as it began, and Will leaned heavily forward, hands bracing himself on the counter to keep his weight off her. He slowly raised his head, his gaze meeting hers.

"Christ," he said. "You okay?"

"Did it sound like I was in distress?" she demanded as she lowered her legs.

"I guess not," he said with that melting, beautiful grin.

She laughed and pushed him back. "I have to clean up, then we can leave."

After she showered and dressed, she fed Caligula, then argued briefly with Will over whether to walk or take his car.

He won, mainly because he claimed to have a lot of equipment and supplies in the trunk that he might need.

"So what exactly does a journalist do?" she asked as she climbed into the passenger seat. "So far, all I've seen you do is hang around and ask questions."

As he turned to check over his shoulder before pulling out into traffic, Mia admired his profile. He had great shoulders buck naked, but somehow a suit made them look broader.

"That about covers it. Journalists, like all writers, observe and absorb, then disgorge."

"I'd like to read a few of your articles. You wouldn't have any copies of older magazines or journals in the trunk, would you?"

"No, but if I come across any extra copies later, I'll let you have them."

"Deal." As he pulled into the small lot, she noticed that Hugh's car was already there. She could count on one hand the number of times he'd beat her into the shop in the last two years. "Hugh must've decided to get in a little early work."

"Unless we're a little late," Will pointed out.

True; such were the perils of kitchen sex first thing in the morning.

Will followed her to the back door, waiting as she entered the security code, and then he pulled the door open for her.

"You take security seriously here."

"We have to. Sometimes we have millions of dollars' worth of art or jewelry on-site."

"Is Hugh the only one who can open the vault?"

It wasn't an odd question, yet she felt a sudden flutter of unease. "Will," she said softly, "that's really something you should ask Hugh, not me. It's not that I don't trust you, but technically I'm not supposed to say—"

He held up his hand. "It's all right. I understand, and you're right to tell me to back off. I have no business asking questions like that."

As they passed Vanessa's empty workstation, he asked, "Do you ever see her boyfriend?"

The question took Mia by surprise. "Of course, though not as much since she moved out. These days, I only run into him when he drops her off or picks her up. Kos puts in a lot of time at work, and I think Vanessa said that he's taken a second job, too."

"Not exactly the social couple, huh?"

Mia shook her head. "Van's really shy. She does all right with small groups of people she knows, but large parties terrify her."

"Must be rough. I take it the two of you don't go out to parties together, seeing as how there's nothing shy about you."

She didn't live for weekends and parties, but the energy sparking through groups of people energized her, and she also liked the conversation, the drinks, and getting dressed up. "She doesn't go with me often, no."

In fact, Vanessa hadn't gone out with Mia to a party or a bar since Kos had moved in. It wasn't unusual for friends to cut back on social activities once they became part of a couple, especially if they weren't very social to begin with, but Will's comment reminded her how isolated Vanessa had been lately. An old, unwelcome pattern Mia hadn't picked up on because Van seemed so much happier this time around.

She also realized that this wasn't the first time Will had shown curiosity about Vanessa and her love life.

When they stopped at her desk, Mia turned, looking him directly in the eyes. "Why do you keep asking about Kos and Vanessa?"

"Curiosity. I'm still having trouble reconciling the two of you as friends."

"What does that have to do with anything?"

He scratched his chin, his expression faintly perplexed. "I don't know. I guess asking questions all the time is one of those journalistic bad habits. I don't even notice anymore when I'm doing it, so if I'm bothering you, just tell me to knock it off."

The explanation made sense, to her relief. "I'll do that, then. Now go pester Hugh before he gets jealous over my hogging you."

With a wink, Will strode across the room. When Hugh looked up, his eyes widened, and he boomed, "Good God, man! What happened to your face?"

"Somebody tried to mug me in the parking garage at the hotel. I wasn't in the mood to be robbed. I won; no big deal," Will said, his tone dismissive, as it had been last night. "I was thinking that I need to add a few general facts to my article. Can you give me your thoughts on the appeal of Byzantine art? And what's your opinion on the reliquary's notoriety? Is it because of the relic, the curse, or something else?"

Once Hugh started talking about the history of Byzantine art and regional differences, a subject he could drone on about for hours, Mia tuned out their conversation. Since she was done with her work, she headed over to Vanessa's table to see if there was anything she could do to help out.

Mia didn't know what was taking Vanessa so long; she was usually a much faster worker. As she turned the reliquary over, she frowned, almost certain the left side of the box had been completed when she'd looked at it yesterday.

But one corner wouldn't take Vanessa long, and she wouldn't need any help. As Mia walked over to ask Hugh what she should do next, the back door closed with its customary heavy thud.

"Morning! I'm so sorry I'm late, but there was an accident on the—" Vanessa stopped short, staring at Will, her eyes widening. Then, looking away, she added quickly, "I apologize. It was rude of me to stare."

"Unless you were the guy who attacked me with a club last night, you have nothing to apologize for."

Vanessa's head snapped up, expression alarmed, before she looked away again. "I was trying to be polite, that's all. Your face is—"

"Believe me," Mia cut in, trying to ease the strain she sensed. "He looks much better this morning than he did last night."

What was going on here? Mia glanced at Will, who was watching Vanessa—until he realized Mia was looking at him; then he turned away and smiled ruefully at her.

"So much for my attempt at humor," he said. "I think I need more coffee."

Mia gave him a warning poke and whispered, "She doesn't deal well with teasing."

Will nodded and returned to his conversation with Hugh. Within minutes they were laughing again like old pals, but Mia couldn't shake a lingering sense of doubt. Something here was not right. She didn't want to admit it, because it was so alien to *her* Will, but there was something distinctly . . . cold about him all of a sudden.

After a moment, she said, "Excuse me, Hugh, but I'm finished with the earrings, and it doesn't look like Vanessa needs my help. Is there anything you'd like me to do?"

"I have paperwork threatening to stage a coup in my office. Could you do filing for me? And open mail?"

Mia shot him an exasperated look—Hugh's paperwork backlog was always threatening him in some way—but said only "Sure."

"And get hold of the security company to confirm the armored truck is scheduled as I requested. I want to get this collection to the Met as quickly as possible once we're done. And then I'm going to sleep for a week straight."

She didn't blame him for pushing all of them so hard; this was their biggest contract to date. It would be a catastrophe for Hugh if anything happened to the Eudoxia collection. "Where's the number?"

"In the address book. I think. If not, check my desk for an invoice."

"Do you want to look at the earrings before I box them up?"

Hugh sighed and sat back. He was carefully adding dents and scratches to the gold chalice to match the original, which had gone through a few adventures after its discovery. "I know you've done a perfect job, because you always do, but it would be remiss of me if I didn't take a peek. Bring them and the originals on over."

Will was quietly watching the exchange, and Mia remembered what he'd said about writers observing and absorbing.

She hadn't told him that she and Vanessa both had access to the vault, but now he'd figure it out. It wasn't anything for her to worry about, but it did make her wonder what else he'd observed while with her.

Annoyed with herself, she pushed the doubts away and went to retrieve the original gold and pearl earrings. She brought the case, along with the reproductions, over to Hugh, then stood aside quietly while he compared the two.

"How do you mark the reproductions?" Will asked.

"We usually add a small logo identification, though sometimes we simply alter an unobtrusive area to make it more easily identifiable as a reproduction. Mr. Toller didn't want that, so we have to mark these as inconspicuously as possible." Hugh slipped on his magnifier loupe, then bent over both pairs of earrings, adjusting each lens as needed. "After that, it's up to the museums and collectors to tag their collections properly."

"It's a tricky business, buying and selling art and antiquities."

"God, if people had only half a clue how crazy it can be." Hugh sat back. "But don't get me started on that."

"Yes, please." Mia nodded vigorously. "It does bad things to his blood pressure."

Will smiled. "I'm fairly up-to-date on that aspect of the business."

Of course he would be; anybody even remotely associated with the art world knew that art theft was big business, right up there with drug and weapon smuggling.

"Sorry," Mia said. "Back when I knew you, you couldn't tell a Fra Lippi from a Degas."

A strange look came over his face, and he shrugged. "Yeah . . . funny, where life brings us."

He sounded regretful, which brought all her vague, uneasy doubts rushing back. Yes, something here was wrong—*very* wrong—and later tonight they were going to talk about it. This time she wouldn't let him distract her with kisses or sex.

Hugh pronounced her work "superb," and she returned both pairs of earrings to their respective places, then went to tackle the stack of filing on Hugh's desk and call about the armored truck and guards.

When she emerged to grab a bottle of water, Will and Hugh were still talking and Vanessa was still toiling over the reliquary copy.

"How about I take everyone out for lunch?" Will offered. "It's the least I can do for getting in your way over the past few days."

"Splendid idea. I make it a policy never to turn down free food." Hugh checked his watch. "I'll have to make it quick, though. I already know Mia's answer. How about you, Van? Up for a lunch on Tiernay here?"

Vanessa stood to look over the partition, her expression uncertain as she glanced from Will to Mia to Hugh. She smiled even as she raised her shoulders in a shrug. "I don't know . . . I have work to do. I should probably stay."

"Oh, come on. You need to eat," Will said, his tone friendly and cajoling. "I'm not going to take no for an answer."

At that, Vanessa's smile faded. "I really should stay. Besides, I'm sure Kos will be coming by to pick me up for a late lunch."

"Invite him along." Will flashed a smile. "Like Hugh said, it's free food."

"Will's right," Mia said, guessing that he was trying to make up for when his attempt at humor had backfired. "Give Kos a call and tell him to meet us."

Vanessa hesitated, then shrugged again. "I suppose I have no good reason to say no. I'll call Kos, but I can't promise that he'll be able to come."

When Vanessa disappeared back behind her cubicle, Will turned to Mia, looking pleased with himself. "It'd almost be like those double dates we used to go on with Kathy and Sam. Remember?"

Memories came rushing back, and for a moment her

niggling little doubts dropped away. "How could I forget? They were always fighting. I used to think they'd never last, but I got an email from her a few months back, and she and Sam just had their fourth baby."

"Really?" Will's face seemed to light up, genuine pleasure warming his eyes. "You've kept in touch with them?"

"Yup. Even Christmas and Hanukkah cards. If you want, I can give you Sam's email address. I bet he'd love to hear from you."

Some of the warmth faded from his eyes, even though the smile remained. "Yeah, I'd like that. Okay, back to the subject. Anybody have a favorite restaurant? Price doesn't matter; the boss owes me a little extra this time around."

"I vote for that wonderful Indian restaurant over on Boylston Street," Mia said. "The curry tastes even better than it smells."

"Works for me," Hugh said.

"Vanessa?" Will called. "How does that sound to you?"

There was a brief silence, then Vanessa's muffled voice answered "Fine."

"My, my, someone's still in a bad mood. I'm going to make sure she eats dessert. She's too damn thin." Hugh winked at Mia. "Me, I like a woman with curves."

"No argument from me," Will said, smiling as he met Mia's gaze. "But I think Vanessa is one of those naturally tall, thin British types. Feed her all the tiramisu in the world, and she'll never look like Mia."

Hugh's eyes twinkled with amusement. "Our resident earth mother pagan goddess. Pity she works for me, or I'd have tried a go-round with her myself."

"Please." Mia closed her eyes, feigning long-suffering patience. "I'm going back to filing. Just knock on the window when it's time to go to lunch, and—"

"Why not now?" Will asked. "It's nearly noon. Mia, go wrestle Vanessa away from that damn box. We can take my car."

Fifteen minutes later, they'd locked away all of the valuables, checked out with the receptionist, and piled into Will's car. Hugh graciously allowed Mia to sit up front as he and Vanessa stuffed their long-legged selves in the backseat.

"It's okay," Vanessa said, when Mia offered to trade places. "You sit with Will. It's a short ride anyway."

"Is your boyfriend joining us?" Will asked as he turned out of the parking lot.

"No, sorry. He couldn't get away from work. Someone called in sick, so they're short-staffed."

"That's too bad. Maybe next time," Will said, then launched into a conversation with Hugh about Boston restaurants, and where to find the best beer in the city.

Mia was content to listen, happy to steal another moment's closeness with Will. Vanessa, as usual, was quiet as the proverbial church mouse.

They were early enough that the lunch rush hadn't started yet and snagged a booth by the window. Conversation continued in the casual vein, local talk mixed in with a little shoptalk, and when the food arrived Mia was too busy eating to do much more than nod now and then.

Being seated next to Will gave her a chance to touch his arm with hers, brush her thigh against his. Beneath the tablecloth, she sought his hand and squeezed it.

He squeezed back—and didn't let go. His thumb traced circles in her palm, and halfway through dessert he moved her hand over to his groin and she nearly choked on her spice cake.

Then she grinned and whispered, "You better not stand up anytime soon."

"Wasn't planning on it," he murmured.

"Hey. Save it for the bedroom, you two," Hugh ordered. "You're embarrassing poor Vanessa."

Vanessa, staring at her plate, said tartly, "Vanessa knows about sex, thank you very much, and isn't so embarrassed as that."

"Then *I'm* embarrassed," Hugh declared. "Christ, *somebody* should be embarrassed. The heat between you two is about to melt the vinyl seats."

Mia stood. "I'll be right back. I want to use the ladies' room before we leave."

* * *

"I suppose it's that time," Hugh said, sliding out of the booth. "Work beckons. Thanks for lunch, Tiernay. Much appreciated."

"My pleasure." As Will looked away from Mia's swaying hips, distracted by how nicely her backside filled out those pants, he caught Hugh's gaze on him and grinned unapologetically.

"I bet," Hugh said dryly.

Will picked up the bill their waiter had left, then leaned across the table toward Vanessa. "You done with your dessert?" he asked in the casual tone he'd used all along.

She met his gaze. "Yes."

"You didn't finish it."

"It was wonderful, of course. I'm simply stuffed. Can't manage another bite." She paused. "But thank you for lunch. It was very generous of you to include me."

Will picked up on her sarcasm, although it sailed right over Hugh's fedora. He didn't enjoy playing the bully, but only he and Vanessa knew that he'd forced her to come along.

She knew why he'd done so; it hadn't escaped his notice that she avoided looking at his face. He had a feeling Vulaj hadn't informed her of the plans for the hotel garage ambush.

"I'm sorry your boyfriend couldn't have joined us. I would have really liked to meet him."

What he really wanted was to force her to tell him

where Vulaj had disappeared to: Claudia had called earlier to say that he'd never shown up at the airport.

"I'm sure you would," Vanessa said, her tone a shade more clipped than usual, but she didn't pull away when he helped her from the bench—and kept his hand on her arm as he guided her toward the cashier.

She stiffened but didn't dare protest or draw attention to his actions.

Hugh headed to the bathroom as well, but when Vanessa made to follow, Will closed his hand more tightly over her arm in a silent warning.

There was another group of business types in front of them, negotiating single checks with the middle-aged female cashier, whose English was iffy at best.

Will turned, moving closer to Vanessa until he forced her into a corner beside the wall that separated the register from the hallway leading to the restrooms.

Leaning toward her, mere inches separating her face from his, he said quietly, "Where's Vulaj? I know he didn't show up for work today, so don't bother lying."

Not only had Claudia reported Vulaj's absence but she'd also told Will that two "large and nasty-looking" men were occupying Vanessa's apartment. If Vulaj was inside, Claudia had no way of knowing, but she hadn't seen any sign of him when she'd knocked on the door and pulled a "wrong address" shtick.

"I don't know where he is," Vanessa said after a moment, hatred for Will burning in her pale blue eyes.

"And even if you did, you wouldn't tell me."

"That's right."

"If you come clean now, I can still help you stay out of trouble, Vanessa."

"I don't know what you're talking about."

"Yes, you do. And I know all about your boyfriend. I even know about the second reliquary and what you plan to do with it."

Her eyes stretched wide, verifying he'd guessed right, and then she looked away. "I have nothing to say to you—except that you'd better let me go before your precious Mia comes back and gets the wrong idea about us."

Your precious Mia.

Will went cold and squeezed Vanessa's arms more tightly. "I have a message for your boyfriend. Tell him that if he comes anywhere near my precious Mia, he'll regret it."

She continued to avoid his gaze, but her body began to tremble. He let her go and stepped back, whispering, "I'm watching you, Vanessa, and I'm very patient. You're not getting away with it."

Vanessa looked up, smiling. "We'll see about that."

So there was steel inside the wilting violet after all.

She pushed past him and walked out to the car just as Mia stopped beside him, her expression puzzled— and wary.

He wasn't sure how much she'd seen, but even a little would be hard to explain.

"What was that about? Are you angry with Vanessa?"

"Not at all. We were just talking, and it was easier to do it here than over by the cash register." He motioned at the group of loud businessmen. "I haven't had a chance to pay the bill yet. Want to wait with me?"

Mia hesitated, then touched his arm lightly. "I'll wait in the car. You're coming over tonight, aren't you?"

"You bet." He kissed her, and she tasted like cream cheese frosting and coffee. "We can leave right after you're done with work, and I'll drive you."

"You don't have to do that," she said. "If you have work to catch up on, I can walk home. I always do."

Which was a problem, now that Vulaj had disappeared.

"Whatever you want," he said, careful not to push too hard. She was suspicious enough already. "Either way, I'll see you later."

"You might want to change into something more casual. I thought we'd take a walk later tonight to the park and talk over a few things. Does that sound okay?"

"Sounds great."

Except for the talk part; that definitely sounded like trouble.

As Will moved to the cashier, he watched Mia walk to the car and join Vanessa. She didn't look back at him.

The rest of the day passed with frustrating slowness. Will took pictures, making sure to take a lot of Vanessa, further aggravating her. When she'd left for a "walk" that afternoon, Will had tried to follow her, but it had taken too long to get away from Hugh, and he'd lost her. When she returned, he'd picked up immediately on her heightened nervousness, and knew she'd met with Vulaj.

The plan was coming together; it wouldn't be long now.

Anticipation filled him, the danger and challenge a heady rush. He'd never known this part of him existed until he got into his first chase as a cop, and there'd been no going back.

Mia headed off early, and he discreetly tailed her until she was safely inside her apartment. Then he returned to Haddington and stayed until Vanessa left. She caught a cab—still no Vulaj—and he followed her. When she got out of the cab, she went directly into her building, not even looking back at him, although he'd made no attempt to hide his tail.

He'd watched the building until Claudia returned from her break to take over. Then he drove to his hotel, changed into jeans and a casual shirt, and five minutes later was on his way to Mia's.

He let himself in, heard her moving around in the bathroom, and called, "It's just me."

"Okay," she said. "I'll be right out."

She didn't sound right, and his inner alarm flared. He'd left his gun behind, since there was nowhere he could wear it without her noticing, and reached for the switchblade in his pocket. His fingers closed over its cool, slim length as footsteps came down the hall.

Mia walked into the living room, putting on earrings, perfectly fine and smiling.

Pulling his hand back out, he returned her smile. Her golden-brown silk tank top brought out the warm browns of her eyes, and her tight jeans did incredible things to her ass.

Grinning, he unfastened the top button on his shirt.

Instead of helping as he'd expected, she turned away. "How was the rest of your day?" she asked.

"Okay, I guess. It's looking up, though."

She didn't respond. Will picked up on the edge of tension, the stiffer lines of her body, and how she avoided meeting his eyes. As he recalled the day's events, he zeroed in on several possibilities for her mood—none of them good.

"Are you mad at me?" he asked at length. "Is it about me standing close to Vanessa at lunch? Because—"

"No, it's not that," Mia interrupted. "Not exactly."

In that instant, he knew she'd figured out he'd been lying to her. How, he couldn't say—he just knew it.

Time to return to role-playing mode. Bluff it out if possible, and if not, he'd play it rougher and find a way to keep her quiet and out of trouble.

Or, he could tell her the truth—as much as was reasonable, anyway—and hope for the best.

Who was he kidding? There wasn't much hope of a "best" here—and this was his chance to make a clean break and get out of her life. Play the bastard, make her angry enough to be glad to get rid of him. She was handing him the perfect opportunity to act it through, right to the bitter end.

Nineteen

"WILL, WHAT WAS ALL THAT EARLIER TODAY, WITH Vanessa? She acted as if . . ." Mia hesitated, frowning. "As if she was afraid of you."

Will's expression was faintly questioning. "I don't know what you're talking about."

She walked over to the window, brushing aside the curtain. Outside, a few cars rolled by, and an old woman moved laboriously along the sidewalk with a panting Pomeranian on a pink leash. "I know you, Will, and there's something not right here."

She waited for him to answer, too nervous to face him but so acutely aware of his presence that she could hear each breath and the slightest brush of denim as he came toward her, then stopped.

"Know me? You haven't seen me since I was twenty-two. That was a long time ago."

Taken aback by his cooler tone, Mia turned. He was standing only a few feet away, hands shoved in the pockets of his jeans.

After a moment, he added more gently, "If anything is not right here, it's probably just me not matching up to the memories."

Could the answer to this persistent sense of unease be so simple? No; it was more than that, more than even what had happened today. Little signs, all along, that she could no longer explain away.

She shook her head. "That was fear in her eyes. Why on earth would she be afraid of you?"

Will shrugged, muscles moving beneath his shirt with fluid strength—and despite her intentions, desire snared her. It was all she could do not to follow that pull and go to him, letting the comfort of those arms chase away her worries.

"You're imagining things," he said.

Mia met his flat gaze. "I saw what I saw. Now answer me."

Silence—and the longer it stretched on, the deeper her hopes sank. If he had nothing to hide, he would've given her an explanation by now.

"You're not really here to do an article on Haddington Reproductions, are you?"

His focus on her suddenly seemed sharper, and his brows had drawn together in a small frown. When she couldn't stand the tense silence any longer, she started to turn away—just as he let out his breath and said quietly, "No, I'm not."

She froze, uncertain she'd heard him correctly.

"I'm not a journalist." Despite his calm tone, the muscles in his arms flexed as he clenched and unclenched his fists in his pockets. "None of it was real, Mia. Nothing I told you was true."

Her mouth was dry, her throat too tight. "So why are you here?"

"I'm investigating a suspected forgery—and a theft that's planned to take place very soon."

Forgery.

An ugly, ugly word; a gross perversion of her work, her dedication to her craft. The implication, and all that came with it, hit her hard. She was trembling from head to toe.

"You're a *cop*?"

"No. Not a Fed, either. I work for a private organization."

It was too much. Mia made her to way to the couch and sank down. She whispered, "Is somebody going to steal the Eudoxia Reliquary? Or the entire collection?"

"We believe so."

"And you came here to catch a thief."

"Yes." Will hesitated, running a hand through his hair, and then backed away from her to lean against the kitchen partition, arms folded across his chest. "To find out who was involved."

Mia raised her head to meet his eyes. "You thought I was?"

"Initially everyone was a suspect. It was the usual process of elimination."

"You slept with me, thinking I was a thief?" Her voice rose, sharpening. "How could you believe that of me?" She squeezed her eyes shut against a rush of angry tears. "How could you do that to *me*?"

A memory echoed, his voice rather than hers. Eyes widening, she made a strangled sound, a bitter laugh mixed with a choked-back sob.

Will must've heard that same echo, because he shook his head and snapped, "No! This wasn't about payback, Mia, and I knew almost right away that you and Hugh weren't involved. What happened between us . . . it wasn't something I planned." His gaze briefly slid away. "It just happened. And you wanted it as much as I did."

"*Almost* right away," she repeated. "But not from the start. You still had sex with me, thinking I was going to steal from my own client! My God, what would you have done if I'd—"

"If you'd been guilty, I'd have taken you down." To his credit, he didn't avoid meeting her eyes and he didn't look happy. "It would've hurt like hell, but I'd have done it."

As if that made it all better.

"I see." Then a sudden, sinking feeling swept over

her. "You think it's *Vanessa?* No, no. It's not possible. I've worked with her for years. She's a friend."

"Mia, the facts are indisputable."

"Facts? What *facts?*"

"I can't share that kind of information with—"

"Vanessa would *never* do anything like that. I don't believe you."

"Not on her own, no. But she's not working alone." He made a gesture of frustration. "You have a lot of reasons to be mad at me, but not for this. You asked for the truth. I told you."

And right now, she wished she'd never asked him anything.

"If you're not a cop or with the FBI, then what kind of authority do you have?"

"I'm in private enforcement." He let out a sigh. "Technically, I'm a mercenary."

Mia stared. "In *Boston?* Don't mercenaries prowl around South American jungles or other third world countries?"

"The people I'm with specialize in retrieving stolen art and antiquities, tracing forgeries, and tracking down organized looters and smugglers, among other things. This takes us from Boston to London to Rome to Baghdad to Bangladesh—all over the world, greed is the great equalizer."

"Then you're not operating within established laws."

"No, but neither do thieves and smugglers," he said tersely. "These people are highly organized, well-armed, and dangerous. They kill and move freely across borders, which makes catching them an international night-mare—and they use that to their advantage. Putting them out of business sometimes requires working outside the law."

"Vanessa—"

"Is a pawn," he interrupted. "She's a weak, gullible woman who got involved with the wrong man, and right now all she cares about is proving to him how much she loves him. Even if that's through grand theft larceny."

"Kos is a thief?"

"Kostandin Vulaj has ties to the Albanian Mafia, and to the black-market art trade both in Europe and the U.S."

Mia went cold. "Has she . . . she taken anything yet?"

"Not that I'm aware of, no."

"Then you can stop her before she does." Mia shot up from the couch, grabbing his arm with urgent force-fulness. "She doesn't understand, Will. I'm sure of it. Talk to her, make her see reason. *Please*."

"It's too late for that. I'm sorry." After a moment, he added quietly, "I need Vanessa to get to Vulaj; he can lead me to the person who set this up. If it's who we think it is, he is a very dangerous individual. These people belong in police custody, and what I'm doing will put them there. Legally."

She dropped her hands and stepped back, staring in disbelief. "You're using her," she whispered. "Just like him, you're using her."

Will's dark eyes narrowed. "You seem to be forgetting she's made this choice of her own free will. No one's holding a gun to her head and forcing her to steal from people who've put their trust in her. I'm not the one in the wrong here."

"You just told me she's been manipulated." She was still close enough that she could feel his heat, and the tension radiating off him so strongly it tingled along her skin. "You don't know what kind of hold he has over her."

"And it doesn't matter. If she'd walked away from this, then I'd have nothing on her and I'd let her go. But she hasn't done that, and she won't. Within the next twenty-four hours she'll make her move, and when she does, I'll be waiting."

"How can you so cold-bloodedly . . ." Mia's voice trailed off, shaking. "All right, I agree she's been stupid; she's desperate to find someone to love her. But is that enough of an excuse for you to let her destroy her whole life just so you can catch her boyfriend? What gives you the right?"

"Jesus Christ, Mia," Will snapped back. "Lots of people have shitty lives, but most of them find other ways to cope than by stealing or killing. Bad luck with men doesn't give anyone the right to steal or kill."

"I am fully aware of that, Will. Don't patronize me."

He shook his head. "You don't know what these people are like, or what they're capable of. I do. Vanessa's not truly your friend. Not anymore."

Memories crowded her: lunches and gossipy tea breaks, shopping and watching movies, long talks on the phone, at the bar . . .

"I can't believe that. She's been my friend for years; it *can't* all be a lie."

"Mia, if Vulaj told her to, Vanessa would put you in harm's way without thinking twice. The girlfriend thing is just an act now."

Anger, irrational and hot, made her lash out. "And you haven't been putting on an act from the minute we met?"

"Who are you really feeling sorry for here? Vanessa? Or yourself, because you've been played for a fool?"

Before she could answer, he pushed away from the wall and moved toward her, so quickly and with such a focused, frightening intensity that Mia backed rapidly away, almost tripping over the coffee table.

Anger flared in his eyes. "I took a huge risk in telling you the truth. I did it because you deserved to know, because I felt guilty for deceiving you, and because once, a long time ago, I loved you."

Will forced her steadily backward, and Mia put her

hands on his chest to try to signal him to stop, that he was scaring her.

It didn't work. She bumped against the wall.

"Giving you this information breaks every rule I've sworn to obey, and puts me in a bad situation. One careless word from you, and it's all over. They'll disappear and surface somewhere else, and there'll be more and more victims until they're stopped. That's the reality," he said, his voice as hard and unyielding as the wall at her back.

She didn't understand how his eyes could be so cold and his body so hot. "There has to be another way."

"Don't even *think* about talking to her. I mean it, Mia. Don't make me regret being honest with you, or trusting you."

Trapped between his powerful body and the wall, she couldn't move, and she gasped when he seized her wrists and pinned them above her head. Fear flashed through her, mixed with anger and the confusing ache of a hot, bone-deep desire.

And, inexplicably, grief.

This wasn't her Ohio boy. She'd wanted to believe he hadn't changed so much, to think it was possible to go back to that magical time and pick up where they'd left off, before things had gone so wrong. But she didn't know this man. There was nothing in him of that sweet, rough-edged boy who'd taught her all about the excitement of falling in love and the wonders of sex.

"What happened to you, that you ended up like this?" she whispered.

"Nothing at all. I just got older. Wiser." With each word, his breath brushed against her hair. "I need you to promise me you won't interfere."

Although furious with herself for still feeling this pang of need, even after what he'd told her, she refused to turn her face away from his. "Let me go. I don't want you touching me ever again."

He went still for a moment. Then his lips brushed against hers and she almost forgot to breathe, her face hot with shame when her body quickly proved her a liar.

He pulled back to look at her, his expression unreadable. "You're angry and upset right now. I can't blame you for that, but I'm not the bad guy here. You need to understand that."

"I understand that what they're doing is wrong, and what you intend is right—but I don't have to like it or approve of how you're going about it. The Eudoxia Reliquary . . . it's old and it's valuable and it's beautiful, but it's just a *thing*." Mia's voice thickened. "Vanessa's a human being, and people have disappointed her all her life. If you were such a good guy," she whispered, "you could've found another way."

After a moment, he said flatly, "Your promise?"

"I promise. Now get out."

Twenty

DOWN THE STREET FROM MIA'S APARTMENT, WILL slumped in his car and rubbed at the dull ache behind his eyes. He'd tried bluffing, tried the truth, and ended up scaring the shit out of her.

"Way to go," he muttered.

Just days ago, he'd swept in full of confidence, certain he could handle anything. Now . . .

Swearing under his breath, he forced himself to focus, to cut through the jumble of emotions and get to the heart of the real threat: Mia was too involved for her own good, Vulaj was missing, and he had to try to second-guess the man.

He pulled out his cell phone and called Morris, who still didn't answer. Will left a terse voice message: "I need another favor, Morris, and I need it now. Call me back."

After a brief hesitation, he dialed Ben's private

number next, and his boss answered on the second ring. "Sheridan."

"Vulaj sent someone after me yesterday."

"Claudia told me. I should've heard it from you first." There was a brief silence. "How did you leave matters?"

"I didn't kill him, if that's what you mean. A woman interrupted the fight and started screaming, and he took off. There was no time to run him down."

"All right. And how are things going with Morris?"

"He's cooperating on the contingency that I don't lose control here, and that's the problem."

"Explain."

"Vulaj has gone missing. Claudia reports that he has a couple friends guarding the apartment he shares with Sharpton. I know where both of the fake reliquaries are located"—a stretch of the truth, but Sheridan didn't need to know that—"and I can get past the security into the Haddington workshop if I need to, but—"

"So what's the problem? It sounds to me like you have matters under control."

"The problem is Mia."

Again, a brief silence. "If she's not involved in the forgery or theft, then she's not a problem."

"She is if *Vulaj* involves her."

"And you feel this is a valid concern."

It wasn't a question, but Will treated it as one. "It would make sense. He's gone into hiding until Vanessa is ready to make the switch. He knows I'm watching her, and I think he's going to try to use Mia as leverage to keep Vanessa safe. Vulaj is aware of my connection to Mia."

"Shit." Ben sounded irritated. "I just had to deal with this in L.A. We're in the business of taking down art thieves and smugglers, not rescuing damsels in distress."

"Even if we're the ones who put them in distress in the first place?"

"I don't want innocent people harmed, but what I want more than anything right now is Kostandin Vulaj in custody and talking."

"Will you settle for the girlfriend?"

"Hmmm." Ben fell silent on the other end, and Will could imagine him sitting at his cluttered desk, feet on its top. "Does she mean enough to him that he'd turn himself in to help her out?"

"Maybe. And maybe she knows something about von Lahr."

"Maybe isn't good enough. If you're going after Vulaj's woman because he's going after yours, that's not good enough, either."

Will's hand fisted tightly enough to show white knuckles. "You knew this would happen."

"No, I acknowledged it as a risk. I gambled on you being able to pull this off without your intentions being revealed. I gambled that your ex-lover was unlikely to be the suspect. I was right on the one, not so right on the other."

"And now she's in danger because of why I'm here."

"I regret that, I truly do, but that doesn't change your objective." A sigh sounded on the other end. "Where will you be tonight?"

"In my car, guarding Mia."

"Will, that is not—"

"Until I can get someone here to take over for me, I'm not fucking leaving. I'm dead serious, Ben."

If you were such a good guy, you could've found another way.

Mia was right; he'd had choices and he'd taken the easiest one. No matter how this turned out, she had helped him remember who and what he used to be, why he'd signed up with Avalon in the first place.

No more sidestepping complications, no more ignoring consequences just because he didn't have to stick around to face them, and no more avoiding questions that should be asked. He'd signed on to make a difference, and he could do that without losing his basic decency and compassion.

"What if Vulaj is counting on you to do exactly that? And he and Sharpton disappear tonight with the Eudoxia Reliquary?"

"Then we track them down later and take it back. But Vulaj isn't going to make his move tonight. There's no way Sharpton can finish the second copy before tomorrow, and Vulaj has to wait until both reproductions are ready. If he's going to risk double-crossing von Lahr, he's not giving up now—not when he's so close to getting what he wants."

"You're sure about that?"

"As sure as I can be about anything."

"You realize that your priorities here are not in line with what you're being paid to do."

He did; but there'd never been a question of which he'd choose if it came down to the job or protecting Mia. Ben *had* to know that. "Yes, I do."

There was a brief silence, then Ben said, "Do the best you can. I'm not happy about this, but I understand. Keep me updated."

After the call ended, Will glanced up at Mia's apartment. The lights were still on, but she'd pulled the curtains closed. He couldn't see any movement inside.

He wanted to talk to her, but she needed time alone right now, and he couldn't blame her. Not only had the news about Vanessa hurt her deeply, but for it to come the way it had . . . Well, if he was keeping score on which of them had hurt the other worse, they were about even.

Will briefly squeezed his eyes shut, then rested his head on the back of his seat.

He could still feel Mia, the warmth of her skin as he'd pressed her against the wall, her trembling. That she'd been afraid of him should've cooled his lust, and he was ashamed that it had had the opposite effect.

What happened to you, that you ended up like this?

Was it wrong to use Sharpton to get to Vulaj and bring down Rainert von Lahr after all this time? Will didn't believe it was—but maybe the issue wasn't whether it was wrong but why it hadn't bothered him. If he caused someone pain, even if that someone was not on his side, he should feel at least a twinge of regret.

And if he were honest with himself, he wanted to be the man Mia had imagined.

"Shit," he muttered, disgusted.

He was sexually frustrated; he'd just told his boss that if push came to shove, he was choosing the woman over the job; and Vulaj's disappearance had jacked his nerves to the breaking point.

Worse, he'd tried scaring Mia so that she would stay out of the way, even lying about the danger of her talking to anyone. Hugh might be a problem, should he learn the truth, but not Vanessa anymore. He should've handled that better, instead of getting angry and shooting off at the mouth.

And his mouth kept saying "no" and "can't stay," yet . . . he *still* wanted a chance to bring Mia back into his life. The realization had hit with crystal clarity the second she'd kicked his ass out. And now that he'd finally admitted to himself what he wanted, it was too late.

His cell phone rang, and he snatched it out of his pocket, trying to squelch the hope that it might be Mia.

"Tiernay, it's Morris. Returning your call."

"I need your help," Will said. "Can you find someone to keep an eye on an apartment for me?"

"Depends. Are there bad guys in this apartment?"

"No." Will rubbed again at his eyes. "She's a woman who means a lot to me, and I have every reason to believe that what I'm doing is putting her in danger."

"And does she know this?" Morris asked after a while, his tone no longer sarcastic.

"No."

"You thinking of letting her in on this little secret sometime soon?"

"I might, if she'll ever let me near her again."

Morris sighed. "Sucks to be a secret agent man, eh? Tell me where you are and I'll send someone over as soon as I can."

"Thanks, Morris. I appreciate it."

"Like you said yesterday, in the end, all that matters is that the bastards go down."

"Yeah," Will said softly. "That's all that matters."

"Van, over here!"

Vanessa barely managed to suppress a squeak; the harsh whisper came from right behind her, and she could've sworn there was no one standing there.

"Kos," she said. "Don't do that!"

He motioned her into the dark shadows of an alley. They were in one of the shabbier parts of East Boston, and it was pitch-black and frightening. Now that Kos was here, though, she felt safe enough to take her hand off the Mace in her coat pocket.

"It's not like I could stand on the street corner and wave you down. I'm sure by now Tiernay or the cops are out looking for me. You sure you weren't followed?"

"Positive. Ari helped me get away from the apartment." She went into his arms and returned his hug. "Are you all right?"

"Yeah. And you? Tiernay's not giving you any trouble?"

Vanessa sighed. "Well, we had an interesting chat at lunch. He got me alone and dropped the act."

His muscles went rigid with anger. "Did he threaten you?"

"Of course he did. What did you expect?"

Kos startled at her retort, then flashed a rueful smile. "Point taken. So what did he say?"

"He knows about the second reliquary."

"What?" His fingers tightened on her arms, though he immediately relaxed his grip at her wince. "How the hell did he figure that out so fast?"

"I don't know for certain. But remember that night when I went back to match colors?" When he nodded, she said, "You wondered if someone had been looking around. Maybe Tiernay was there that night."

"I didn't see anyone. You looked around, didn't you?"

"Not thoroughly. There were places he could've

hidden that I didn't check as completely as I might have. If he was by the lumber, it's such a mess back there that it would've been easy to miss him. He could've overheard our conversation. But even if he wasn't in the shop then, he could've . . . figured something out."

"How could he have gotten inside?"

"Mia."

"Would she do that? You always say how good a person she is, how honest, how she can't lie to save her life—"

"I think where Will Tiernay is concerned, she'd do just about anything." Vanessa pulled back. "What are we going to do? There's no doubt Tiernay knows about our plans. He must know your partner as well." And Kos's refusal to give her details about the man he was working with seemed pointless now. "Who *is* this person? It's time you told me."

"It is best that you do not know."

When he was under stress, Kos's accent became more pronounced. It was the surest way to judge his moods. "Yes, but since we're in considerable danger at the moment, what can it hurt to give me his name?"

"He wouldn't like it." Kos had withdrawn farther into the alley, where a weak shaft of light from a back door provided just enough illumination to see his face—and she was shocked and worried at how tired he looked.

"You have to understand, Vanessa, this man is wanted by many countries. He has managed to stay one step ahead of cops all around the world for fifteen years, and he's done that by being very clear about expectations."

"And yet you plan on pulling this trick on him? He sounds more dangerous than these Avalon people you've been telling me about."

Kos smiled morosely. "I don't want to cross either one; I have no doubts about what would happen to me. But we're not crossing him, exactly. We're just creating a new opportunity. If he does learn about the second copy, he won't be angry with me. It's not as if he came as far as he has by playing fair. As long as he doesn't lose face, he won't come after us."

He sounded so sure, she wanted to believe him. Maybe there was some truth in that old saying about honor among thieves.

She hoped so. This wasn't what she'd dreamed of doing with her life, but she had found no love or honor among the "good" people who were supposed to care for her and love her. Instead she'd found that with the "bad" people, and while the price she was paying for happiness was a high one, she no longer regretted it.

"How long are you going to be hiding out? Why don't you come back to the apartment? Your friends are there. The police can't search it without a warrant, and they can't get a warrant without evidence, so—"

"Avalon isn't the cops, that's why. Nothing's stopping Tiernay from breaking in. For all we know, he already has. You're sure the reliquary is still safe in the fridge?"

The possibility of that man having been in her apartment, having searched through her intimate belongings, left her cold. She nodded. "I checked before I left. It's safe."

"How much longer until you're done with the other one?"

"Tomorrow morning. Then all I'll have to do is remove the Haddington mark and patch it, but I can't do that until after Hugh has inspected it. I'll just take what I need to fix that when I leave."

Kos nodded. "And the jewelry?"

"I switched everything tonight, before I came to meet you. No one was in the workshop. I searched it thoroughly this time."

"Did you find any bugs or cameras?"

"I think so. I got rid of them, like you told me to."

"Good." He touched her face and gave her a kiss. "You're doing very well."

"But I'm so terrified, I can hardly think straight. And now I'm even more worried about *you*. What are you doing? What's next, and—"

"I will be fine. This isn't the first time I've had to hide out from a little trouble, and I've faced bigger problems than this man," Kos said, giving her a reassuring squeeze. "You do what you need to do tomorrow, and once you switch the reliquary, slip it into a shopping bag and no one will notice."

"What about Tiernay? He'll be watching for—"

"I have a plan in place that will keep Tiernay out of our way."

Dread settled over her, cold and heavy. "I saw his face, Kos. I don't like people being hurt."

"Tiernay was tougher than I expected. I underestimated him. I won't do that again."

Vanessa chewed on her lip. "You wouldn't hurt Mia to keep him away, would you?"

He stared at her, eyes suddenly harder and colder than she'd seen them for a long time, reminding her with a jolt of the life he led in the real world outside her bedroom. "We've been through this before."

"I *know*. I just hoped it wouldn't come to that."

"It's what he would do if our places were switched. He'll know that."

For a moment, she forgot to breathe. "You mean he'll expect you to go after Mia? This is insane, Kos! There must be a better way for us to get away and be together. Maybe it seemed like the only way when we started, but—"

"No," he interrupted again, his tone cold and firm but tinged—with regret? Maybe, but perhaps, like Mia, she saw only what she wanted to see in the man she loved.

"For me, there is no other option. You know what I am, what I've done. Nobody would give me a second chance, and the people who helped me come to this country, they wouldn't let me alone. If I have more money, more power to bargain with, then I can make a better life for you. It won't be an easy one, but it'll be better than what we have here."

"I know. I was just . . . being a coward, as usual."

Why had she even brought it up? Once he came clean about why he'd hooked up with her, Kos had never been anything but honest. She had made her choice; there was no going back to the old life.

"I promise to do my best not to harm her. I will scare her a little, because if she's scared she will do as I tell her, but I won't hurt her. If Tiernay does what he's told and leaves you alone, then he'll get her back. He'll co-operate with me because he'll think he can either second-guess me or track me down later. All I have to do is stay one step ahead of him. If my partner has been able to do that for so long, then I can."

His words were oddly comforting. Kos had no compunctions about using violence, but never against innocent women or children. Like most of the men in his line of "business," he avoided trouble with regular people. Killing or harming them guaranteed the police would come after you with everything they had. When one mafioso knocked off another, the police didn't get as worked up.

"You okay with that now?" Kos pressed.

Vanessa nodded. "Yes. I don't much like it, but you know I'll go along with whatever plans you make. We can't lose now."

"And we won't." He kissed her again, a long, hot, possessive kiss that made her dizzy and breathless and very nearly distracted her from her worries.

After all, Mia always landed on her feet. She was obscenely lucky. Everybody liked her, she was successful at everything—except marriage, but that was just a quirk.

Envy, resentment, anger . . . they helped keep guilt at bay. Mia, always telling her what she should do, always doing things "for Vanessa" without ever asking if Vanessa wanted them done, or thinking they might not be what she wanted or even needed. Mia, always trying to mold her into another version of herself without understanding that it wasn't possible.

Mia, who suspected Kos was leeching off her because he was young and good-looking, and of course, a young and handsome man wouldn't ever want anything to do with the likes of *her*. Mia, the one with the family who always sent pictures and cards and emails, who called and said "I love you" so naturally.

Mia had so much, and it came to her so easily. God, how Vanessa resented her, seeing her now with clearer eyes.

"I almost wish I could be there to see everyone's reactions," Vanessa said, smiling a little. "They'll be so shocked. I'll have achieved notoriety. They'll talk about me, about how they never imagined I'd do such a thing."

Kos grinned. "You can get to like that notoriety. I know."

"And maybe I'll get to like it, when I'm not throwing up out of sheer terror."

"You have nothing to worry about. I promised to take care of you and protect you, no matter what I have to do. I will be there for you. Please trust me." He cupped her cheek and kissed her, and she melted against him, love and lust and fear and excitement mixing in an intoxicating rush. So much so she would've made him do her right there in the alley, but he pushed her away.

"Time for that later. I have to go, and you need to go back to the apartment. I won't see you again until we meet at the factory tomorrow night. You have the addresses I gave you? The paper with the phone number?" When she nodded, he added, "No matter what happens, find a way to the house I told you about. After that, we're all but home free."

Twenty-one

❖

MIA HOPED THAT WHEN THE OTHERS SHOWED UP AT work she could act as if nothing was wrong, even when everything was *so* wrong.

What was she going to do? She was no good at lying; the instant Vanessa laid eyes on her, she'd guess that Mia knew the truth.

Maybe she could tell a partial truth: that she and Will had had a fight and she was upset. No one would ask too many questions after that.

At least she wasn't shaking anymore, or feeling the need to cry. She'd hardly slept and had finally resorted to pet therapy, scooping up Caligula to cuddle. That had calmed her enough that she could think straight. She'd deliberately not answered Will's three calls because talking with him would just upset her all over again.

Especially once she'd realized the real reason for the

bruises and cuts on his face, and that he was in very real danger.

For hours she'd replayed in her mind what Will had said, and had finally given up trying to find excuses for Vanessa's betrayal. She didn't want to believe it, but all the little signs were there. And then there was Kos—who was certainly living down to her expectations.

Ten minutes after Mia arrived at work, Hugh showed up, full of himself because they'd met the deadline and life was good.

Or so he thought.

It seemed so wrong not to tell him about Will, about Vanessa, to pretend that his entire livelihood wasn't about to be destroyed by someone he'd trusted for years. He would be devastated when he learned the truth.

"You look awful," Hugh said, leaning down to look closely at her. "Tell Will he needs to let you get more sleep."

"I'll tell him." Mia smiled and hoped it looked convincing.

It didn't.

"Why the long face? I'd think you'd be happier. Today we wrap up and send off the whole bloody lot of it. Instead, you look like . . . Oh, I say, you and Will haven't gotten into a row, have you?"

"We did have an argument last night." Obviously

she couldn't hide her mood even from Hugh, the least intuitive man on the planet.

He looked surprised, then awkward. "A bad one?"

"Yes."

"I'm sorry to hear it."

Just wait until you hear about Vanessa. You'll be even sorrier to hear that.

When Vanessa came in Mia headed to Hugh's office to file and that way also avoided Will, who came in on Vanessa's heels.

Hugh, showing more sensitivity than usual, didn't ask her what she was doing. Instead, he struck up the jovial old friend routine, keeping Will close to him when he tried to follow her into the office.

A few minutes later, when she glanced out the office window, Mia met Will's direct, intense gaze. She looked quickly past him—and caught Vanessa watching Will.

It looked like the fun was already starting.

Her hands shook as she picked up a pile of folders, and when the office door opened with a sharp click, she was so rattled that she dropped them.

"Mia, we have to talk."

"I think we did all the talking we needed to do last night."

"Look at me."

His voice was calm but firm, and she reluctantly looked up, torn between wanting to tell him to leave her alone and wanting him to say something—any-thing—to make this all go away.

He looked so tired that she had to check the impulse to soothe away the lines of strain etched around his eyes and mouth—the mouth with the cut she'd fussed over, which wasn't caused by a common mugger.

"What do you want?" she asked wearily.

"I tried to call you last night."

"I didn't want to talk to you."

"Too bad, because I could've saved you a walk into work today."

"What? Why would I—"

"You need to go back to your apartment and stay there. Wait, just listen to me." He held up his hand, halting her retort. "Please. I know you're angry with me, and you have every right to be. If you ever give me a chance after this is over, I'd like to explain a few things that might make me look like less of an asshole. Right now, I need you to believe that I have your safety in mind."

"My safety?" Mia stared at him. "What does that have to do with this?"

"Kostandin Vulaj has pulled a disappearing act. He and Vanessa know why I'm here, and I'm concerned that he might use you to get to me."

Mia glanced out toward Hugh, who was failing mis-erably in his effort not to be obvious about staring into the office. Vanessa was out of sight at her desk.

"Why?" With a shaky sigh, she stood and walked over to Will, turning her back to Hugh and blocking his view of their conversation. "Why would he want to harm me?"

"To force me to do as he wants."

"Wait a minute. Last night you told me I couldn't say a word to Vanessa because I might give you away, and now you're telling me she already knows? It was just another lie!"

"Mia, I—"

"No." She held up her hand. "I can't really be angry about that, can I? All things considered, I don't have the right to be angry."

To her surprise, anger flared in his eyes. "Bullshit! Yes, I lied, but as I said last night, it wasn't to get back at you for something that happened years ago. I thought if I scared you enough, you'd stay the hell away from Vanessa and listen to me. I don't have time for finesse here, Mia."

Desperation sharpened his voice, and that, more than anything else, cut through her anger and confusion, driving home the seriousness of the danger.

"It was a mistake on my part, I know. And if you hadn't thrown me out or had picked up my calls, I would've told you so, and then told you why I need you out of here."

She motioned to his face. "You weren't mugged."

"No."

That was it; no other explanation was forthcoming.

"I don't understand. Why don't you just arrest her now? Why go through all this?"

"I can't arrest anyone. I'm not the police anymore."

Before she could ask what that meant, he added, "I have to catch them in the act. I need her to take me to Vulaj, who is smarter than I anticipated. She'll make her move today, and I want you safe. I have someone watching your apartment; he'll have followed you here today, too."

"I never noticed." She swallowed, going cold. "I didn't . . . I'd never know, would I? By the time I realized someone was following me, it would be too late."

"Yes, it would," he said quietly. "Tell Hugh you're not feeling well and need to go home. You're done here, and he told me you'd said we had a fight. He'll just assume you're upset and let you go. The man who's been watching over you will pick you up and take you back to your apartment. He'll also stay there with you. It may not be necessary, but I'd rather err on the side of caution."

Dear God . . . he was dead serious about all this. And if she stayed, she'd only get in Will's way. As much as she hated what he was doing, she wouldn't stupidly jeopardize his, or anyone else's, safety.

"All right," she said. "I'll go home."

The rigid set of his shoulders relaxed. "I am truly sorry for what's happened. I never wanted you to be hurt like this. Before I leave Boston, please let me come by to talk with you."

She didn't answer. Instead she asked, "And what about Hugh? Will he be safe?"

"I have no personal connection to him, which makes him less valuable as a bargaining chip. He should be okay, but I promise to keep watch just to be sure. The police are aware of what's going on, and my outfit has sent someone in to help me. The minute I've contained Vulaj and Vanessa, the police will move in and finish up. After that, you and Hugh are in the clear, and you won't see me again."

Unless you want to.

Although unspoken, Mia still heard the question in his tone. But she wasn't sure if she ever wanted to set eyes on him again. Being together seemed to be like walking a tightrope: moments of exhilaration, feeling so high and free and alive, then the sudden, painful plummet without a safety net.

"Thank you," she said after a moment. "I'll tell Hugh I need to go home."

"The man waiting for you will be standing outside a black BMW. His name is Swanton."

She nodded and walked out of the office without looking back.

Will had nailed Hugh's reaction to her request. He assured her it would be no trouble and even offered to drive her to her apartment. "It's okay," she said, realizing all over again that he was a really great guy and she was lucky to have him as a boss. "I feel like walking anyway. I need to think through a few things."

With a look of concern, Hugh asked, "Are you okay? He isn't being a bastard, is he? Because if he is, I'll throw his ass out of here. I don't need the publicity that bad."

Mia smiled. "Thanks, but that won't be necessary. Do me a favor, though, and stick close to him today. Talk his ears off." Hugh gave her a questioning look. "I want you to keep him so busy, he won't have time to call me or come knocking at my door. I'm sulking, and I want him to squirm a little."

Hugh winked. "Consider it done."

As Mia passed Vanessa's workstation, anger surged again, gathering into a tight knot in her chest. Last night with Will, she hadn't had time to be angry with Vanessa. After he left, however, she'd had plenty of time to think. There was nothing she could do, really, but she couldn't just walk away without saying something.

She stopped, and Vanessa looked up, her gaze flat and watchful. "Is something wrong? You look terrible."

"I'm not feeling well."

"Oh." Vanessa stood. "Sorry to hear that."

Mia could hardly believe it. She sounded and acted just like Vanessa, and if it hadn't been for Will's revelation, Mia wouldn't have noticed the hint of wariness . . . or the colder light in her blue eyes.

She could feel Will's stare boring a hole through her back. "Will and I got into a fight last night and I didn't sleep well, so Hugh said I could go home."

"Oh," Vanessa said again. "What a shame. I hope it wasn't a serious fight."

Mia took a deep breath. "I hope so, too. There are some mistakes you can't ever come back from. You know what I mean?"

Vanessa went very still. "Can't say that I do."

Mia wanted to grab her and shake her, to make her see reason. She whispered, "I know everything, Van. I won't ask why, but just . . . don't do it. He's not worth it."

Vanessa's expression flattened. "Good-bye, Mia. I hope you're feeling better later."

Mia turned, hot tears pressing at the back of her eyes, and left the workshop.

In the sun's glare, with tears in her eyes, it took her a moment to find the car. It was parked right in the lot, and the driver wasn't even trying to be covert. He was an older man, but despite the graying hair, he looked like someone she wouldn't want to confront in a dark alley.

"Ms. Dolan? I'm Mark Swanton. Mr. Tiernay will have told you about me."

Nodding, she got into the car. He didn't say a word

during the drive to her apartment, which she appreciated since she wasn't in the mood for small talk.

They were at her apartment door before he spoke
again. "Excuse me, ma'am, but let me go in first."

Her hands shaking, Mia handed over her keys. He
opened the door slowly and slipped in—and somewhere between leaving the stairwell and opening her
door, he'd pulled out a gun.

Her knees almost gave way. She could deal with guns
just fine in movies, but this was too real.

Swanton eased farther inside, turning on the lights,
and motioned her to wait. She wanted to warn him
about the ferret, to be careful not to let Caligula run
out, until she realized how absurd it would sound.

This man had a gun. There might be people trying
to harm her. Someone had attacked Will, maybe even
tried to kill him. A sneaky ferret was the least of her
worries right now.

After a quick search of the apartment, Swanton motioned her inside. "You can come in now. Please shut
the door and lock and chain it. I'll need to use your
phone and—"

A man emerged from the hall with a gun. Before she
could scream a warning a muffled pop sounded, then
another. Swanton dropped with a grunt of pain, and
then was absolutely, chillingly silent.

Even as she watched the pooling blood, Mia couldn't

believe this was happening. A dizzy faintness warred with her heaving stomach, and she grabbed for the wall for support.

"Hello, Mia." Kostandin Vulaj's deep voice was pleasant and friendly.

"Sit down and be very quiet," he said, turning the gun on her. "And don't do anything stupid."

Twenty-two

❖

SOMETHING WAS WRONG.

It had been twenty minutes since Mia had left; Swanton should've called by now to let him know everything was secure and Mia was safe. Will checked his cell phone, but there were no missed calls listed.

He looked across the room at Vanessa. She'd finished with the reliquary only moments before, and Hugh had approved it. Now she was cleaning up her bench, working calmly—and neither the fake reliquary nor the original, which had been on the bench just moments before, was anywhere to be seen.

As if sensing his gaze on her, she looked up—and smiled.

Fuck. Will turned to Hugh. "I need to use your office to make a private call. I'll be right back."

He didn't give the man a chance to refuse, just

moved quickly inside and shut the door. Still watching Vanessa, he punched in Mia's number.

The phone rang. And rang . . . And with every ring, he had to fight to keep from putting his fist through the office window.

On the sixth ring, someone finally picked up.

"Mia?"

"It's about time. I've been expecting your call, Mr. Tiernay of Avalon."

"Vulaj." Will dropped onto the desk chair, his heart pounding so hard he could hear each beat in his head. "I take it we are about to enter into negotiations."

"You aren't going to ask if your girlfriend's okay?" Vulaj asked, his tone faintly mocking.

"If she weren't, you wouldn't be talking to me now."

"So we understand each other. Good."

Will took a deep breath and let it out slowly, trying to cut through his raw rage. It was the last thing Mia needed from him right now. "What do you want, Vulaj?"

"I think you can guess. I'm going to call you tonight at nine o'clock. I'll give you an address, and you'll go there immediately. Time will be very important, so no side trips to pick up reinforcements. No police. All you will bring with you is Vanessa and the shopping bag she'll have with her. Once Vanessa is with me, I'll tell you where to find your girlfriend. Again, time will be critical. You won't have any chance to chase after me if you want to find her alive."

"If she so much as suffers a scratch, I'll—"

"You'll what, kill Vanessa in retaliation?"

For a split second, Will envisioned it. Then, swallowing, he said, "No, but I'll kill you. Count on it."

"Good," Vulaj said after a moment. "Then we truly understand what is important to each of us. And to be as clear as possible, if Vanessa suffers so much as a scratch, as you say, I *will* kill Mia and then I will kill you."

"You sonofabitch." If he could get someone over to Mia's apartment . . . Claudia was too far away; he could get there faster himself.

"Keep your phone on. Again, I will call you at—"

Will cut the call short, yanked the office door open, and ran, ignoring Hugh's shouted questions, barely registering the terrified look on Vanessa's face.

He shoved the door wide and raced to his car, cranking the ignition even before he had the door closed. Then he went speeding down the street in the heavy traffic.

Within minutes, he braked hard in front of the apartment, double-parking and paying no attention to the irate honking that erupted around him. He bolted up to the second floor, slowing when he saw Mia's door ajar.

He pulled his gun, advancing carefully, breathing hard. He nudged the door open and went inside, gun sweeping the living room—and saw the body lying on the floor.

"Jesus."

He went immediately to Swanton, gun still in hand. Crouching, he gently rolled the man over, feeling for a pulse . . . and found it. Feeble, but there. He quickly grabbed a handful of towels from the kitchen drawer, using them to apply pressure to the wound.

He put down the gun long enough to call for an ambulance, and then he called Morris. "Get your ass over to Mia Dolan's apartment, fast. Vulaj shot your buddy and took Mia. The guy's alive, but barely. I called an ambulance, but I can't be here when they arrive."

"Dammit, you can't just— All right, I'm on my way. But you and me are gonna have a talk real soon, because this has just moved into the streets of my city, and I told you what I'd do if that happened."

"I know. Just get the fuck over here!"

By then neighbors had started gathering around the open door, and several rushed in, asking Will if he needed help.

"I called an ambulance. You!" He pointed to a middle-aged man who looked calm enough to handle the situation. "Stay here, and keep the pressure on the wound. I'm a cop, and I'm going after the shooter."

He still walked the walk and talked the talk well enough that he didn't have to flash a badge. The man nodded, bending over Swanton as the distant wail of a siren sounded outside.

Will ran back to his car, pulling away seconds before the first squad car arrived.

Even if they'd caught his license plate number, Morris would take care of it. Right now he had to go back to Haddington, because there would be questions to deal with. Lots of questions.

By the time he pulled back into the parking lot, he'd bottled up his fury and regained his calm as best he could. He double-checked to be sure he'd wiped all the blood off his hands. His black suit hid bloodstains fairly well; that was why he owned so many of them.

"Will!" Hugh stood and hurried toward him. "Are you all right? Did something happen? You ran out of here like you had a thousand devils at your heels. Is it Mia?"

Will smiled and laid his hand on Hugh's shoulder in a comforting gesture. "It's okay; false alarm. She thought someone was trying to break into her apartment, but it was just her ferret. Sorry for the drama. Everything is fine. I tucked Mia back in bed and put the damn thing back in its cage."

Hugh frowned. "That's not like Mia to overreact."

"She's not feeling well and was upset, not thinking too clearly." Will turned his attention to Vanessa. She'd also come to her feet and was watching him with a guarded expression. Fake knew fake, after all. "I better go reassure Vanessa that Mia's okay and I'm not crazy."

Vanessa sat back down as he approached and made no attempt to hide her fear of him.

Smiling, he leaned over her. "You knew this would happen."

To her credit, she didn't pretend to misunderstand. "He won't hurt her unless you force him to," she said, her voice barely audible. "Do what he says, and she'll be fine."

"You'd better be right. Because if anything happens to her, I will gut your boyfriend from groin to gullet." He continued to smile his friendliest smile. "And then I'm coming for you."

Knowing that he couldn't do much by staying at the workshop, Will told Hugh he had to head to his hotel to check in with his editor about a new assignment. "I'll be back later to finish up the interview, take a couple photos, and then I'm done."

He returned to his car and drove only a short distance, since he still needed to watch over Vanessa and the building. Then he called Claudia and quickly filled her in.

"What do you want me to do? This sounds like it could go bad real fast, Will."

"I'd say it's already beyond that." He massaged his brows, where the dull ache seemed to have taken up permanent residence. "Right now there isn't a lot you can do. I have to wait for Vulaj to call again, and that's when I'll need you to back me up."

"Where are you now?"

"Sitting in my car across from Haddington."

There was a pause, then she asked, "You have anything to eat yet today?"

Had he? He couldn't remember. "I don't think so."

"I'll swing by with something and keep you company."

"I'm not hungry," Will said.

"Ha! You just don't want to be stuck with me for the rest of the day."

"That, too."

"Tough. You need to eat, and all things considered, it's better that I be close by. Tell Morris to find someone to watch the goons at Sharpton's place."

"All right. See you in a few." Next he punched in Morris's number and went through the same briefing routine. "How's Swanton?"

"In surgery. Looks like it's gonna be touch and go. It's a good thing you got there when you did, though it did cause me some trouble in having to explain your presence. Several concerned citizens called in your license plate number, seeing as how you parked illegally and forgot to be all covert and shit."

"I was in a hurry."

"Yeah." Another sigh. "I'm sorry about Ms. Dolan."

"Me, too. Look, if you can spare someone to watch Sharpton's apartment, that would be a big help. My backup is joining me now, but I'd still like to keep an eye on those two in the apartment, on the off chance they might lead us to Vulaj's location."

"I can do that," Morris said. "And then we'll have that talk I mentioned earlier."

"I'm outside the Haddington building. Get here as soon as you can."

In a few minutes it was going to be downright cozy in this car, although the atmosphere would be anything but warm.

Staring across the street at the plain brick building, Will tried not to think about what Mia was going through.

And failed. "Hold on," he whispered. "I'll be there."

Twenty-three

"WHERE ARE YOU TAKING ME?" MIA ASKED AS CALMLY AS she could. It was hard not to be terrified when one was sitting in a locked car, hands and feet tied, with a crazy man carrying a gun.

"Here and there," Kos answered. "It's not time yet to meet your Will."

He was driving the big SUV Vanessa had bought for him, and he stopped for all the red lights, didn't speed, did nothing that would draw unwelcome attention.

By now, Mia had also noticed a pattern. He would drive for an hour or so, then stop and park for another hour, moving her into the backseat whenever he stopped. He didn't even let her out to go to the bathroom—he'd given her a peculiar-shaped bottle that she understood, with distaste, was her only choice unless she wanted to pee her pants.

At first she'd been too frightened to consider ways to

escape. She couldn't stop remembering that man in her apartment falling in such an awful way, with hardly a sound. She kept seeing the blood slowly spread out from beneath him, and all she could think about was that she didn't want to die like that.

But after the initial horror, a muffling calm had slowly spread through her. Maybe it was only shock, but it kept her from giving in to hysteria.

That was when she started to think about how she might get away from Kos. While she knew Will would come for her, she didn't want to just sit and wait. Not if she could rescue herself.

Unfortunately, it was impossible for her to do *anything* with hands and feet tied, buckled into the backseat, out of view. Because the back windows were tinted, she couldn't even try to catch the attention of passengers in the cars whizzing past.

Now, with the sun setting, she'd grudgingly admitted that she wouldn't have a chance to escape until Kos stopped at their final destination and removed her from the SUV.

God, her wrists and ankles hurt. He hadn't tied her tightly enough to cut off her circulation, but she had to keep shaking her hands and feet to prevent them from going numb, and every time she did so, it hurt like a bitch.

"There's no way you'll be able to get away with this, Kos," she said quietly. "You killed that man in my apartment, kidnapped me . . . add that to stealing the Eudoxia collection, and everybody will be out hunting for you."

"That possibility has occurred to me," he said dryly. "But thank you for pointing it out."

Anger spiked. "I don't understand why you're doing this. It's wrong."

"It's wrong," he mimicked her, his tone mocking. "Yeah, I know that, too."

"Stop it," she snapped.

"Then stop talking to me like I'm stupid," Kos snapped back, his gaze meeting hers in the rearview mirror. "I know you never liked me, never thought I was good enough."

"And I was proved right."

He laughed. "You thought I was bad for Vanessa, but it turned out I was bad for her in all the right ways."

Arrogant prick.

The arrogance wasn't surprising, since he'd been blessed with those dark, sulky good looks. Ancient Greek statues had profiles like Kos's; the Christos of Byzantium shared the same intensely dark eyes—a pity that such a pretty package concealed such a rotten core.

"You used Vanessa."

"She didn't seem to mind." He grinned lazily. "It's true that I picked her out to help my cause, but I told her the truth. She knew from the start what I wanted. It's what she wants, too."

"I don't believe you."

"You don't believe what? That I love her?"

"Of course you don't. If you loved her, you wouldn't have dragged her down with you."

"You seem to think she's helpless. Why do you find it so hard to believe she is with me, working with me, of her own free will?"

The question took her by surprise, then she retorted, "Because Vanessa isn't stupid! She'd know this would ruin her life, everything she's worked so hard to achieve and—"

"And what has she achieved? She's had a hard life, as a child and as a woman. She wanted a chance to have something more, and I gave that to her."

"It's *stealing*! What you're giving her is not, and never has been, yours to give."

"I'm not keeping that box and all the jewelry. I'm selling it. It's the money I want."

The logic of that left her momentarily speechless; then she said coldly, "God forbid you just get a job like everyone else."

Kos pulled off in a small parking lot, stopped a distance from most of the other cars, then turned in his seat to look at her. "I have a job. I have several. You know nothing of me, of my life before I came here, what it was like to live where I did. You read about it in the news and shake your head and think it's so sad, but you don't really care because it doesn't touch you."

"And so you bring it all with you when you come to this country, instead of trying to get away from it? Nothing you've told me makes me feel any sympathy for you, or changes the fact that you're breaking the law."

"I think we already agreed on the part where I'm morally inferior to you." He smiled again, teeth flashing white. He could've been a model in a magazine, he was so striking. "Not that I care."

She stared at him, then demanded, "Do you really love Vanessa?"

Kos raised a brow. "I already said I did. Why would I lie to you about it?"

Mia shook her head in disbelief. "I can't believe it. I just can't."

"Vanessa was right about you. She told me that she couldn't be herself around you, because you were always telling her how she should act and think, making her feel like there was something about her that needed fixing."

Stung and shocked, Mia wanted to deny his words vehemently, but couldn't find her voice to do so.

"But she isn't you and doesn't think like you. She is her own person, and she didn't need fixing. She just needed someone who could accept her and take care of her, who would give her love and accept her love in return. She's a good woman. You have no idea how good."

Dear God . . . she'd thought for sure he was lying, but that wasn't it at all.

"She deserves so much more," Kos continued, his gaze intent and direct. "No one has ever cared for her the way I do, looked after her or protected her. I give her something no one else has ever given her, something that I've never given to anybody else. For her, I am her hero. Do you understand?"

Mia looked away so he wouldn't see her sudden welling of pity. "Yes," she said quietly. "I understand."

It was clear now why they loved each other. Both of them needful, feeding off each other, trying to fill the empty places inside that couldn't be filled. Mia had always feared something like this for Vanessa, even when it seemed she'd escaped the cycle and had put her life together.

Maybe Vanessa *did* resent her. All this time, Mia had thought she'd been supportive, a good friend . . . had she instead only added to the problem?

So now Vanessa had given Kostandin Vulaj the role of hero that he needed to play, the chance to style himself as a good guy who was merely misunderstood. In turn, he made Vanessa feel important and valuable, desired and loved, everything she'd hungered for all her life.

Silence enveloped the SUV for what seemed like

forever. The sun had set, and darkness settled over the parking lot, its white lights cold and harsh.

"It's time to go," Kos said quietly and turned the ignition.

"It's getting late." Claudia's husky voice came from behind him. "When are you going back inside Haddington?"

Will glanced over at her. Orange-red wasn't her natural hair color, but it looked great against her dusky skin. In tight, low-slung jeans and a black hoodie, she looked like just another young urban woman hanging out in a car with friends.

"Not until Vulaj calls," he said. "If I keep going in and out, Haddington will start wondering what the hell is going on."

"Hang in there. It's almost time." She leaned forward, bringing with her a whiff of thick, sensual perfume. "Here comes Morris again."

"The man's punctual," Will murmured. "I'll give him that."

"He's been pretty decent, all things considered."

"That's because he doesn't have anything to work with. We'll see how nice he plays after I get Vulaj's call."

And it had better come soon. The hours of waiting, not knowing—

He cut the thought off, refusing to give fear a foothold. He couldn't afford to.

Morris parked in the empty lot of a hair salon, then dodged traffic as he crossed the street. He climbed in the back of Will's car. "The two of you aren't being very stealthy. I thought you should know that."

Will shrugged. "Stealthy is pointless now. I'm in wait mode."

"No call yet, huh?"

"No."

"Christ, I hate the waiting," Morris muttered.

Will glanced back at him. "How's your buddy?"

"Out of surgery and stable. It could be touch and go for a couple days. He lost a lot of blood, and he's not as young as he used to be."

"Good to hear he's doing okay, though," Claudia said. "I don't think Ben was expecting this one to end up such a mess."

"I don't know where I went wrong," Will said. Except that he should've spent less time in Mia's bed and more time tailing Vulaj, but that was twenty-twenty hindsight. "I did everything I thought needed to be done. I knew Mia would be in danger, but I didn't think Vulaj would get that much of a jump on me."

"Her apartment showed no signs of a break-in. I say he had a key," Morris said.

It's the only spare key I have left . . .

"Dammit, I should've asked about that," Will muttered, angry with himself. "Before she moved in with

Vulaj, Sharpton roomed with Mia, and Mia probably never asked for the apartment key back."

Claudia checked her watch for what had to be the hundredth time. "Learning the hard way not to trust people is a bitch."

"Yeah," Will said, staring at the traffic but remembering the hurt and anger in Mia's eyes during their last conversation.

Morris leaned forward. "So what the hell is Sharpton doing in there?"

"My guess is that she's waiting on her ride—which would be me—to meet her boyfriend."

"So what are your plans?"

"I don't know yet." Will turned, facing Morris. "But you and your people are going to have to stay clear. Vulaj almost killed once today. He's going to be desperate, and I don't have to tell you that desperate people and hostages are a bad combination. I don't want Mia's life endangered any more than it already is."

"You're not gonna let them just walk away," Morris said sharply.

So much for Morris being cooperative. "I can and I will, *if* necessary."

"And you're not going in there alone," Claudia said flatly. "That's just asking for disaster."

"Look, I don't have a firm plan yet because I don't know where the fuck he's taken her," Will snapped. "If it's a location that's too open, any interference will get her killed. Right now, I'm leaning toward going after them once I have Mia safe, but to get to her, I'll have to meet Vulaj. Alone."

"If you can get me in there, and Morris here can find me a rifle, I can take him out at a signal from you."

"You're a shooter?" Morris asked.

Claudia nodded. "Pretty good shot, yeah. Not sniper material, but if you get me close enough and if you give me a clear shot, I'll always hit what I'm aiming for."

"That's a lot of ifs," Will pointed out.

"You got a better idea?"

The conversation was circling on itself, and Will didn't bother to answer.

"Ten minutes to nine," Morris said softly.

As if Will wasn't watching every second click over on his watch's digital display.

At three minutes to nine, his cell phone rang. He immediately answered. "Tiernay here."

"I have instructions for you."

"I'm listening." At Morris's questioning look, Will nodded, then pulled out his notebook and pen. "Talk."

"First, time is very, very important. You won't have an opportunity to do anything more than what I tell you to do."

Will did not like the sound of this. "All right. What else?"

"As I said earlier, you will take Vanessa and her bag

and drive her to where I'm waiting. It's an abandoned building just outside the city limits."

He liked the sound of this even less, but said nothing as he jotted down the address. Both Claudia and Morris leaned forward to read it; Morris grimaced.

"Again, you are not to bring anyone with you, and you're not to involve the police. I'll be waiting for you when you get here. When you hand over Vanessa and the bag, I'll let you go to Mia. If you do everything I tell you to do, you will have just enough time to take her to safety before the bomb detonates."

Will froze, his fingers closing hard around the pen.

"I learned many interesting skills as a kid where I grew up. It's a homemade bomb, but it'll get the job done."

It took a moment for the red haze to clear, then Will relaxed his grip on the pen. He ignored Claudia's sharp, suspicious look. "I understand."

"Make sure you do," Vulaj said coldly. "Don't fuck with me, Tiernay. I'm not some stupid street punk. And I have powerful friends."

"How will I know she's all right?"

"You'll be able to see her and hear her talk. I don't want to hurt her, and I won't unless you leave me no other option. I'm playing straight with you here. After all, you have someone I want very badly, too."

"How much time do I have to get there?"

"Enough." Humor tinged the cold tone. "I don't

want to blow myself up; I have plans that don't include dying. I'm sure you do as well, so don't do anything crazy. If it looks like you've lied to me or not followed my exact instructions, I'll detonate the bomb myself."

Vulaj ended the call.

Will sat unmoving, trying to rein in a rising fear, to think of what to do—and knew he had to do exactly as Vulaj demanded. He had no other choice.

"Is she all right?" Claudia demanded, alarmed. "What's going on? You don't look so good."

"This should never have happened, and it's my fault that it did. Sheridan is gonna nail my balls to the floor for this."

"Not likely," Claudia said. "And it's not entirely your fault, although you probably should've kept your pants zipped until you had Vulaj in custody."

"So what's the plan?" Morris asked. "You got one now?"

"I do what Vulaj told me to do, or Mia dies. You people stay the hell away from this. He's not bluffing."

For a split second he considered telling Morris about the bomb, but if he did, and Morris brought in the SWAT team, it'd end up a goddamned war zone. People would die, and the first would be Mia.

"I know that place," Morris said, motioning to the address on the notepad. "It's an old fish canning factory, abandoned back in the sixties. It's in a remote area off the interstate; if something happens, the police won't be able to respond right away."

Exactly what Vulaj was counting on.

"You can get your people in the area, but don't go near the factory itself," Will ordered flatly. "If the situation gets out of control, you'll be close enough to respond. But if he sees anyone but me, he'll kill her. And if she dies because you gotta play cowboy, I will hunt you down and make you pay. Are we clear on this, Morris?"

"Crystal," Morris said stiffly as he exited the car. "But I want a piece of this little shit. You owe me that."

"Once I have him, he's all yours. Can you get Claudia a rifle?"

Morris nodded curtly, then stalked off.

Claudia said, "Tell me what's wrong, Tiernay. Don't you try to bullshit me."

"It's a bomb," Will said, his voice tight. "Vulaj has a bomb."

"Jesus!"

"Praying might not be such a bad idea." Will opened his car door. "Get your ass over there, but the same instructions apply to you. Keep out of sight, find a good shooting spot nearby, and stay in touch. If it looks like we need to take him out and I can't do it, it'll be up to you."

"Got it."

Will ran across the street to Haddington.

"You're back?" Hugh said, looking up from packing the last of the Eudoxia collection into its crate for the pickup. "It's a little late for journalistic activities, I think."

Vanessa was helping with the packing. Her face was so pale, she looked ill. If Haddington didn't notice, he had to be blind.

"I'm here to pick up Vanessa. I was with Mia when Kos called her. He has to work late and asked if Mia would pick her up and take her home. Since she's not feeling well, I said I'd do it."

"Why didn't Kos call here?" Hugh asked, pushing back the brim of his fedora to meet Will's gaze head-on.

Will read the suspicion in the man's eyes and wished Haddington had remained oblivious for just a little longer. He didn't have time for explanations; he had to grab Vanessa and go.

"He called here earlier, while you were in the vault," Vanessa said. "He said he might have to work late but wasn't sure. I told him that Mia went home early, so I said he should call Will over there."

That seemed to appease Haddington. "And speaking of being sick, *you* look ghastly."

"I do feel a little off," Vanessa admitted. She was turning out to be quite the accomplished liar.

Haddington sighed. "You better go home then, and stay home tomorrow if you need to. I can finish the packing, and the armored truck's coming first thing in the morning. I may make an early day of it tomorrow myself."

"Are you sure?" Vanessa asked.

"Yeah. Go on."

"I'm in a hurry to get back to Mia." Will grabbed Vanessa's arm tightly. "Let's get your things."

Vanessa bit her lip as she walked with Will, although when she approached her workbench, she whispered tightly, "You're hurting me!"

"Tough. I'm in a fucking bad mood, and you damn well know why, so shut up and get this bag of yours. I'm on the clock here."

She gave him a look that made him wonder briefly if she was entirely aware of Vulaj's plans, but it didn't really matter.

Soon after, Vanessa slid into the front seat of his car, clutching a large canvas shopping bag on her lap.

Will pulled back his suit coat to reveal his shoulder holster. "I'll use it," he said, his voice tight with the fury he no longer had to hide. "So don't try anything."

She wisely said nothing.

Will took off, driving slightly above the speed limit, concentrating on getting out of the congested city and onto the interstate as quickly as possible.

"Do you know where I'm taking you?" he asked at length.

"Yes. Kos said it was a meeting place." She sounded subdued. "I didn't know he'd do anything like this or—"

"Don't give me that shit. You knew he was going to use her to hamstring me, and you didn't do anything about it. Jesus Christ—she thought you were her *friend*, and you let this happen to her."

Vanessa stared straight ahead. "If you hadn't interfered, nothing would've happened to her. The minute you made our business your business, she was fair game."

"If you hadn't decided to rip off your boss, a rich businessman, and a major museum, I wouldn't have *had* to make you my business in the first place. You messed up, Vanessa. Whatever he's giving you, it's not worth this."

"How would you know? You're not me."

If she had any qualms about throwing her lot in with Vulaj, they'd long since disappeared. He'd seen this sort of thing often as a cop. White-collar crime was different from generic street crime in its genesis and mechanics. So many times, he'd seen apparently ordinary men and women throw away nice, comfortable lives because of poor money management skills, a need for instant gratification, or because they couldn't resist the temptation to make a quick, illegal buck.

Some took to their new lives with an unexpected flair, and it looked like Vanessa Sharpton was one of them.

"He's got her by a *bomb*. Is he such a good fuck that it's worth blowing up an innocent woman? Because the world's full of men who know how to fuck, Vanessa—

and most of them aren't likely to die young or spend the rest of their lives in maximum security."

The look of horror in her eyes proved she hadn't known about the bomb. "Kos isn't a killer."

"Tell that to the man who nearly died in Mia's apartment. If I hadn't arrived when I did, he would've bled to death."

"That man had a gun. Somebody would've ended up shot, and Kos wasn't about to let it be him."

"So that makes it okay in your book?"

"No, it makes it a necessity." Vanessa looked away. "Don't mistake me, Tiernay. I don't like this. I don't want people hurt. But if it happens, it happens."

Whatever happens, happens had been his own philosophy far too often. He made an effort to relax his grip on the steering wheel. "It's not too late for you to pull free, Vanessa. I offered to help you earlier, and I'm offering again. But this is the last time."

Even before she shook her head, he knew he was wasting his breath.

"I'm going with Kos," she said quietly. "But the offer of help goes both ways. If you want to just walk away, you can do it. Kos won't hurt Mia unless you do something to me, or try to double-cross him. What does it matter to you that we take the reliquary? Why do you even care?"

The raw frustration in her voice took him by surprise. "I care because betraying the people you work for, the people who trust you, is wrong. I care because stealing is against the law, and I believe that laws are the foundation for decency and fairness."

"The law was never much help when my old man used his fists on my mother or us kids. Laws weren't much use when a boyfriend decided to knock me around or steal everything I owned. So you'll have to forgive me if I don't hold the law in such high esteem as you do."

"It's easy to blame it all on somebody else—and convenient as hell, too. I used to be a cop. People were always telling me it wasn't their fault. It was Mom and Dad's fault, the economy's fault, the bitch who couldn't keep the house clean." He glanced at her. "A lot of people have rough lives, Vanessa. They cope. Some of them cope with the help of meds, but they do it without victimizing anyone else."

The interstate was dark, the lanes constant streams of headlights and taillights.

"Victimizing?" Vanessa made a contemptuous sound. "Please, who exactly is being victimized? Malcolm Toller, who has more money than he knows what to do with? The Met? Do you have any idea how many museums the world over have fakes in their collections? And yet they manage. Or do you mean the hordes of tourists? They wouldn't know the difference between the real deal and a fake anyway, so how are they victimized? The

Met gets its money's worth whether tourists gawk at fakes or the real thing."

"Is this how Vulaj convinced you to go along with him?"

"Partially," Vanessa admitted. "But it's the truth. Nobody cares that much if art goes missing. Working sods don't have much sympathy for some rich bloke who loses a couple trinkets. Not even the police."

"Bullshit," Will said quietly. "If a rich man is shot dead and a bum is knifed, they're both dead and they're both victims. If a prostitute is raped by her john and a college girl is raped by a frat boy, it's still rape and they're still victims. If a little old lady is robbed of her pension check and a rich entrepreneur is robbed of some ugly statue worth hundreds of thousands of dollars, it's still robbery and they're still victims. I don't treat them any differently, and I never will."

Silence settled over the car, except for the hum of the tire treads on the pavement. After a minute, Vanessa said, "Well, you get points for passion. Not that it'll do you much good against all the people who don't really give a shit. It's why you and your people never will make any headway. It would be so much easier if you'd just look the other way, take Mia with you, and let me and Kos go."

She glanced at him. "Kos and I are going to use this money to start a new life. He's going to get out from under the thumb of his bosses and make the business work for him instead of the other way around. He has passion, too." She sighed. "Is it really so bad, what we're doing? No one had to be hurt. No one would even have known what happened if you hadn't come here."

Briefly—for only a second or two—he almost agreed.

But then the image of Mia, alone and frightened, held captive in an abandoned factory with a bomb close by, came rushing back.

"Save it for your lawyer," he said harshly. "Because I'm going to take you and your boyfriend down. If not tonight, then I'll hunt you down another day. For what you did to Mia, I will never forgive or forget."

Vanessa studied him, her expression solemn, as he turned down the off-ramp to head for the factory. "That, at least, I can understand and respect. You love her and will do anything for her. It's the same for Kos and me, although you'll never admit that to yourself."

Twenty-four

❖

MIA WAS TIED TO A PEELING RADIATOR IN AN ABAN-
doned building in the middle of nowhere. The radiator
was near a broken window, so she could see outside and
not be completely in the dark. Kos had also left a small
flashlight, for which she was grateful. Even if she didn't
like what little she could see, the alternative—pitch
blackness amid rustling creatures of the darkness—
would be far worse.

God, she was still as frightened of the dark as when
she'd been a little girl. She'd thought she'd outgrown
it, but her own dark bathroom was a far cry from a
derelict old building, where there was a man with a
gun nearby who wouldn't hesitate to kill her.

Kos had taken her up a stairway, the handrails so
rusted that metal flaked off where she gripped them.
She was on the second or third floor; it was hard to tell

since the main floor had such a high ceiling. There had been an elevator shaft, the elevator itself long dead, and the stairs weren't safe, either. She'd passed rusty old machinery, gears and pulleys, levers and things she couldn't identify in the dim light.

There were a lot of windows on the main floor, high and narrow, broken or boarded up, but this room was darker. The warped wood and peeling paint were covered in so much mildew that the walls were nearly black. Shards of glass glimmered in the low light, and broken wood, nails, and bits of furniture lay scattered across the floor. Kos had carefully cleared a place for her, even spreading his sweatshirt on the radiator for her to sit on when she tired of standing.

A strange gesture of kindness to a woman he'd threatened to kill.

From the creaking of the floorboards, she knew he was close by, out in the hall. The floor was so rotted that every time she shifted, she feared the wood would give way and she'd plummet down to the main floor.

She fantasized that happening to Kos, hoping it would kill him, even though the notion of being trapped here alone terrified her.

And what if he *did* leave her here? What if no one found her in time? She could starve, be attacked by a wild animal or some serial killer. It looked like the kind of place that would attract violent people who needed to hide. Or she might freeze to death. The

April nights were cold, which would quickly take its toll, along with the lack of food and water.

Sitting alone in the darkness, night after night—

No! She was not alone; people were out looking for her. Will was coming for her; he'd get her out of this.

God, please, let him come soon.

Mia shifted, jostling the flashlight, and its weak beam flared on a long, jagged shard of glass. Her breath caught.

If she could reach it with the tip of her shoe, maybe she could pull it toward her and use it to cut the ropes tying her hands.

Careful not to make the floorboards creak too much, she extended her leg toward the shard until she touched it, then, gently nudged it with the side of her shoe back toward her.

The floorboards gave a loud groan, and Mia froze as she heard footsteps moving closer.

Dammit!

She leaned against the wall and radiator just as Kos walked in, a black shape casting a weak shadow in the flashlight beam.

"Hey," he said. "You're doing okay?"

Mia glared at him. "I couldn't be more comfortable. Thank you ever so much."

He laughed softly. "It won't be long now. Your Will is on the way."

"He's bringing Vanessa?"

"He agreed without an argument. It seems you're very important to him."

"And will you let me go when he gets here? You won't try to hurt him?"

Kos leaned back against the wall. The leather coat he wore over a dark T-shirt and black jeans looked a little worse for wear, smeared with dirt and rust stains. "It depends on what he does. I'm prepared to play fair, but I don't think he will."

"Why do you say that? He's—"

"You have no idea who or what he is," Kos interrupted angrily. "These Avalon people are just hired guns. They have no loyalty to a cause, no allegiance to family or friends. They'll do anything for money."

"If you're trying to make him look bad, that's not going to convince me."

"I'm not trying to make him look bad. I'm saying that he's not the saint you seem to think. This group he's with is no better than me; only they have the money and power behind them to keep them out of prison. You don't think they kill? You don't think they lie and cheat and break laws? Ask him. Dare him to tell you the truth."

Mia looked away. Her instinct told her Kos was just trying to excuse his own actions, but his words bothered her, since she suspected Will's methods *were* less than proper.

"He won't expect you to play fair, either."

Kos shrugged. "Probably. Except he has something very important to me, so I'm not going to do anything that will put her in danger, either."

Using the other's lover to ensure good behavior had at least evened the balance, or put them in a stalemate—maybe enough of one for her to reason with Kos.

"If you love Vanessa, don't take her with you. She still has a chance to get clear of this, but if she leaves with you, it's all over. Do you really want her to have that kind of life? What chance of a normal life can you give her while running from the law?"

"So much concern for Vanessa. None for me?"

Mia didn't know what to say to that.

"No? I didn't think so. I'm not worth second chances, worth believing in." He dropped his head back against the wall, regarding her, the low light casting his face in shadows and angles. "I have dreams, too, you know. Things I want to see, to do. Where I came from, there was nothing. Here there's a better chance."

"How can you possibly believe fencing stolen art is a better chance?"

"You haven't lived my life. People like you have opportunities, you have choices and never think about how lucky you are. I never had anything but poverty and a homeland torn apart by war. I come to America, and I'm looked down upon because I'm not one of you.

I'm just another foreigner, stealing your jobs and living off your taxes. But at least no one is shooting at me, so it's not so bad."

"Will said you were with the Albanian Mafia. Is that true?"

Kos shrugged. "I'm family, that's all. I didn't like it. I'm tired of answering to others. The work is all the same—the whores, the drugs, dealing with troublemakers. The cops get you for all that. Art pays better, and it's not so much of a risk."

"Prostitution, drugs . . . how can you justify any of that?"

"Supply and demand. As long as there are men, there will be prostitutes. Me, I don't even smoke, and I believe drugs are bad, but there's good money in it if you can stay out of jail. It's not a life I want for myself or Vanessa."

Mia wasn't sure if she should feel pity or contempt for his strange vision of the good life. "I still think you're making a mistake."

"Maybe, but it's worth the risk." He pushed away from the wall and walked toward her. Alarmed, Mia scooted back as far as she could. "Are you one of those people who gives up just because the road gets rough? Because it might take work or effort, or you might have to bleed for it? Vanessa and I are stronger than that. And that's why we'll win."

The chance of them winning in any sense of the

word seemed slim to none, and pity won out over contempt.

"You should've called it quits with the reliquary. You should have known, once Will arrived, that things wouldn't work out."

"Who says they won't? He's on his way now. He's agreed to my every demand. I forced him to choose between you and his work, and luckily for you, he chose you." He tipped his head, studying her. "And I can read your face even in this light. Don't pity me. I don't want or need it. I know what's at stake, and even if I can't win, I won't go to prison."

She had no difficulty understanding the coldly fervent gleam in his eyes. "You'll kill me."

"If I can't win, no one wins." He went still, turning slightly, as if listening for something. "I'm going downstairs. Stay quiet until I say otherwise."

As his creaking footsteps faded, Mia squeezed her eyes tight to hold her fear. Her breathing rasped loudly in the silence, and then she heard the crunch of tires on gravel as a car slowly approached.

She had never been religious, but now she whispered, "Please keep him safe. Please."

The thought that she'd never get to see Will again terrified her more than her own danger. Their last conversations had been so full of anger and recriminations—and she'd never gotten a chance to tell him that she still loved him.

Loved him?

Shock quickly faded, replaced by an acceptance that calmed her and renewed her strength. How could she ever have doubted that she'd fall in love with him all over again if given a second chance?

A few hours ago, she hadn't believed she could find anything in him of the man she used to love. Preoccupied with his revelations, she could see only the negatives. She had been selfish, naïve, and foolish. He was still the man she'd loved in all the ways that truly mattered.

What Will did was important, and Kos was wrong about him having no cause. Not compared with her own complacency, only working to pay the bills, the days simply passing by, month after month, year after year.

What kind of life was that? If she walked out of this alive, with Will, that would change.

Mia might not like what Vanessa had done, but she began to understand what drove her. Stability, safety, and contentment were all good but sterile, without a flash of passion or risk.

In a way, Kos was right. He'd just taken control of his own life in all the wrong ways.

She heard the slam of a car door and looked outside to see Will standing by the car.

"Oh, God," she whispered, as the fear came rushing back.

* * *

When Will pulled onto the broken, weed-choked road that led to the canning factory, the first thing he noted was that it was the only way in or out. A small river ran behind the factory, and beyond that stretched acres of dark, tangled woods. What made it difficult to get to also made it difficult to escape.

It was the first good news he'd had in hours.

The building looked ready to collapse, the old mortar crumbled, leaving cracks and gaping holes. Much of the roof was gone, sagging where it was still intact, and the windows that weren't broken were boarded up.

The idea of Mia in there somewhere left him cold. A couple of miles away, nearly invisible in the dark, Morris and several patrol cars were ready to intercept Vulaj once he escaped. Claudia would have moved in closer, ready to back him up.

What he feared most now was that Mia, as a hindrance, was already dead. Vulaj wouldn't have expected him to hold up his end of the bargain; in reality, Vulaj had no reason to hold up his end, either.

It was a risk, but double-crossing Vulaj before Vulaj could double-cross him was the only way to get Mia out of there. Will was prepared to take Vulaj alive, as he'd been ordered, but if Vulaj had killed Mia, he wouldn't walk out of that factory alive. Fuck Ben's orders and catching Rainert von Lahr.

"There's Kos."

Vanessa's quiet voice directed his attention toward the back of the factory, where the car's headlights barely illuminated a man emerging from a doorway.

Before they'd gotten out of the car, Will had slipped his gun from its holster. Now he held it at the side of her jaw. Vanessa gasped and went stiff.

"Let's go," he said quietly.

He walked forward holding her in a tight grip, and she stumbled along with him, not even moving her head.

At the halfway point, Will stopped. "Come into the light, where I can see you."

Vulaj hesitated, then moved forward. Slowly, details became more distinct: dark hair, dark clothes . . . the gleam of a gun pointing at him, barrel unwavering.

"Let her go, Tiernay. Now."

"Not until I talk to Mia and know she's unharmed."

Without taking his gaze from Will or lowering the gun, Vulaj shouted, "Mia! Let Will know where you are."

"I'm up here! I can see you . . . I'm okay!"

Relief flooded through Will as he caught a flash of movement, a pale face behind the broken glass.

It was her, and she was alive; Vulaj was playing fair so far.

"What do I do next?" Will asked.

"You send Vanessa and the bag over to me. Then you throw your gun into those bushes, lie down, and put your hands behind your head. Vanessa and I will get in my car and drive away. When I turn off the service road, I'll honk the horn. That will be your signal to go inside for Mia."

Beyond Vulaj, Will could barely make out the hood of a vehicle parked in the tall grass and weeds.

"What's to stop you from shooting me in the back?"

"Nothing but my word that I won't, as long as you don't try to shoot me," Vulaj said.

"Do it," Vanessa whispered through tight lips. "He means what he says."

It was either get down or shoot Vulaj right now—and pray the man didn't live long enough to detonate the bomb. Not his idea of favorable odds.

With Claudia, Morris, and six cops waiting, there was no way Vulaj would get far. But Will would have to move very, very fast once Vulaj drove off.

"All right," he said, tossing the gun into the bushes, hoping his cooperation would keep Vulaj from ordering Vanessa to search him—and find the other gun holstered at his back. He held up his hands. "I'll do it your way. Go, Vanessa."

She edged away from him, fear in her eyes as if she expected him to stop her. When she was out of arm's reach, she ran for Vulaj, who moved her protectively behind him.

Will glanced toward the window again. All he could make out was the pale blur of Mia's face watching him.

Then he lay down in the dirt and laced his fingers behind his head. He couldn't see much through the grass and weeds, but he could hear Vulaj and Vanessa running. A moment later an engine roared, then a big SUV sped past him, so close that the tires kicked up gravel against him.

He rolled to his side, hands still behind his head, and tracked the red taillights as they disappeared around the bend in the road.

Then he leaped to his feet and ran for the factory, slowing only to grab his gun from the bushes. "Mia! Keep calling my name so I can find you!"

He could hear her doing as he ordered while he fumbled for his cell phone and dialed Claudia. "They're gone, but don't do anything! I haven't got to Mia yet. Let him go, and pass the word to Morris."

He slammed open the door where Vulaj had been standing, pulled a small flashlight from his back pocket, and swung it around, revealing a wide-open space full of debris, old machinery, broken furniture—and ahead, a stairway.

"Will, are you here?"

Her voice was muffled, but he could hear her more clearly. Sweat trickled down his spine.

"I'm here," he shouted as he took the stairs two at a time, ignoring how they protested under his weight. "Keep talking!"

At the top of the stairs was a long, dark hall lined

with doors. Mia was singing "Yellow Submarine" off-key at the top of her lungs.

He found her in the room at the end of the hall, and the instant she saw him she started to cry, then laugh. "I *knew* you'd come for me! I knew it."

"Careful; don't move. It's hard to see, and I don't want to hurt you." Pulling out his switchblade, he cut the ropes binding her wrists.

When she was free, she flung herself against him, and he caught her as she sagged. "Hold on. We're not in the clear yet," he warned.

Grabbing her hand, he ran for the stairs. No sooner had they reached the second landing than a barrage of distant gunfire brought him up short. Mia bumped into him from behind.

Cold fear washed over him. "Oh, *fuck*."

"What's wrong?"

Pulling free from Mia's hand, he grabbed the edges of the stairwell window, heedless of splinters and broken glass digging into his palms, and kicked at the remaining glass and boards.

"Will! What's wrong?"

He kicked harder and knocked the boards loose. The next kick cleared the window.

He seized her arm. "We gotta go now!"

"Out the window? But—"

He pulled her, resisting, with him as he jumped. She screamed the entire six-foot drop to the ground.

The grass and weeds cushioned their fall, but as he landed, something gave way in his ankle with a hot stab of pain. Mia landed on her hands and knees, crying out, but he didn't give her time to recover. Ignoring the pain in his ankle, he grabbed her hand again and ran for cover behind an old flatbed truck tipped on its side.

"There's a bomb in the factory!" Will shoved her flat to the ground. "Keep your head down!"

"Did you say a *bomb*? Oh, my God, I can't believe—What's that sound?"

"A car," Will said, grimly. "Vulaj is coming back."

Twenty-five

◆

Mɪᴀ ʜᴀᴅ ɴᴏ ɪᴅᴇᴀ ᴡʜᴀᴛ ᴡᴀꜱ ɢᴏɪɴɢ ᴏɴ. Sʜɪᴠᴇʀɪɴɢ, ꜱʜᴇ moved toward the solid, comforting warmth of Will's body. "Why is he coming back?"

"Because the cops were waiting for him, and this is the only road away from them."

She looked up at him. "That wasn't part of the deal."

"So I lied," he said tersely, holding a gun with shocking familiarity as he pulled out his cell phone. "Claudia? Yeah, I know. I have Mia. We're behind an old truck that's lying on its side, by the back entrance. You see it? Where are you?"

The car sounded as if it was almost upon them, and Will's mouth tightened. "You'll need to move in closer. I'm not sure I can get a clear shot from where I am . . . Okay, good. Be careful."

"Is there really a bomb in the factory?" Mia asked.

"That's what Vulaj said. There's only one sure way to find out, and I'm not eager to give it a try."

She pressed against him, and the hard tension of his muscles vibrated all along her skin where they touched. "What is he going to do?"

"He's probably hoping to catch me off guard and take one or both of us hostage. Or maybe he thinks he can lure the police here and take them out in one big explosion. There's no way he's getting out down that road now, and he knows it."

A flash of light arced across the building: headlights approaching fast.

Will suddenly kissed her, hard. "Here we go. Stay down!"

The SUV pulled in, engine protesting as Kos pushed it hard. Tires skidded against the ground while the car came to a halt, brakes squealing. A door slammed, then Kos screamed, "Tiernay, you fucking sonofabitch! Where are you?"

"Kos, get back in the car," Vanessa's voice begged. "Please get back in!"

The rage and panic in their voices made Mia feel sick. "How come he didn't suspect you'd bring the police?" she whispered.

"I guess he thought he could trust me." He spared her a quick glance. "Don't feel sorry for them, Mia. Just don't."

A staccato burst of gunfire split the night, and he

added grimly, "Sounds like the gloves are off. That's an assault rifle."

Very bad news, since Will had only a handgun.

"Tiernay! I'll blow it up if you don't come out and face me—I'll fucking do it, I will, and I'll keep shooting until I kill you both!"

Mia shivered. If there really was a bomb and it went off, would this old truck provide enough protection?

"Stop it and get in the car!" Vanessa sounded frantic, tearful. "We have to try again!"

Will's face looked so forbidding and resolute that it sent a chill through Mia. "What's going to happen?" she asked.

He didn't answer right away. "I've seen this play out before. It usually doesn't end well."

He didn't need to spell it out further. "Oh, my God."

A single loud shot cracked out, followed by a scream, and Will lunged upward and started firing.

A spray of returning fire peppered the ground and truck, and Mia dropped flat with a harsh gasp, covering her head and squeezing her eyes shut. Will dropped beside her again. His hand kept her down, but he lowered his mouth to her ear and whispered, "My backup just took a shot at Vulaj. Winged him, and he's spooked. They're hiding behind their car now. The police are on the way; hear the sirens?"

She did.

And so did Vulaj, because he left the cover of the

SUV. Another single rifle shot cracked, followed by another high-pitched scream and the deadly *rat-tat-tat* of the assault rifle spraying the thick underbrush and woods.

Will slid a fresh clip into his gun, then scrambled around the truck, motioning for Mia to stay still, totally unnecessary because she was frozen with terror.

He stood, firing the gun with a double-handed grip, mouth pulled in a tight line, his face harsh and alien in the filmy glare of the headlights.

From her hiding spot beneath the truck, Mia glimpsed Kos on his hands and knees in the grassy open space beside the factory, Vanessa huddled over him.

She closed her eyes, not wanting to watch, then forced herself to open them. This was part of Will, who and what he was. She would not close her eyes to it.

Will fired again, and Kos toppled over into the long grass.

"Stop," she whispered, her fists closing tight. "Please stop."

Another shot rang out. Vanessa ducked, throwing her hands over her head. Then she pulled at Kos, trying to get him to his feet. It looked as if she was arguing with him, or pleading.

The sirens drew closer. Any second now she'd see the flashing lights of the squad cars, and it would be over for good.

Kos struggled to his feet, swaying as he pushed

Vanessa away. She seemed to hesitate, then started running for the other side of the factory, toward the heavier brush and woods. Kos went in the opposite direction.

"Goddammit," Will snapped. "He's making a run for the factory!"

Again he fired, and Vanessa stumbled but didn't stop. As the darkness of the trees swallowed her up, Kos sprayed bullets toward the truck. Will dropped down over Mia, holding her protectively.

And then the whole world erupted.

A blinding flash, followed by a deafening roar and a blast of heat, hit her like a monstrous fist. She screamed, the sound muffled against the ground and Will's chest.

Seconds later, Will dragged her to her feet and ran back toward the main road, putting distance between them and the burning factory. The dry brush, grasses, and trees around it had quickly caught fire, lighting the sky an angry orange-red. The sound of the fire itself was a horrible, otherworldly roar.

Even from a distance, Mia could feel the ferocious heat.

She clung to Will's arm, partly for comfort, partly to reassure herself he wasn't hurt. Rivulets of sweat made tracks in the dirt on his face, but she didn't see any blood.

"Are you hurt anywhere?" he demanded, running his hands over her face, her body, checking for injuries.

"No, I don't think so." Her voice was flat, dazed. "Are you?"

"Messed up my ankle when we jumped. Other than that, I'm okay."

She reluctantly looked toward Kos, who lay unmoving. "Is he dead?"

"Looks that way. I'll check for sure. You stay right here." He maneuvered her behind a large tree to keep her hidden.

"Is it safe? The fire—"

"It won't take me long."

Will ran with a marked limp toward Kos, his gun out, just as the police pulled up. There were several squad cars and one unmarked car with a light on its hood. A plainclothes detective and two patrolmen ran toward Will, but they were too far away for her to hear what they were saying. The detective didn't look happy. He bent over Kos, and Mia saw him shake his head.

Will then pointed in the direction where Vanessa had fled, but the flames had spread so rapidly that it wasn't possible to follow. Will tossed a canvas shopping bag at the detective, then bent and grabbed Kos by the coat collar and dragged him away from the fire.

Mia couldn't help glancing at the body, and before looking away again she had a quick impression of open, staring eyes and a lot of blood.

Kos had shot a man in her apartment, had kidnapped her, tied her up, threatened to kill her, planted a bomb—and yet his death seemed such a terrible waste.

When Will returned to her, leaning heavily against the tree, she asked quietly, "What about Vanessa? I saw you shoot at her."

He dropped his head back, briefly closing his eyes. "I didn't try to hit her. I was hoping she'd stop running."

"If she had, she would've been caught in the explosion."

"She might have been anyway. She was too close."

Pity, mixed with horror and anger, swept over her, and she turned toward Kos. Bracing herself, she knelt and closed his eyes. Will watched, his expression stony, but said nothing.

The detective headed their way, stepping over Kos. "Jesus Christ, what a mess. I don't think that woman made it out, but we'll have to wait until the fire's under control before we can start searching. We better pull back. It's been so dry that this is all gonna go up fast."

Will pulled Mia close as they followed the detective and other police officers.

"Can you walk, or do you need help?" the detective asked.

"I can make it," Will said. "You have the reliquaries?"

The man held up the bag Will had tossed him.

"Right here. There's also a gold cup thing and some jewelry. Sure as hell didn't look like anything worth dying over."

Mia glanced from the detective to Will. "Reliquaries? As in plural?"

Will sighed. "It's a long story. I'll explain later."

A woman with a rifle emerged from the darkness of the woods. Mia saw her first and grabbed Will in warning. He turned, tensing, then relaxed.

"It's okay," he said. "Claudia's my backup. She took those first shots at Vulaj."

"Who, I take it, is dead." Claudia fell into step beside them, glancing back at the two cops carrying the body. "He don't look too lively."

"He's dead."

"So much for getting the information we need." The woman eyed Mia, unsmiling. "What about Sharpton?"

"She made a run for it right before the explosion. I doubt she survived."

"You at least got the reliquary back?"

Even as stunned by the events as she was, Mia didn't miss the sarcasm.

"Yes, I did manage not to fuck that up."

"Well, that's a relief. Time for cleanup, then. Not my favorite part."

"No," Will said quietly, glancing at Mia. "Not mine, either."

There was a moment of confusion as everyone tried

to maneuver vehicles out. Will's rental had a bullet hole through the back window and was covered in dust and soot. Will helped Mia into the front seat, and Claudia got in back.

Catching Mia's look, she said, "I'm parked way out by the main road. Like hell am I walking."

"Of course not," Mia said and turned around in time to catch Will's grimace of pain. "Are you okay to drive? If that ankle's broken—"

"I can drive."

The tone of his voice warned her against pressing the issue. As their convoy retreated from the factory, Mia turned to look back at the flames flaring upward. And then she started shaking in earnest, so badly that she slipped her hands beneath her thighs to keep Will from seeing, since everyone else was so calm.

No one spoke the rest of the way to the main road. By then, the county sheriff's department and state patrol squad cars had pulled up. Fire trucks arrived right on their heels, sirens wailing and horns blaring, then disappeared down the service drive. One of the fire department vehicles stopped, and Mia saw the detective talking with a state trooper, a deputy, and the fire official.

To her surprise, the detective waved Will past. The trooper started to protest, but the detective must've said something, because he backed down.

"Why did they let us go?" Mia asked, astonished.

"Shouldn't they talk to us? Won't they want to talk to me?"

"Later. Morris, the detective, will take care of it."

"What do you mean, take care of it?"

"Tonight was a drug bust that went bad," Claudia said, her tone flat. "A little territory dispute between the Albanians and the locals. Somebody got carried away. It happens."

Mia twisted around to stare at her. "But that's *not* what happened!"

Will sighed. "No, but that's how we handle these situations. Morris will return the stolen items, and no one will know they were ever missing."

"But Vanessa . . . What will you tell Hugh? It's not like he won't notice, and there was the man shot in my apartment." She turned back toward Will. "Did he die, too?"

"Last I heard, he was recovering from surgery with a guarded prognosis. The only person who ended up dead tonight was Vulaj—and probably Sharpton. The wages of sin, and all that," Will said.

"Everyone in my apartment building, in the neighborhood, knows about the shooting. What am I supposed to say when people ask questions? How—"

"Mia, take a deep breath and let it out. Then do it again. I'll worry about Hugh. Morris will take your statement about Vulaj. There will be a brief, vague report in the news, and that will be the end of it."

The end of it?

She couldn't stop thinking of Vanessa, of Kos lying in the grass with those open, dead eyes. And Hugh . . . What was Hugh going to do? Then she thought about her apartment, the blood soaking her living room carpet, and felt sick all over again.

"This is where I parked." Claudia slid across the backseat as Will slowed down and pulled to the side of the road. "If you need me, call my room. Otherwise, I'm flying out tomorrow."

"Will do. Thanks for the help, Claudia."

"All in a day's work. Take it easy and get that ankle checked out by a real doctor." She got out of the car, taking the rifle, then eyed Mia. "And good luck with . . . everything else."

After Will pulled back onto the road, Mia asked, "Where are you taking me?"

"To my hotel. You can't go back to your apartment yet. It's a crime scene, and the landlord will need to have it cleaned up."

The words "crime scene" and "cleaned up" brought unwanted flashes of images, and she seized on normalcy. "What about Caligula? He'll need to be fed. I can't leave him alone."

"Caligula is in the care of your next-door neighbor, Mrs. Kinski. I'm sure he's not a happy ferret at the moment, but he'll be okay with her for the next few days."

"Oh." She let out her breath, then sucked in another to calm down, as he'd suggested. It helped clear her head a little. "I still can't believe all this happened. I keep waiting for hysteria to hit. I saw someone die. For real."

"You're not the hysterical type. Though if you wanted to let go and have a good cry, I wouldn't blame you."

Maybe she would later, when this empty exhaustion faded. "What I want most is a long, hot shower. I'd rather not walk through a hotel lobby like this. The desk clerks will take one look at us and call the police."

"There's some paper towels in the back. We'll stop at a gas station and clean up as best we can."

"Your suit looks like it's been in a battle. There's no way to clean *that* up."

He kept his attention on the road, his expression unreadable. "We had a little too much to drink, and played an impromptu game of football with some friends in a park. They won't question that."

"And if they do?"

"I'll take care of it," Will said wearily. "It's what I'm paid to do."

Twenty-six

THE WALK THROUGH THE HOTEL LOBBY WASN'T AS BAD as she'd expected. While the desk clerk on duty looked startled, she only smiled and asked if everything was all right. When Will assured her that there was nothing wrong, the woman nodded and didn't press the issue. Of course, that was what she was paid to do.

The moment Mia was inside the room, she turned on all the lights and sank down on the chair by the small table, hands clenched tightly in her lap. Will slid the security chain in place, then stripped off his tie and ruined suit coat, leaving him in torn pants, the remains of his shirt, and leather holsters.

"Can you take those off?" Mia asked quietly. "I've had my fill of guns tonight."

He removed the holsters and shoved them under the clothing in his suitcase, out of sight.

"We should probably talk," he said. "But it can wait

until after you shower. Go on. Take as long as you want. I'll go after you're done."

Mia appreciated that he didn't press for a resolution right that instant; she felt too brittle to think rationally. She was also relieved he didn't offer to shower with her; she needed time alone. Maybe he did as well.

Standing under the hot shower, she scrubbed her skin until it was pink and tingly, and washed her hair several times. She could still feel the grit, smell the stink of mildew and rot, the acrid smoke of the fire, as if it had seeped into her skin and follicles; she couldn't seem to get it out.

She sagged weakly against the tiled wall. Will had *killed* a man. In self-defense and justified, yes, but only now did she comprehend the reality, the finality, of what he'd done.

There were laws to handle these things, and even if the shooting was in self-defense, the law should deal with it. That was not to be the case here, and it troubled her. Nor could she forget Kos Vulaj's bitterness about how the law didn't work the same for everyone.

He was right in more ways than she wanted to admit.

No matter how she came at the problem, she couldn't find any comforting answers. "He had it coming" certainly wasn't right. She wasn't sorry that the police wouldn't be involved, but if they had been, it might have brought some sort of catharsis. Anything would be better than this disquieting sense of sweeping violent death under a rug.

And God, what was she going to do with Will? What did she want from him?

She finally stepped out of the shower and returned to the main room, towels wrapped around her body and hair.

Will was on the chair where she'd sat before, elbows resting on his knees. He'd taken off the shirt, his shoes, and socks, and she winced at the cuts and bruises marring his skin. His right ankle looked puffy and purple. If it wasn't broken it had been badly sprained, and all that scrambling and running had only added to the damage.

"My clothes are a mess. I don't have anything else to wear," she said at length.

"I'll ask Claudia to pick up something for you before she leaves Boston. In the meantime, you can wear one of my T-shirts. Take whatever you want from the suitcase."

"Thanks." She sat on the bed. "You should have that ankle looked at. It's really swollen. And it must hurt."

"I'll wrap it up and have it checked later. I don't think it's broken."

Did men think they got extra machismo points for bullheadedness?

"The cuts and bruises don't look very good, either. I hope your tetanus shots are up-to-date."

That made him smile a little, and he slowly stood, favoring his injured leg. "The job comes with full medical. If you want anything to eat, just call room service. It all goes on my expense report."

He limped past her to the bathroom, grabbing clean boxers on the way.

Mercenaries had *expense reports*? Mia imagined line items for room service and police bribes side by side, and wondered if his paycheck was docked if he killed someone.

Just how powerful was this secret organization, that they could manufacture stories for events that included shootings, forgeries, kidnappings, blown up factories, and dead mafiosi? How could they possibly explain all of that away? And while she was inclined to keep quiet and try to forget it all had happened, what about Hugh? He was going to notice when one of his two employees didn't show up.

With sudden grief, she realized that when she returned to work, she'd have to pass by Vanessa's empty desk. They'd never talk on the phone again, run out for a quick lunch together, gossip, or tease Hugh about his inability to make a decent pot of coffee.

Whatever else she'd been at the end, Vanessa *had* been a friend, a co-worker, and a part of her life for over five years. And now all that was just . . . gone.

Mia didn't even realize she was crying until the tears fell on her bare thigh, warm and wet, and she sniffed, wiping her eyes. Crying wouldn't make any difference or change anything.

Except she would miss the Vanessa who'd been her friend. And if she *was* dead, to die in such an awful way . . .

This time she didn't hold the tears back, wrapping her arms around her middle, rocking back and forth. Finally, when the tears had run their course, Mia pulled the towel off her hair to wipe at her eyes and face.

She was still holding the wet towel when Will came out of the shower, wearing only his boxers. He didn't say anything, but the mattress dipped as he sat beside her.

Then, quietly, he began combing out her hair. He was gentle, even while tugging at the snarls, and the feel of his fingers in her hair, on her face, soothed and comforted her. She couldn't resist the pull of his body's warmth and leaned against him.

"I am so tired and sad," she said, staring at the drawn curtains as he worked the comb through her hair.

"I know."

"And I keep seeing it, over and over. I'm glad it wasn't me, but it still hurts."

"I know," he repeated, softly.

Mia pulled back, searching for any hint in his carefully neutral expression of what he might have been thinking or feeling. "Are you?"

"Tired and sad?" He paused, then said, "Yes."

"Good." She leaned against him again, closing her eyes as he resumed combing her hair. "If you weren't sad, there would be something very wrong with you." She fell silent for a long moment, then added quietly, "He didn't want to go to prison. I think he preferred to die instead."

His chest rose and fell as he let out his breath in a long sigh. "The possibility had occurred to me."

"It's not your fault."

"Yes and no. To say this assignment didn't go well is an understatement. And I put you in danger. That was inexcusable. It was just a matter of time before Vulaj realized who I was, and by sleeping with you, I put you right in his crosshairs. I should've known better. I *did* know better, and still couldn't stay away." He sighed again. "You always did drive me crazy."

He stood then and moved back to the chair. "I can give you the room and find somewhere else to sleep."

Mia glanced at the clock. "At this time of night? Where will you go?"

"Claudia's down the hall. I can crash on her floor if you want to be alone."

That didn't sit well at all.

"No. I don't want to be alone tonight, Will. And like you said, we need to talk."

He looked at her, then dropped his gaze to his hands. "Then maybe you should put on some clothes. You're very distracting like this."

Mia stood and tossed him a T-shirt. "So are you."

As he slipped the shirt on, she went to his suitcase and pulled out another plain white undershirt. Her bra and underwear were soaking in the bathroom sink, but the shirt went to midthigh—and it wasn't as if he weren't familiar with every inch of her already.

She pulled it on and sat down again, tucking the hem of the shirt under her bottom. She had a million questions about this Avalon, about his so-called work, about how he felt about her. The more she thought it over, the more hopeless she felt.

How could she deal with not knowing what kind of danger he was in? It would take an enormous amount of trust between them to make it work—and their track record in the trust department wasn't so great.

Presuming, of course, that he wanted to stay with her.

As the awkward silence stretched on, Will's agitation charging the room as physically as a touch, Mia recalled what Kos had said to her in the factory.

If someone like him could feel such devotion and love, and fight for it, shouldn't she be able to do the same? What would it say about her if she let Will fade out of her life again because there were complications to being together?

"When I was in the factory with Kos," she said, finally breaking the silence, "he talked to me about taking risks for something you believe in, about not giving up just because the going gets a little rough."

Will was watching her with a quiet intensity.

"He was kind of right—and I realized that, while I have a nice life, it's missing passion. It's missing risk."

"Life can't be all about passion and risk. It can't be all action and adventure," he said. "You'll burn out too fast."

Mia nodded. "Balance. I know. But the point is, I was having these fantasies about getting back together with you, of picking up where we'd left off all those years ago, and making up for the mistake I made in letting you go. Except I kept thinking of you like you used to be, not like you are now."

"And what do you think of the man I am now?"

"Well, on the positive side, you can finally tell a Degas from a Fra Lippi."

That brought a small smile to his face. "There is that."

"On the negative side, you're involved in something that's not only highly dangerous but shady as well. You shoot people. You get mixed up with people who make bombs, who work for organized crime. And you bribe the local law enforcement."

"There was no bribe. Morris owed my boss a favor."

Mia took a deep breath, then plunged straight to the heart of the matter. "Do you love me?"

"Yes," he said simply. "The you from back then, the you of today, the you of tomorrow and the tomorrow after that."

"Why?" she asked bluntly. Because he didn't *know* the current her very well, except for the obvious fact that they still enjoyed sex with each other.

The question clearly wasn't expected, and he frowned. "I'm not sure I can . . . When I'm with you, life just shines a little brighter. You were always like that for me. I know it sounds stupid, but maybe that's all love is—making someone's life better, brighter. I don't know."

"And you could use a little more brightness in your life? Is that what you're saying?"

"Yes, but not just any brightness. Only yours."

And just like that, her anxiety and doubts faded. Though joy surged through her, she asked calmly, "Then how will we make this work?"

Twenty-seven

Zákynthos (Zante), Greece

DAWN WAS BEAUTIFUL ON THE IONIAN SEA, COLORING the sky and water and sand, tinting the whitewashed villas pink. Rainert could appreciate the beauty, even as tired as he was after a sleepless night of waiting.

There had been no call from Vulaj.

Rovena came out to the patio, her eyes puffy and red from weeping, bringing with her a pot of strong coffee. A light, warm breeze carried the sharp scent of it toward him as he leaned over the balcony.

Rainert took the cup she handed to him, her hands trembling. "There is a chance it wasn't him."

"You know better than that," she whispered.

A call had come a short while ago from one of the men who'd been waiting to help Vulaj and the woman get out of the country on a plane to Athens, then Zákynthos. The news hadn't been good.

First came sketchy information regarding a shooting in an apartment at the address Vulaj had provided for the other female assistant working for Haddington Reproductions. Later, even sketchier details about an explosion at an abandoned factory, some five miles from where Vulaj was to meet his contact. A fatality was reported, an unidentified male.

No one had heard from or seen Vulaj since that explosion.

"Explosion," Rainert said, after draining his cup. "What the hell happened, that there was an *explosion*?"

"I don't know. Kos is young and impulsive but always careful. I can't imagine what went so wrong."

"Young and impulsive" was probably all the explanation required. He'd known Vulaj had a tendency to overreact, but this . . . even he hadn't anticipated it.

"There hasn't been a positive identification yet. He could still be alive. Facts are easily confused in these situations, and there are always rumors."

Though he felt compelled to say the words, they rang hollow. He didn't believe Vulaj was alive, any more than Rovena did.

The job had been so simple, a standard switch. The Eudoxia collection wasn't that high-profile, the security at Haddington was merely adequate, and the help of an insider had all but guaranteed success. So what had gone wrong, as in spectacularly-exploding-buildings wrong?

Bombs were not a usual part of Avalon's repertoire. They tended toward skulking and snipering, seduction and infiltration, and the occasional out-and-out assault. Secretive as they were, they avoided drawing attention to their presence: blowing up buildings was surely not something Ben Sheridan, their very capable Kommandant, would approve, either.

Rainert's people had already cleaned up, going through the apartment Vulaj shared with the woman, removing any traces of evidence that would link them to Rainert. If Vulaj *was* alive, he would have to lay low for a long time.

Either way, everything Rainert had worked toward these past few months was gone. It was a good thing he'd taken the time to enjoy that sunrise—the rest of the day would quickly turn ugly.

Rainert poured himself another cup of coffee. "I'll stay here this morning, in case there are any more calls. I can't stay longer than that. I have people to meet, people who won't be happy to hear there will be no merchandise."

Rovena grabbed his arm, sharp nails digging into his skin. He looked from her dark red fingernails to her angry, tear-streaked face.

"He was my older sister's son, her youngest son and my favorite nephew. How will I tell my sister what's happened? What will you do to make up for his loss? I hold you responsible for this, Rainert. He was young. You swore it would not be dangerous—"

"Stop it." He knocked her hand aside, then forced her down on a deck chair. "What we do always involves risk. Don't pretend it has ever been otherwise. Your nephew knew this, and I warned him about Avalon. More than that, what could I do from half the world away, eh? Nothing."

"That is *not* good enough!"

Anger rose at her shout, and he slammed her chair back against the wall. Not too hard, but enough to gain her full attention. "I'll do what I can—but for my own interests, no one else's. Not even your nephew's. Do you understand?"

Rovena nodded, then burst into loud tears. Rainert immediately stepped away. Emotional women made him feel useless; he never knew how to deal with those messy tears and that nerve-racking wailing.

As he turned, reaching into his pocket for a cigarette, he spotted the little girl. Frightened and bewildered, Anna watched her mother's breakdown; then her face crumpled and she started to howl.

Rainert quickly picked her up, the small body in his arms stiff with distress, and patted her back, speaking in a soothing voice even though she wouldn't understand him. "Hush, hush. Don't cry, your mama is sad, but it's okay. Hush now."

He turned to Rovena with a furious glare. "Pull yourself together," he ordered, his tone clipped. "For the sake of the child. Now."

Rovena gave a watery gasp, then took in a long, shaky breath and wiped away her tears. She smiled and held out her arms, talking softly as he handed over the girl, who soon stopped wailing.

"You are good with children," Rovena said, her voice still thick with grief as she rocked her daughter. "You should find a nice girl and get married. Start a family. It would do you good."

"I think the chance for that has passed me by. Family would only hold me down now."

Silence fell between them and Rovena continued to rock her daughter, stroking her dark curls until the little girl's eyes drooped, then fluttered shut. "When was the last time you talked to your parents?"

Rainert went back to the balcony, looking out over the sea. "The police watch them. If I call, they will only be upset with me."

Rovena wisely dropped the subject, and he lit up a cigarette and watched a flock of birds soaring and dipping above the waves.

"She's asleep. I'm going to put her back to bed." The chair creaked as Rovena stood, and he heard her quiet footsteps as she came up behind him. "What are you going to do?"

"I won't allow these people to interfere in my business any longer. But I'll need your help. This isn't something I can do alone."

"Whatever you need, I will make sure my husband provides. And my family. For Kos's sake."

"Good." Rainert turned to face her, resting his elbows along the balcony rail. As he flicked his cigarette butt over the side, a strong breeze swept across the patio, ruffling his hair, his open shirt. "If they can field a secret army, so can I."

"You're going after Sheridan?"

"Yes, but not just him. I want the puppet master. Cut the one holding the strings, and they'll all go tumbling down."

Twenty-eight

❖

MIA WAS HANDLING THE SITUATION WITH AMAZING
calm. Most women would be in shock, yet she just sat
on the bed—looking incredible in only his T-shirt—
asking how she could remain a part of his life.

"That you can ask that," he said, sitting beside her,
"even after all you've seen tonight, isn't what I'd expected."

"What I saw tonight was a man who risked his life
for me."

"Mia, I would've risked my life to save anyone
caught up in that mess, because it was my mess, my responsibility."

"I know, but it told me everything I needed to
know about *you*—and I'm not wrong to love you."

Hearing her say she loved him allayed his uncertainty, but she still needed time to think this over rationally.

"The best chance we have of making things work would be for me to quit my job, and I can't do that." Because he really did believe in Avalon's mission, even if he didn't always agree with how it was handled. "My work is dangerous, I won't deny that. The smartest thing you could do right now is to tell me to walk out that door and give you a few months to get your feelings straight. You're not thinking with a clear head. In the excitement of the last few hours—"

"Will," she said, her tone gentle but firm. "If you can look me in the eye and say that you really want me to tell you to leave, then I'll accept it—even though I'd think you were an arrogant jerk who has no right to make my decisions for me."

Jerk? He was trying to *protect* her, and . . . and dammit, she was right. He was trying to force her to make the decision *he* thought was right, not what she thought was right.

Will met her gaze, seeing patience, strength, and acceptance in her dark eyes. "What I really want is to lay you down on that bed, take off that shirt, and look over every inch of you to make sure you're okay."

"Scrapes and bruises, nothing more. We match now," she teased.

His emotions zigzagged between anger and gratitude, fear and relief—and desire, God help him. And the more he tried to suppress the need, the more urgent it grew.

"Why do I get the feeling you're trying to comfort me, when it should be the other way around?"

"If you could see your face and the look in your eyes," Mia said softly, "you'd know why."

And just like that, his doubts and uncertainties vanished.

"I was so afraid I'd lose you, Mia. I couldn't allow myself to feel the fear until you were safe, and now . . . Jesus, I don't *ever* want to go through that again." He flopped back on the bed, resting his arm over his eyes. "I'm as afraid of letting you go as I am of letting you stay."

But she'd said she loved him. Maybe she would regret that a few months down the line, but maybe not. The one thing he knew for certain was, this was the only second chance they'd ever get.

"Before I started to work for Avalon, I was a detective in Seattle," he said, his arm still over his eyes. Somehow, it was a little easier if he didn't have to look at her. Or at the faint curve of her breast under the shirt, the press of her nipples against the white knit. "Do you know why I became a cop?"

"No."

"Because of you. I'm in this room right now because you dumped me twelve years ago. After I got off the phone with you that night, I was pissed. I called some buddies to bitch about you, and the next thing I knew, a couple of them dragged me off to the bar. I ended up drunk and got into a fight, and the cops were called in. One of them, an older guy, sat me down for a long talk. God knows what I said, drunk as I was, but he kept talking about positive attitudes and turning negatives inside out to find opportunities. Nothing profound, but for some reason it got to me. I really admired him for taking the time to talk me through a bad night, and I chucked my plans to go into teaching and became a cop instead."

He could hear Mia, breathing quietly, and feel the warmth of her skin where her thigh brushed along his—but either she didn't know what to say or he'd bored her to sleep.

"So I became one of Columbus's finest, and met a woman I liked enough to move in with. A few years later, her job required her to relocate to Seattle—you already know how that ended. But I did well working for the police. Well enough to catch Avalon's eye."

He pulled his arm away from his eyes. Mia was sitting with her legs tucked beneath her bottom, watching him with a thoughtful expression.

"You're probably wondering if there's a point to any of this."

She smiled. "Beyond the whole life-is-full-of-surprises kind of thing? The answer would be yes."

"It's like fate."

Her brows arched.

Will raised himself on his elbows. "If you hadn't

ended the relationship while you were in Italy, we would've eventually gotten married. Instead we drifted apart, and because I got drunk, met a good cop, and joined the police so I could help people in a more direct way, I ended up in Seattle and was recruited by Avalon, and then met you all over again. No matter what, I'm tied to you. It just took me a decade or so to find my way back."

"I think maybe you hit your head when we jumped out that window." She was smiling but eyeing him with a little confusion as well.

Embarrassed, he flopped back on the bed. "It made perfect sense to me two seconds ago."

Mia leaned against him, and he inhaled deeply, taking in her scent and the fresh, clean smell of soap. "I kind of like the idea of fate. It has a certain romantic appeal."

His gaze kept straying to the teasing shape of her nipples outlined beneath the T-shirt, and he felt like a dog. She wanted a cuddle and comfort. That was all.

"So the whole reason you became a cop was that you were fighting drunk and got lectured?"

"It was more complicated than that. I *did* want to help people, to achieve some tangible good so I wasn't just sucking up space. I believed it then, and still do. But I was also feeling sorry for myself and figured dealing with other people's misery would make mine look like nothing in comparison." He paused. "It worked. I was only twenty-two when I joined up, and being a cop was a hell of a maturing experience."

"If you liked the job so much, why did you quit?"

"Money. Cynicism. The law doesn't always deliver."

Mia gave a long sigh. "The laws do seem to be rather . . . opaque in certain situations."

"Yeah, the world's a grayer place than I ever imagined when I was a kid, that's for sure."

"How do you deal with that? Doesn't it bother you?"

"Sometimes." He remembered Vulaj screaming his name, feeling again the twinge of regret that he hadn't played fair when the other man had. He was supposed to be the good guy, after all. "Sometimes more than others. Knowing these people get what they deserve makes it worthwhile."

"Did Kos and Vanessa get what they deserved?"

"Yes, and then some," he said, quietly. "They were small-fry. What they did wasn't worth dying over, but I guess Vulaj didn't see it that way."

Silence fell between them again, and Will reflected on what Mia had said earlier about Vulaj's talk with her at the factory before all hell broke loose.

"You had a good point," he continued. "Vulaj might've gotten everything else in his life all wrong, but he was right about taking the chance for who and what you believe in. About being strong enough to take the good along with the bad. You and I got it wrong back then, because we were too young to understand how much work it takes to make a relationship last. But we're older now, tough enough to ride out the bumps. Jesus, after what we just went through, we should be able to handle anything life throws at us."

"You mean that?"

"Absolutely." Mia was back in his life, and he was going to get it right this time. He needed her brightness and love, and the reminder of the man he needed to be again: a man who wanted to make a difference, plain and simple.

"Some Avalon operatives are married and have kids. We can do it, too—but it's not going to be easy. I'll be gone a lot, sometimes for months. There will be times when I won't even be able to tell you where I am."

"It sounds like being with one of those top-secret military forces."

"That's not a bad comparison." He ran a hand through his damp hair. "After I talk with Hugh tomorrow and try to explain what happened—even though I'm not supposed to and my boss will be pissed—maybe you could ask for a few days off and we can spend some time together. Right now, neither of us is up to making life-altering decisions."

But he *was* feeling up to something else. Especially since she was touching him, stroking him beneath the boxers.

"What I want right now," Mia said, nibbling kisses along his lower lip, "is to be with you. No bad memories, no past, no worries about tomorrow or next week. I just want you to make love to me."

He wanted that, too. And he wanted to let her brightness chase away the dark.

Will eased Mia back onto the sheets, kissing her. He slipped his hand beneath the T-shirt, playing his thumb across her erect nipple, and her sigh of pleasure sent hot desire racing straight through him. He was already erect, needing to be inside her so bad, he could hardly think straight.

And she wasn't wearing any underwear. Again.

"Tiernay."

Will turned at the sound of Morris's voice.

"I was just over at Haddington, talking to Mr. Haddington and Ms. Dolan. She told me you were looking for a picture Sharpton took of you. That true?"

"Yeah."

"Did you find it?"

Brow raised, Will gestured at the mess that was Vanessa Sharpton's apartment. "What do you think?"

"I think somebody cleaned up before you got here."

Will looked over at what was left of the computer that had been on the living room desk. "I should've anticipated this."

"But?"

"But I was otherwise engaged in offering comfort to Ms. Dolan all night."

Morris gave a bark of laughter. "If it helps, there wasn't anything to find. The two men staying here made a run for it while we were blowing up factories. A couple of uniforms gave chase but lost them. By the time we got in here, the apartment was trashed."

Will glanced at the other man. "Decoys."

"Looks that way," Morris said ruefully. "Is this picture really that big a problem?"

"It is when you're working for a secret organization."

Morris shoved his hands in his pants pockets, balancing on his heels. "I see your point. But between you and me, that whole 'secret' thing is hard to pull off in this day and age. Maybe you guys should give it up."

"I agree. But it's not my decision to make." Will stepped over a pile of dirt, broken clay pot, and wilting leaves that had been a spider plant, and walked over to the detective. "Any news on Sharpton?"

Morris shook his head. "It took hours to contain the fire, so if she survived the explosion, she would've had time to get out of the area. We found old drainage pipes leading from the factory to the river, big enough to crawl through. Some were damaged, but a few were intact. There's a slim chance she had time to get to one of them. The search teams used dogs, but didn't pick up her trail."

Will wondered if she'd been smart enough to follow the river. She didn't seem like the type who'd know such things, but maybe she was a fan of old Westerns or movies about fugitives.

"We brought out a couple helicopters, but again, nothing. By the time they were in the air, she could've gotten to the highway and hitched a ride, or just hid out. We've got an APB out on her. Maybe we'll get lucky; maybe someone saw her and will call it in."

"You really believe she lived through that?"

"No. I think some guy out fishing or walking his dog is going to have an unpleasant find one of these days, but we'll keep looking anyway. What's your next step?"

"Haddington was pretty shaken when I told him what happened. After sending off the Eudoxia collection to the Met, he's closing up shop for a long weekend. I'm taking Mia back to Seattle with me for a few days. I think a break away from here will do her good."

"Not to mention safer, just in case."

"That too. By the way, thanks for your help in handling the cleanup duty."

"No problem. I don't care much for your sort on principle, but you're okay. You screwed up, but you admitted it. I respect that." Morris let out a long sigh. "I wish we could've taken him alive, though. It would've meant a hell of a lot less trouble and paperwork for me."

"Ben's not going to be happy about it, either."

"From what we can tell, it looks like the explosion's what finished him off. If you were having a crisis of conscience about that, I thought you should know."

"I appreciate the thought." Explosion or gunshots, it didn't matter: Vulaj was dead because Will had messed up. "Out of curiosity, what excuse did you give for letting me leave the factory last night?"

"I told them you were all undercover. *Deep* undercover, and it was critical that as few people see you as possible."

"And they believed you?" Will asked, incredulous.

"I doubt it, but they didn't question it, which is the only thing that matters. By the way, are you done here?"

"Yeah. Why?"

"Technically, it's a crime scene. You should probably get lost before I have to explain your presence again. Three times is pushing it, Tiernay."

"I'm gone." Will headed toward the door, picking his way over shredded cushions and broken photo frames, including one of Vulaj and Vanessa.

He picked the photo up, then set it back on the bookshelf where he'd first seen it.

At the door, he turned. "I hope your friend is out of the hospital soon. And again, Morris, I appreciate your help. I couldn't have done this one without you."

"Damn straight. You tell Sheridan we're even—and I don't want to hear from him ever again."

"Consider the message delivered."

"Excellent. Now get the hell out of my crime scene—and take it easy for a few days. You look like shit."

Twenty-nine

WILL GLANCED AT MIA DOZING IN THE SEAT BESIDE HIM, her head on his shoulder. Outside he could see the familiar approach to Sea-Tac, and he slipped the Balestrini murder file back into his briefcase.

"Mia," he whispered. "We're getting ready to land. Time to wake up."

She made a soft little sound, eyes opening, and the familiar sensation of being lost in those dreamy, heavy-lidded depths swept over him.

"Already? How long have I been sleeping?"

"A while. You needed the sleep."

Drawing back with a yawn, she brushed her hand over the shoulder of his suit coat. "I didn't drool on you, did I?"

"No." He grinned. "And you didn't snore, either."

"So what did you do all the time I was zonked out?"

"Read a little paperwork. Nothing too taxing. I'm tired myself."

Mia peered out the airplane window. "I've never been to Seattle. I hope you'll have time to show me a few sights."

"I'll make time," Will promised. His gaze moved along her profile, the curve of her nose and roundness of her lips, and he realized all over again how beautiful and sexy she looked in red.

"Once we land, we'll catch a cab to the hotel. I have to check in at work, but I won't be gone too long."

"I really can't come with you?"

Will shook his head. "Not this time. If I take you along, my boss will want to see you and ask a bunch of awkward and annoying questions, and I'd rather not have you deal with that yet. And *I* don't want to deal with that yet."

Mia eyed him. "He can't be that bad."

"No, but he didn't get where he is today by being a nice guy."

"All right," she said. "Does your boss know about me?"

"He always knows about everything. That's why he's the boss and I'm the peon. I also left a message updating him on the situation. He's not the type to appreciate surprises."

"Well, I'll be happy to stay in the hotel and take a

nap. I've had enough excitement for the past few days."

The pilot came over the intercom, announcing their imminent landing and the local time and weather. Will leaned toward her and said softly, "Will you be all right going back to work on Wednesday?"

She nodded. "I'm pretty much over the shock, and it's not like staying away will make things any better. Besides, I'm all Hugh has now. We'll have to start thinking about hiring a replacement."

She'd never asked if Vanessa had been found. He supposed she didn't want to know and trusted him to tell her if there was any need to be concerned.

With Vulaj dead, Vanessa missing and likely dead, the Eudoxia collection safely in the depths of the Met, and the reproductions on their way to Malcolm Toller's estate, Will had no fear of retaliation against Mia. Still, it never hurt to remain cautious, and she understood that.

After the plane landed and they collected their luggage, they took a cab to the hotel, holding hands like newlyweds. He liked the feel of her hand in his, soft yet firm, the skin a little rough from the work she did. She was self-conscious about that, but he found it sexy and teased away her embarrassment by telling her it was every red-blooded-man's fantasy to hook up with a girl who knew how to handle power tools.

And when she ran her hands over his skin and muscles, the rougher touch aroused him, tingling along all his senses.

His body responded just to the thought of it, and he decided his meeting would be short and sweet.

Once they were in the room, he dumped their luggage in the nearest corner and took Mia in his arms, kissing her hungrily. She responded with equal urgency, and he didn't even remember pushing her down on the bed—only that he had his hand inside her red silk shirt, working at the fasteners of her bra, when she suddenly laughed and pushed him back.

"Enough of that! You have a meeting, remember? I'm in no hurry, and we'll have the rest of the day to ourselves."

Feeling a little sheepish at having lost his control so quickly, Will stood and tucked his shirt back into his pants, then smoothed back his hair.

"Keep that thought," he said. "I'm holding you to it."

Ben Sheridan was signing invoices when Ellie buzzed him on the intercom. "Will's here. Should I send him in?"

"Yes, please."

He sat back with a sigh, hoping Tiernay's temper had improved since the last time they'd talked. He wasn't in the mood for drama.

"And I should warn you," Ellie added with amusement, "I have his expense report. It's been a while since we had a two-suiter."

"Goddammit," Ben snapped as his office door swung open. "I'm not paying another couple thousand dollars for suits!"

"The hell you aren't," Will retorted as he entered. "You owe me and you know it. Don't even try to talk your way out of it."

Even through his irritation, Ben noted that the tie wasn't as perfectly knotted as usual, and that Will had the contented look of a man who'd spent a lot of time in bed with a woman he was crazy about. Good: a sexually satisfied man was less likely to get pissed off or pick a fight.

"If you're going to make a habit of getting into brawls—"

"I never *brawl*, Ben."

"—then at least wear cheap suits. Or cheaper suits," he added, at Will's offended look. "Sit down. How was your flight?"

"Not too bad, even if we didn't rate the company jet."

"Budgets aren't glamorous, but they're a necessity. You'd do well to remember that moderation is your friend. Speaking of immoderation, where's Ms. Dolan?"

"At the hotel." Will sat in the chair across from the desk, but despite the casual sprawl, his eyes held a hard edge, emphasized by a truly impressive set of cuts and bruises. "I don't want you trying to contact her. When I'm ready, I'll introduce you. Not before then."

"How much does she know?"

"Enough so she understands, though not enough to make me feel less like a bastard for holding back so much."

"The rule of silence protects everyone."

"I understand that." It looked as if he might say something more, but instead Will changed the subject. "So you were right and I was wrong about this mission being complicated."

"Partly my fault, as you know."

"I'm still pissed about that, but we already covered it. And I didn't get you Vulaj. I'd say that makes us even at screwing up." Will took a quick breath, then let it out. "I lost control of the situation."

Ben waited for more, reading the frustrated look on Will's face.

"And I had a clear shot at Sharpton, but I couldn't . . . I just couldn't take it."

How had things come to this, that one of his men felt as if he had to apologize for not shooting down an unarmed woman? "It's good that somebody in this outfit still has a conscience."

Will frowned slightly. "Vulaj kept one step ahead

of me the entire time. The Eudoxia collection is safe, but other than that the mission was a failure, and I take full responsibility for it."

Will was a good man, in every way that counted. "It wasn't a failure. The collection is secure. You extracted a hostage safely from a dangerous situation. Your cover wasn't wholly compromised. It could've gone more smoothly, I agree, but all in all, I consider it a success."

Will dropped his gaze briefly. "About my cover . . . Sharpton took my picture. I went to her apartment to retrieve the digital camera and files, but somebody beat me there. It was cleaned out, and what they didn't take, they destroyed."

"We'll deal with it. It's not the first time something like this has happened. As for the apartment, it sounds like von Lahr wanted all traces of his connection to them removed. This has his style written all over it."

Ben rubbed his chin, thinking. "Even though we don't have Vulaj, we can try working backward from there. I'm going to send you back to Boston, but only for gathering intel. I don't want you in any confrontational situations. Find out who Vulaj was working for, and any other contacts. Morris's information indicated Vulaj was busy in Queens before he left for Boston, and I think we'll find a Greek tie. If that's the case, I can send someone to Greece to find out who von Lahr was using as an intermediary."

Will looked pleased at the order, which Ben had expected. And he saw the instant Will realized what else it meant.

"You're sending me there for a couple more weeks so I know for sure Mia will be safe. And to give us a little more time together."

"I'm not a total bastard, Tiernay. And it *is* a real assignment. The follow-up work needs to be done."

Will nodded. "I'll have a complete report for you tomorrow."

"Good. Now, I can tell you're anxious to get the hell out of here. Is there anything else you need to talk about?"

"Yeah." Will leaned forward, his gaze sharp. "I was taking notes on the Balestrini file on the flight here, and a couple things you said have been bothering me."

"Ask away."

"It's not a question so much as a clarification. You told me you were looking into an older disappearance in the hope of solving a more recent one."

Ben hadn't expected Will to make the connection this fast—nor had he expected to feel so angry and defensive at the prospect of discussing it. "Just get to the point."

"I checked up on you before I joined Avalon. Your family made its fortune in logging and shipping, and you have an older sister who married into the family of an English baronetcy. She married a cousin or something."

Ben shoved aside piles of papers so he could rest his elbows on his desk, his steepled fingers supporting his chin. "That's all public knowledge."

"Yes, and I remembered you were friends with the heir to the baronetcy, who was a couple years older than you. You went on a fishing trip with the baronet and his son in Malta. They disappeared while out on the chartered yacht. You weren't feeling well that morning and stayed in the hotel. No one ever saw the baronet and his son again. Or the yacht and its crew."

"Foul play was never an issue. They were presumed lost at sea in a freak accident. These things do happen."

"And their disappearance fits the time frame when you first became active in Avalon. Am I right in assuming that the newer disappearance you mentioned referred to the baronet and his son?"

"Yes." Ben returned Will's stare without blinking.

"Why didn't you just give me their names? You should've known I'd figure it out almost right away."

"As I said, I wanted you to approach the investigation with fresh eyes. I kept expecting the connection to start with them, but that led nowhere. I was hoping if you started from a completely different direction, that you'd have better luck. That's all; there were no ulterior motives."

Except one, but with any luck it would take Will weeks or even months to make a few other connections.

"So you don't want me to start by looking into the disappearances of Sir Arthur Whitlea, Fourth Baronet of West St. Aubry, and his son, Gareth?"

It had been so long since Ben heard anyone say those names. Almost twenty years now, and he still felt the loss.

"No. I want you to start with Maria Balestrini."

Will's expression was quietly speculative. "All right then. I just wanted to make sure."

Ben smiled faintly. "I appreciate your thoroughness." In a brisker tone he added, "Now get out of here. You don't want to keep her waiting."

Will stood, his smile warm and genuine. Seeing it brought a kick of emotion—but Ben wasn't keen on examining his reaction too closely.

After Will left, Ben turned to his computer, clicked on his email program, and typed:

Tiernay has made the Malta connection.

The terse update was all that was required, but he added, as he always did:

I await your orders. Tell me what you want me to do.

He waited only fifteen minutes before the expected answer came:

I will send my response by courier. Stand by.

Ben deleted the email, clicked on the Empty Trash icon, and murmured, "Stand by . . . that's all I ever do these days."

Thirty

❖

Mia sat in the terrace restaurant of the Hotel Rialto, soaking up the sun and enjoying the view over the Grand Canal and the Rialto Bridge. It had rained earlier that morning, bringing a fresh scent to the air.

The midmorning light warmed the city's brick and stucco façades, in their time-worn palettes of red, rust, pink, and gold. Gothic to modern, classic to Baroque, it was one of the most beautiful cities in Europe.

It was good to be back in Venice, even if only for a few days, hearing the calls of the boatmen, the chug of ferry engines, and the multilingual hum as tourists and locals rubbed elbows at the markets and shops. Water buses, ferries, and black gondolas glided by, and the

smell of the city—damp stone and wood and sea—
hinted at age, long use, and gentle decay.

It was Venice. Not only one of the most beautiful
cities in the world, but also one of the most romantic.

Hands suddenly covered her eyes, and the warmth
of a body moved close behind her. "Guess who," whispered a deep male voice in her ear.

She leaned back and made a low, appreciative sound.
"Mmmm, you're late."

"Sorry. I had a hell of a time finding a parking spot
at the Tronchetto. I should've left the car on the main-
land; it would've been quicker."

As Will removed his hands, Mia turned and slipped
her arms around his waist. "This isn't a vehicle-friendly
city. Will, we can . . ." She trailed off and sighed, helpless against the warm, liquid tug of desire. "You look
wonderful."

"Isn't that supposed to be my line?" His tone was
teasing as he bent to give her a kiss.

Not a quick peck in deference to the packed restaurant, either, but a full-on, hungry kiss with tongue.
And his hands dipped low, fingertips sliding along the
curve of her bottom.

Lust, embarrassment, and delight twined together;
then she returned his kiss—briefly—and gave him a
push away. "Not here!"

A man behind her gave an enthusiastic shout of approval, to the effect of "More, more!"

Will laughed. "The Italians live up to their reputations. I don't think they mind the show."

"Well, I do." She poked him, smiling. "Quit distracting me. I was busy telling you how delicious you look. It's been almost a month since I've seen you. Let a girl have her simple pleasures."

In deference to the July heat, he was wearing a loosely tailored suit in tan linen with an off-white cotton shirt and a print tie of khaki, tan, and brick red. She never tired of how he always looked so confident and in control, so at ease even in a full suit and tie.

And half the fun of the suit and tie was getting him out of it.

"First things first. What's with wanting to meet in Venice? A last-minute trip, all expenses paid for me . . . I appreciate the grand gesture, but why?"

"Shall we go for a walk and talk? I've been sitting in planes, trains, and automobiles all day, and I need to stretch my legs."

His hands were in his pockets, and when he crooked an elbow at her, she hooked her arm through his. "Sure. I want to show you off anyway. All the women in this city are going to hate me."

"I was just thinking along the same lines myself."

"Oooh, you sweet-talkin' man, you."

"Is it working?"

Mia laughed. "It's completely unnecessary, but I love it anyway."

As they headed down to the Grand Canal, she noted how his gaze roved appreciatively over her T-shirt—red, because he had a thing for red—and denim skirt, which was snug against her hips but flared out around her knees. Her toenails, with their bright red polish, made the sensible walking sandals look sexier.

"I like the pedicure. The red's a very nice touch."

She hugged his arm against her breasts. "All for you."

"Really?"

She grinned. "And for me, too. I like to pamper myself as much as the next woman."

They strolled along the busy street and headed for the Rialto Bridge. Will steered her up the stairs to the main inner walkway, which was lined with cramped little shops hawking the usual tourist wares, including lots of Murano millefiori glass paperweights. Mia loved the glasswork's bright colors and the unique irregularities that came from its being handblown.

"We should go to Murano and buy a couple of wineglasses," Will said, as she turned a paperweight from side to side. "In case there's a need to celebrate something later."

"Hmmm, you seem to have plans."

"There are indeed plans behind this grandiose gesture; I chose Venice on purpose."

Suddenly feeling a little light-headed, Mia went up

on tiptoe to kiss his cheek. "You're the most romantic man I've ever known."

"It seemed symbolic."

Suspecting where he was going with this, she held back a smile. His cheeks seemed slightly flushed, which was sweet and amusing.

Bending lower, he murmured, "And along with all this grandiosity comes the expectation of getting you naked real soon. What are you wearing under that skirt?"

"A red thong. It matches my nail polish."

He briefly closed his eyes and swallowed. "Maybe we can find a nice pair of wineglasses here and skip the trip to the island."

"I think that's a very good idea. It's been so long."

Over three weeks, with only four phone calls, and she had no idea where he'd been during any of those calls. She didn't even know where he'd flown in from today, or where he was going afterward.

It wasn't easy, as he'd said, but moments like this made all the difference in accepting it.

"Hey, when do I get to meet this Sheridan guy, anyway?"

"Maybe the next time we get to Seattle. By now he probably knows everything about you, your family, every man you ever kissed, and your penchant for rodents. By the way, who's rodent-sitting?"

She suspected he was developing an attachment to

her ferret. "Hugh. He and Caligula hit it off pretty well."

"There may be something profound in that," Will said thoughtfully, "but I don't think I'm going to look for it."

They crossed the Rialto, and she led him to one of the nicer gift shops, where Will found a pair of wineglasses from one of the best Murano factories—beautiful clear glass layered with stripes of many colors, not a perfect match, although a pair.

As they headed back to their hotel room, Will steered her into a canal-side café.

"There's one last thing to take care of, since I don't want any distractions later." He leaned over their table, lowering his voice. "There's something I'd like you to do while you're in Italy. It won't take long."

Mia leaned forward as well, picking up by his body language that this was a sensitive subject. "What do you have in mind?"

"How's your Italian?"

"A bit rusty, but I can still speak and understand it."

"Good, because there's a village I'd like you to check out for me. It's a place outside Orvieto, in Umbria, called Corbasa. Well away from the usual tourist haunts."

"Okay," Mia said, puzzled. "Can I ask why?"

"Of course. That side project Ben gave me to work on—it's something I'd like you to help me with."

Eyes wide, she scooted even closer and whispered,

"But isn't that against the rules of your secret mercenary brotherhood?"

"It's not directly involved in anything we do. It's about the unsolved murder of a twenty-year-old woman back in 1943."

Whatever she'd expected, it wasn't this. "Wow. That's a long time ago."

"Yes, which is part of the problem. There's a chance she's connected to an unsolved disappearance shortly before World War Two, which in turn is connected to the disappearance of a British baronet and his son on a fishing vacation in Malta twenty years ago."

She eyed him uneasily. "Is this dangerous?"

Will shook his head. "I wouldn't involve you if I thought it was. Her murder may have nothing to do with anything, but Ben seems to feel it's worth checking into."

By now, Mia knew a few of Avalon's people. Ben Sheridan was the one who gave orders, ran damage control, pulled intel together, and signed paychecks—and grumbled frequently about Will's expense reports. There were also two secretarial types, Ellie and Shaunda. If she ever found herself in trouble, she wasn't to hesitate to call any of those three.

"It's a small village, and if I go in there and start asking questions, I'll draw too much attention. In my experience, people will talk more freely with a strange woman than with a strange man."

Mia nodded. "You just want me to look around?"

"Basically, yes. I want as much information as you can get me about the town and its history. And I need to know where the girl is buried; that information's not in the file. Either Ben never had it, or it just wasn't included for some reason. I think you can do all this without making it look like you're snooping around."

"Locals love to talk about their history and their families, and I love history. I can do this for you. Do you want me to take pictures or write notes, or—"

"No," Will said, shaking his head. "That'll draw too much attention. Just get the basics. For now, that's all I need."

"Does Ben know you're asking my help?"

"Nope."

Again, not the answer she'd expected, and she shook her head in amazement. "I don't want you to get into any trouble over this. Maybe you shouldn't have involved me." She paused. "Why did you, anyway?"

"Because it's an issue of trust, and I trust you." He took her hand from across the table, playing with the bracelet she wore. "And it's about involving you instead of shutting you out. If Ben has a problem with it, then we'll deal with it one way or another."

Hearing him say he trusted her brought tears to her eyes, but while she was grateful for what he was offering, it worried her, too.

"And what would Ben do to you if he found out?"

"I have no idea. It would be interesting to see, though."

"Will!"

He laughed. "Honestly, Mia, I don't know. I've shared a few beers with the guy, even played a few rounds of golf with him, but I don't really know him."

He grew serious, his thumb tracing lines on her palm. "I never believed Ben was with Avalon out of a great passion for saving art, and I know he's not in it for the money."

Mia mulled over his words, picking up on what he wasn't saying. "You think it has to do with this baronet and his son?"

Will nodded. "Which raises even more questions, but we can talk about that later. Are you still okay with helping me with this case?"

"If it means more time with you, how could I not be? So what will I do after I'm finished in Corbasa?"

"Your flight back to Boston has a stop in London. I'll meet you there, and you can tell me what you found."

"You have everything planned. I'm very impressed. And I feel a little like that sleuthing couple from the old thirties *Thin Man* movies." She smiled. "Although they were a *married* sleuthing couple."

"A minor detail, easily resolved." He flashed a sexy half smile, then signaled for their waiter. "Let's go back to the hotel."

* * *

She'd barely managed to close the drapes on the window overlooking the Grand Canal before Will grabbed her by the waist and deposited her, laughing, on the big four-poster bed.

The first time was hard and fast to take the edge off, and he didn't even give her a chance to get him out of that suit. Naturally, she'd ended up completely naked.

The second time was more gentle, slower, giving her time to remember that he'd always had a knack for paying attention to the little details, which she was learning to appreciate more and more.

After the third time, they lay entwined in the big bed, Mia drowsily cuddled against him. "I was so happy to see you, I forgot to ask how you've been. You look like such a normal kind of guy that it just slips my mind to ask if anybody's tried to shoot you or blow you up lately."

His chest shook as he laughed. "No, it's been a quiet month for me. I've missed you. I wish I could get back to Boston more often."

"I know."

"How are things going with Vanessa's replacement?"

Hugh had hired a fresh-faced kid with a shiny new M.A. from Boston University. "Pretty well. He has a lot of enthusiasm, and he's willing to work overtime, so Hugh's amenable to letting me take off on impromptu trips to Venice. Plus, I think he feels a little indebted to you."

She pushed up on her elbows. "How long will you be able to stay? The room's booked for a week."

Regret shadowed his face. "Only a couple of days. Sorry."

Mia didn't hide her disappointment; it would be dishonest to do so, and she didn't want that to tarnish their relationship. "Well, it's better than no days."

"And since we don't have a lot of time, I'm going to get straight to the point."

Mia went still, certain she knew what was coming next.

Will rolled over to his elbow, propping his chin on his palm, his face so close to hers their noses almost touched. "Marry me?"

Mia blinked. She'd expected something a little less . . . direct. "You weren't kidding about getting straight to the point."

He shook his head, trying to look calm, but uncertainty showed in his eyes.

She leaned into him, her lips brushing against his as she whispered, "Yes. Yes, yes, yes. You have no idea how happy I am to hear you ask me that question."

"Again," he reminded her with a smile, all the shadows gone.

"Again," she agreed, then kissed him gently. "And

this time, I have a feeling we're going to do just fine."

They celebrated by ordering the most expensive bottle of champagne from room service, and the staff member who delivered it didn't even blink an eyelash when Will answered the door with only a sheet wrapped around his waist.

They christened the new glasses, made love again, and took a bath together. Then, after nightfall, they found a cozy little canal-side bar where they could sit and relax.

"I don't suppose you can tell me where you're going next," Mia said.

"Not in exact terms, no, but I'll be in London for a couple weeks. If you want, while we're in London we can look for a ring. Or we can wait until I see you again in Boston. After London, I'll be heading to Amsterdam for another side job. After *that*, I'll talk to Ben about time off for a wedding."

A wedding. She was sitting in Venice on a warm summer night with the man of her dreams, discussing a wedding! Even the champagne hadn't made her feel this giddy. "When did you think a good time would be?"

"As soon as you'd like. If you want a big wedding with the dress and cake and church, you've got it. If you want a quiet civil ceremony, that's all right by me, too. Mostly, I just want to get you legally naked in my bed."

Mia arched a brow at that. "I didn't think legality

made such a big difference for you, but I'll think about it and get back to you with specifics. In the meantime, how about we head back to our hotel and get illegally and immorally naked again?"

He leaned across the white tablecloth and gave her a long, hungry kiss. "I love you, Mia," he murmured over the sound of water lapping in the canal. "Just in case I haven't said it enough lately, and because I can't always say it when I want to, or when you'll need to hear it."

"I know. And I love you, too." She kissed him back, then stood and took his hand. "Let's go. I think we can find enough magic in this old city to make the next couple of days last a little longer."

Epilogue

❖

Rio de Janeiro, Brazil
The following day

THE MUSIC IN THE CLUB ASSAILED HER EARS, VIBRAT-
ing unpleasantly through her body as the flashing
light show over the dance floor assaulted her eyes. As
she sat at the far end of the bar, looking down at its
gleaming black surface and nursing a highball of "sex
on the beach," the stiff lines of her body warned off
most men.

Vanessa hated bars: the noise, the smell, the press
of strangers' bodies, the underlying pulse of desperation. London pub, Boston brewery, or Rio nightclub,
she hated them all.

She'd sat in this wretched club, in roughly the same
spot at the bar, for the past six nights. Each night she
hoped the person she'd been told would meet her

would actually show up. Each night she'd left the bar alone.

Patience worn thin, she'd sworn this would be the last night she'd hang around like a fool for someone who probably never intended to meet her. It was nearly midnight, two hours past the supposed meeting time.

"Enough," she muttered, drained what was left of her drink, and stalked out, slapping aside the hand of a man who grabbed for her ass.

In Rio, the City of Fun, where having a good time was a thriving industry, tourists were plentiful, so not even tall women with British accents drew much notice. Nonetheless, she'd cut her hair and colored it brown, and she didn't talk to anyone unless she had no choice. It worked; most people looked right through her and, when they noticed her at all, didn't pay her much attention.

No one screamed and pointed fingers at her, calling for the police to arrest her. She kept expecting it; the fear lived like a parasite inside her, whittling down her weight and adding years to her face.

Some days she truly felt invisible, as if she were just a ghost now, not the flesh-and-blood woman who'd lost everything that mattered that night at the factory.

She still had nightmares about it, waking in a cold sweat, gulping for air, hearing the explosion and the roar of flames, feeling the searing waves of heat. If she hadn't stumbled into one of the waste pipes Kos had told her about, she never would've made it out alive.

And she still grieved, tears coming whenever she thought of Kos—bloody, barely able to stand, promising he'd create a diversion so she could get away and then meet up with her later.

He'd lied about that—and he'd left her alone. So utterly alone.

As she walked away from the nightclub, her head lowered, she kept to well-lit streets until she turned the corner that led toward her hotel. It wasn't in one of the nicer parts of the city, but it was all she could afford. Her funds, as careful as she'd been, were nearly gone.

Knowing she had to eat something besides bar snacks, she stopped at a corner grocery and bought fresh fruit, a little cheese, and a bottle of water.

Drinking on an empty stomach was never a good idea, but she had to order drinks or the bartenders would throw her out. Feeling fuzzy-headed and a little nauseated from the alcohol, she headed for the alley behind the grocery, in case she was going to be sick.

She sat on the back steps, lowered her head between her knees, then closed her eyes and took in slow, deep breaths until the nausea faded.

Even after she raised her head, she couldn't find the energy to get up and walk again. The hate and fury that had fueled her, and kept her alive in the weeks after Kos had been killed, was running on empty.

In her purse, she still had the slip of paper he'd given her their last night together. It even had his fingerprint on it, smudged now. On the paper was a telephone number, and he'd told her to call it if anything happened to him. He'd made her promise. He'd also said that someone would help her if she asked.

So she'd called, left a message, and a cold-voiced woman who barely spoke English had called back, given her the address of a nightclub in Rio de Janeiro, and told her to be at the bar by ten o'clock and someone would come for her.

But no one had.

What was she going to do? The temptation to give up and turn herself in grew stronger every day. But Kos had died so she could escape; how could she betray his sacrifice by giving up now?

"Strong," she whispered. "Be strong."

It was the mantra she'd been repeating to herself ever since Kos's companions had dumped her in Indiana with a fake ID and a wad of cash. Kos had told her where to go to meet his contacts, but they hadn't been very helpful. She supposed she was lucky they hadn't just killed her. Without Kos, their only reason to help her was a sense of duty.

She should have stayed with him, even if it meant dying. She hadn't wanted to leave; she'd been terrified to see him hurt, certain he couldn't follow—but he'd insisted, swearing that every second she delayed put him in more danger. So she'd run, and hadn't stopped until she got to Mexico.

And now here she was, sitting in an alley in Brazil, still alive, still too guilty and angry to give up.

He'd promised to protect her . . . and he had, although she would give anything to have him back. She missed him so much, lying against her at night, talking with her, kissing her.

Closing her eyes, Vanessa ran the tips of her fingers over her lips, trying to remember the taste of his kiss, the feel of his mouth. Tears leaked from beneath her tightly closed lids, streaking down her cheeks. She didn't want to forget, she didn't want—

"Vanessa Sharpton?"

With a gasp, Vanessa opened her eyes, staring at the man standing a short distance away. She hadn't seen or heard anyone; it was as if he'd appeared out of thin air.

He slowly walked into the light of the back door, hands up to assure her he meant no harm.

"That's close enough," she said, clutching at her purse. She had a gun in it, but she probably couldn't pull it clear before he jumped her.

Obediently, he stopped, "Are you Vanessa Sharpton?"

He had a faint accent, and he was very tall and very good-looking, with white-blond hair and clear blue eyes. He wore a gray suit, with a white shirt and a pink-and-gray striped tie. Everything about him said he was not a man who frequented alleys.

"Who are you?"

He didn't look like a cop, but neither had Will Tiernay. Avalon was worse than the cops, and she couldn't be too careful.

"Someone who is here to help you. Did you not call for help?"

She stared narrowly at him and sniffed. "You're a little late, aren't you? I've been coming here for days."

"And so have I."

"Then why didn't you—"

"I had to make sure you weren't followed." He hunkered down to her level and held out a neatly folded handkerchief. It was only then she realized, with a jolt, that he'd come within inches of her. How had he . . . *when* had he moved? Why hadn't she noticed?

Warily, she took the linen from him and dabbed at her eyes, avoiding that disturbingly pale blue gaze.

"My name is Rainert von Lahr," he said softly. "I'm sorry about Kos."

Tears threatened again, but she held them back.

"Thank you," she said, still not sure if she should

say even that much. Those Avalon people were sly as snakes. What if this was some kind of trap—

"Do you want revenge against those who killed him?"

The question was so unexpected that Vanessa could only stare at him for a long moment. Then she whispered, "Yes."

He held out his hand, a long-fingered, clean, and strong-looking hand. "Then come with me."

Dear Readers,

Thank you for buying *Tough Enough*, from my Avalon series. I hope you enjoyed Will and Mia's story and will check out the next book, in which the audacious Claudia Cruz tangles with the sexy FBI agent Vincent DeLuca, and all sorts of romantic mayhem ensues.

You might be wondering, what's Avalon and what's the series about?

Avalon is a secret organization of mercenaries whose operatives track down stolen art and looted antiquities, chase down art thieves and forgers, and manage to fall in love along the way. More romantic mystery-adventure than romantic suspense, each book of the series features a romance between an Avalon operative and a love interest met while on assignment.

In addition to sizzling-hot romance and a spice of adventure, the series includes two ongoing subplots. One involves catching Avalon's longtime nemesis, the art thief extraordinaire Rainert von Lahr. The other surrounds a World War II–era murder mystery that will shed light on Avalon's hundred-year-old history, how Ben Sheridan came to be involved in the organization, and the truth behind his relationship with the person who is really in charge of it.

And now you might be wondering, What's with the ongoing subplots?

Well, I read books from lots of genres. A week doesn't go by that I don't read a book or two, and the majority of those books and graphic novels are ongoing series. The nonromance series I've read usually had each book dealing with a mystery, a crisis, or some plan to destroy the world. At the end of the book, the mystery, crisis, or looming apocalypse was always resolved, but there was often a strong romantic subplot that continued through the series.

I wondered what would happen if I flipped those plots and subplots around—and the result was Avalon, Ben Sheridan, Rainert von Lahr, and mercenaries with an eye for art and romance.

The idea has been developing over time, and if you're new to my books, you might want to check out *One Way Out*, in which Sheridan and von Lahr are first mentioned, and *Hide in Plain Sight*, in which the Avalon operative Griffith Laughton falls in love with the woman he's protecting from von Lahr.

Best wishes and happy reading!

Michele Albert

Enter the world of
Michele Albert's Avalon series!

Turn the page for excerpts from

ONE WAY OUT

featuring Cassie Ashton and Alex Martinelli

and

HIDE IN PLAIN SIGHT

featuring Fiona Kennedy and Griffith Laughton

Available from Pocket Books

ONE WAY OUT

CASSIE ASHTON SHADED HER EYES WITH HER HAND and squinted up at a man dangling halfway down the face of a bluff, twenty feet off the ground. The guy in the climbing harness wore jeans, heavy boots, a long-sleeved blue shirt with the sleeves rolled up, and a very familiar battered white Resistol hat.

She'd finally run her quarry to ground.

Grinning, she tipped her head back and watched as he braced one gloved hand on the rock and worked the ropes with the other. She waited until he'd secured his footing, then cupped her hands around her mouth and yelled: "Hey, Martinelli!"

The white hat dipped as he looked down, and even though he was too far up for her to hear it, his lips formed a coarse word she easily recognized. "What the hell do you want?" he shouted back.

"Gotta talk to you!"

"In case it's escaped your notice, Ashton, I'm kind of tied up at the moment."

She'd noticed, all right. The leather straps and ropes nicely framed the best, and the most arrogant, ass in all Wyoming.

"Whatever's in that rock has been there for over sixty million years, and it's not going anywhere now. What I have to talk to you about is important."

"Christ, couldn't you once call ahead for an appointment?" He twirled above her as he repositioned himself, muscles pulling at his cotton shirt, straining its seams. "Now go away, call my department, and leave me a message."

Which he wouldn't return. Cassie grinned. "I don't think so. Get your ass down here, Professor Martinelli, because I'm not going anywhere until we talk. And you know I mean it."

"Don, what the hell is she doing here? Why didn't someone stop her before she got this far?" he demanded.

"Sorry, Alex. The new kids on the crew don't know her," answered a familiar gravelly voice. "And I was busy working on that hadrosaur leg we found yesterday. I guess she slipped right past me. . . . You want me to throw her in the creek? I'd really enjoy that."

"You're welcome to try it, Igor." Still smiling, Cassie didn't bother turning around to face Don Cleary, the wiry old man she'd teasingly nicknamed Igor because he was Martinelli's second banana.

Above her, Martinelli called, "That's a pleasure I'm reserving for myself, Don."

Cassie's smile widened into a grin. "Come on, Martinelli. Are you just going to dangle up there, safely out of my reach, or come down here and face me like the big ol' manly man you are?"

She couldn't resist the "manly man" bit. With his half-supported stance against the rock emphasizing his lean, strong build, he looked like a poster boy for a wilderness outfitter advertisement.

For a moment Cassie thought Martinelli would refuse the challenge, but after another mouthed curse he began lowering himself, working the lines and pulleys with an expertise that came from years of climbing mountains and cliffs the world over, hunting fossils, looking for that elusive "big find" that would put his name in the history books.

Too bad for him that she'd just beat him to the finish line.

As he descended, Cassie couldn't help focusing once more on how the harness cradled his rear and groin over the worn denim of his jeans, revealing a most impressive package, front and back.

Mortal enemies they might be, but she could still appreciate what he had to offer a woman. It just wouldn't ever be her, not in a million years.

Martinelli advanced, moving with the confidence of a man who looked good and knew it. He pulled off his Resistol, slapping it against his thigh to knock off the dust before he wiped the sweat from his face with his forearm, then quickly unbuttoned his sun-faded chambray shirt and stripped it off. Without looking away from Cassie, he grabbed a large bottle of water from the cooler by the table, twisted off the cap, then dumped the entire contents on his face and chest.

He had a lean, spare build, the sinews and tendons neatly outlined beneath sun-browned skin, and the water made tracks in the grit on his face, flattened the dusting of dark hair on his chest, and gleamed wetly along the hard lines of his chest, ribs, and belly.

Cassie laughed, knowing this show was all for her benefit.

He flashed the grin that had probably broken legions of coed hearts and mucked up the academic careers of a few earnest graduate students as well. Then he settled his hat back on his dark hair, pushed his sunglasses up his nose to hide his eyes, and strode toward her, arms outstretched as if they were two old buddies about to embrace. "Cassie, Cassie."

Cassie allowed Alex to take her by the arms and position her at a safe distance from him. The palms of his hands were dry, rough, and warm against her bare skin.

"And how," he asked as he released her, "are you going to make my life hell today?"

Cassie shoved her hands into her back pockets. "You sure know how to make a girl feel special, Martinelli."

He gave her an unsubtle once-over, his gaze lingering on her breasts beneath her camouflage-print T-shirt. "What's with the G.I. Jane look? Going for a sneak attack? Didn't work, but it's a good look for you. Kind of cute."

To her eternal annoyance, she was doomed to be cute until she grew old and wrinkled—and even then she might not escape it.

"Martinelli, I'm cute like a rattler is cute."

She seized Martinelli's belt buckle—a calculated familiarity to piss him off—and hauled him a short distance away. "I have news . . . and it stays between you and me. I mean it. I don't want even a single word of what I'm about to say shared with anybody else."

Martinelli knocked her hand aside, then shifted to put the sun behind him—so it shone directly in her eyes and obscured his face. The bastard wasn't above a low trick or two.

"It's something big," he said.

At the guarded, tired tone of his voice, a faint discomfort prickled over her, but she shook it off. "Oh, yeah. *Hugely* big, and I want you to see it. You were my first choice to verify it, Martinelli. As always."

"Because that way you can twist the knife just that much more." He stepped closer, then leaned down until they were almost face-to-face. He smelled like wind and earth and wholly male. "Not interested."

Cassie smiled, unperturbed by the crackling intensity of his hostility. "You might want to wait until you hear what I've found." She inched closer until she could feel the heat radiating off his body, glanced around to make sure no one else was within hearing distance, then lowered her voice. "I had a tour group digging at a private ranch up toward Thermopolis, at what used to be an old riverbed. We found an infant rex, Martinelli. I think it's nearly intact . . . and you damn well know what this means."

His face went slack in shock. A second later his jaw tightened, muscles working beneath the dark beard stubble, and she could imagine the emotions in the eyes behind those sunglasses: anger, envy, regret, longing.

After a moment, she said quietly, "You want to talk about this or not?"

He gave a short, taut nod.

"I thought so. I'll meet you at the Dip Bar tonight. Eight o'clock. I'd come earlier, but my ex is picking up my kid for a visit and I need to be there."

"I bet he's looking forward to another round of emasculation by Ashton."

His flat, unflattering comment stung, but Cassie flashed him her sweetest smile. "No doubt. So you'll be at Dip's, right?"

"I'll be there."

"Alone and sober?"

"Not if I can help it," he said with feeling.

"Either way, I'm sure we'll find common negotiating grounds. Bye, Dr. Martinelli. Have a nice day . . . and I hope you find something interesting up there in that old slab of rock."

Flushed with triumph, she walked away, aware of his furious stare boring a hole in her back as she headed back to her truck.

But when she inserted her key in the ignition, her hands were shaking so bad that it took her three tries to get it right.

HIDE IN PLAIN SIGHT

Fiona's muscles were paralyzed in terror. She'd never heard him move, but she could feel his heat behind her, hear his soft breathing. Smell his cologne and a hint of perspiration.

Despite his nearness, he didn't touch her. "Don't make this more difficult than it needs to be. Stay quiet and do as I tell you, and you'll be okay."

She stepped away, trying to stay as far from him as possible. The young man was sitting up, shaking his head groggily and rotating his jaw as if to test it. He watched Fiona and Griffith, and whenever his gaze fell on Griffith, he looked wary.

"That was stupid," Griffith told him as he slowly pushed to his feet. "You're damn lucky you kicked the little bastard, or I'd be tempted to give you another black eye to match the one you've already got."

The younger man said nothing.

"If you know where your gun is, get it. And for being such a dumb-ass, you get to stay behind and clean up the mess."

The kid took a quick, deep breath. "Yes, sir."

"You got the number for the janitorial help, right?"

"Yes, Mr. Sh——" At Griffith's glare, the kid broke off, glanced at Fiona, and then swallowed. "Yes, I do."

Griffith turned and took her arm. "We need to leave, Fiona. You're in danger."

"Oh, that's rich." She shook free from his hand, and he was smart enough not to try to touch her again. "No one shot at me until *you* did."

Beyond him, she could see Bressler trussed on the floor, unconscious and still bleeding. The nameless kid was standing over him, pointedly not looking at either her or Griffith. More quietly she added, "And you *did* shoot *him*."

"Because it was him or you. Don't be stupid about this."

It didn't escape her notice that he offered no other excuses or explanations. "And now you think I'm going to be thankful and consider you my hero, simply because——"

"Look, I'm not a hero and never claimed to be. But I'm your best chance of staying alive." Still holding Fiona's gaze, he added, "Hey, Noonie. Ms. Kennedy's cat is hiding somewhere. Make sure he's fed and taken care of."

"Yes, sir," the younger man said in a subdued voice. "Anything else?"

"Yeah, watch your ass. Both targets are here and probably close by. Try not to get yourself killed; I don't want any more rookies dying on my watch. Got that?"

Noonie nodded but wisely said nothing.

"Bring me the briefcase. It's by her desk chair."

Fiona watched Griffith through the entire exchange, understanding that something very strange was going on and she was central to it. The manuscript, that call from Richard, if it was indeed Richard. . . . While none of it made sense, it was all connected through *her*.

"I've been ordered to keep you under constant surveillance and to keep you safe," Griffith told her. "I realize you have no reason to trust me, but I'm your only option at the moment. Do exactly as I say and speak to no one. I'm taking you to a safe place. Once we're there, you can ask me all the questions you want and I'll do my best to answer them."

So calm. So polite. So *false*.

Fiona swung her fist and hit him square on the

side of his mouth. Pain radiated up her arm, and her knuckles burned.

Noonie, returning with the briefcase, stopped in his tracks and stared.

She'd hit Griffith with all her strength, and he'd reacted with only a faint grimace.

"You *bastard*. All along you lied to me. You used me!"

A drop of blood welled on his lip as he smiled. "That pretty much covers it."

"You're not a cop."

"Nope." He wiped the blood away. "But I am fighting for truth, justice, and the American way, so you can consider me one of the good guys."

He took the briefcase from Noonie, then pulled her after him out the back door and into the service alley.

He was stronger than she was, and armed, and as much as she hated what he was doing and distrusted him, she wanted to believe he was looking out for her, even if he was being a total bastard about it. And he'd ordered that kid to feed her cat.

Rain drizzled down on them as he led her toward a small, beat-up car that no one would consider out of place parked in an alley.

After a quick check around and under the car, Griffith unlocked the door and pushed her inside, buckling her up—and handcuffing her to the door handle in a quick move.

Staring down with disbelief at the circlet of metal

around her wrist, she said, "You have all sorts of surprises in that jacket of yours."

"Tricks of the trade."

He shut the door and jogged around to the driver's side, and within seconds, he had the car moving. With a dull surprise, she noted that the engine sounded much more powerful than she would've expected from the car's dilapidated appearance.

Even his car was a liar.

Griffith didn't have to look at his reluctant passenger to gauge her mood; anger and contempt radiated off her in waves so strong he could feel it.

He didn't expect anything else, and because he'd known all along how this would turn out, a perverse part of him had been even colder to her than necessary. If she was going to hate him, he might as well give her a good reason to hate him with every cell in her body.

Putting up the wall up between them was better for her, better for him.

He was still running on an adrenaline high, his heart pounding. What a goddamn mess. He'd been so focused on Fiona, standing pressed against Bressler with a gun to her head, that he hadn't had time to really think about Noonie's close call with disaster.

Damn kid. Having to take care of Bressler, feed

the cat, and explain to Ben what had gone wrong would be punishment enough.

Jesus. His hands were shaking. When was the last time he'd felt like this?

Again the image of Fiona with the gun to her head flashed to mind. As angry as he was at Noonie, Griffith knew he'd messed up as well. Bressler would've killed her if he'd had the chance, and Griffith had all but given him that chance on a silver platter.

He'd gotten too involved, too distracted. And not only had he failed to protect Fiona when it mattered most, but he'd probably blown his chance to get to von Lahr.

Uneasiness nagged at the back of his mind, and his instincts warned him that he couldn't relax his guard at all, not even at the safe house.

Which might be a good thing. If nothing else, it would keep him too busy to focus on the regret that stung like a bitch whenever he glimpsed the hurt and anger in Fiona's eyes.

As he entered the freeway on-ramp heading out of downtown L.A., the silence grew so thick that he couldn't ignore it any longer. "Fiona—"

"Don't." She turned her face toward the window. "Whatever you're going to say, I don't want to hear it. Nothing will ever excuse what you've done to me."

She was right.

What was done was done; the best he could do for her now was to get her back to her quiet life as quickly as possible, then disappear.

Inexplicably, that hurt. And he didn't dare consider why.

Fall in love

with bestselling romances from Pocket Books!

~~~~~~

Impulse • JoAnn Ross
A haunted man...A hunted woman...
Together they must stop a madman before he kills again.

BAD Attitude • Sherrilyn Kenyon
Sometimes even the good guys need to have a BAD attitude...

The Seduction of His Wife • Janet Chapman
He set out to seduce her for all the wrong reasons—
but fell in love with her for all the right ones.

Thrill Me to Death • Roxanne St. Claire
When a Bullet Catcher is on the job, he'll always watch
your back. But you better watch your heart.

Dirty Little Lies • Julie Leto
She's a sultry Latino bounty hunter armed with
sex, lies, and other deadly weapons.

~~~~~~